Dear Readers,

The last rose of summer may be fading, but Bouquet romances bloom all year long! And for this back-to-school month—which often means more reading time for Mom—we've got four delightful, heartwarming stories to enhance those late-summer afternoons in the hammock, the porch swing, or even the rocking chair.

After 25 Harlequin novels, it's high time for Vanessa Grant to grace Zebra with **If You Loved Me.** When Emma's 18-year-old son goes missing on a kayaking trip in the Northwest wilderness, Emma has no choice but to put herself at the mercy of onetime lover Gray McKenzie—an outdoorsman with his own plane. He knows every inch of the territory—but can he find his way back into Emma's heart?

It's a long way from high society Boston to Little Fork, Wyoming, but Caitlyn makes the trip when she inherits half a ranch, never dreaming that a sinfully handsome partner will be part of the deal. And who would have dreamed that **Caitlyn's Cowboy** would melt the ice around her heart? Gina Jackson makes her Bouquet debut with this captivating tale of magical love.

Newcomer Susan Hardy sweeps her readers into the breathtaking North Carolina mountains, where free-spirited Clementine "Clem" Harper is reluctantly swept into the arms of city slicker Will Fletcher. Will soon discovers that it's not easy to win the heart of a mountain gal . . . until he learns the secrets of **Mountain Magic.**

Veteran romance writer Judy Gill's **All in the Family** features two meddling daughters who can't resist "fixing up" newly divorced dad Jed Cotts with one of their teachers. Karen Andersen is reluctant at first, but somehow this handsome, athletic, warm-hearted man makes her feel cherished for the first time in ages. Maybe matchmaking isn't such a bad idea after all!

Kick back, slip off your shoes, and settle down for a nice, long read. Let your eyes follow your heart into these four enthralling romances . . . and before you know it, it will be next month—and time for four more. Enjoy!

The Editors

# WILL HE? WON'T HE?

"Good-bye, Karen," Jed said, his voice as stiff as his manner. "Take care, okay?"

Damn it, why didn't they call his flight? He'd said good-bye. She'd said good-bye. They both stood silent for several minutes.

"Jed—"

"Karen—"

"You first," she said.

"You'd better go now. Find a cab and get home. You don't have to wait until my flight goes."

"I know." But Karen didn't move.

He frowned, listening to the loudspeaker announce his flight. "Okay, gotta go." He bent, grabbed his bag. "Bye, Karen."

He strode away, then spun back, dropped his suitcase, and pulled her into his arms. He tilted her head back and fastened his mouth over hers, kissing her until her head roared and her knees turned to jelly.

"Oh, God," he groaned, holding her tighter, "I want to drag you away somewhere."

He kissed her again, deeply, and in moments she'd all but forgotten they weren't alone. . . .

# ALL
# IN THE
# FAMILY

## JUDY GILL

Zebra Books
Kensington Publishing Corp.

http://www.zebrabooks.com

ZEBRA BOOKS are published by

Kensington Publishing Corp.
850 Third Avenue
New York, NY 10022

First Printing: September, 1999
10 9 8 7 6 5 4 3 2 1

Printed in the United States of America

# ONE

"No. Absolutely not." Jed Cotts glared at his middle daughter. "I am forty-five years old. I am a grandfather. I do not go on blind dates! Not for a cup of coffee, not for an evening, and certainly not for an entire long weekend. If your teacher wants to go to her ex's wedding—though personally I think she's nuts—she can do it without me. End of discussion, Cecelia." He picked up his suit jacket and briefcase, turned, and strode out quickly before the tears shimmering in her big, blue eyes could overflow. Nothing made him feel lower than female tears, especially when that female was his nineteen-year-old daughter.

Against his will, Jed wondered if Karen Andersen, one of Ceil's college teachers, was tall, blond, and Nordic, as her name suggested. Undoubtedly, which was why Ceil was trying so hard to fix him up with the woman. Ceil knew enough to be aware that people were attracted to types, and her mother, Crystal, was tall, blond, and Nordic. As always, there was a sting in the thought of his ex-wife, who had left him for his former business partner five years ago.

Resolutely, he put them all out of his mind—Ceil, the doubtless delightful Ms. Andersen, and Crystal. He had more pressing matters to consider. He was a past master at losing himself in his work, and proceeded for the rest of the day to do so.

When he arrived home that evening as dusk deepened into darkness, Ceil's car was parked in the drive, crookedly as usual, beside Wes's van and a battered yellow four-by-four that blocked his access to the garage. *Hell!*

He was beat from spending most of the afternoon and half the evening trying unsuccessfully to track down a missing shipment of silk flowers, as well as dealing with the wholesaler who'd been expecting the consignment. The last thing he wanted now was to have to be polite to Ceil's and Wes's probably beered-up buddies. His home had recently become the hangout of choice for friends of his daughter and her fiancé. He didn't want to have to be polite to guests.

Too weary and disheartened to bother demanding the little yellow wreck be moved out of his way, he backed up and pulled in behind Ceil's car. He always left before she did in the mornings, anyway.

With an enormous yawn, he stretched, then slid out of the car, jerking his jacket from the back of the passenger seat. Draping it over his shoulder, he tugged his tie loose, then pulled it free as he bypassed the front door. He unbuttoned his shirt and stripped out of it as he walked around to the back of the house, pushing his way past the drooping fronds of a weeping willow overhanging a flight of moss-edged stone stairs.

He liked his house. He'd designed it himself, created it out of his mind and imagination, and had it built on a raw acre of soil and rock in West Seattle on a hillside overlooking Puget Sound.

In the cabana, he hung up his clothing and dragged on a pair of swimming trunks. The heat of the early July day had lessened with the onset of evening, but the water felt good as he dived in and began his customary laps.

Finished, he floated on his back and watched the stars overhead. Would it have been so bad, a weekend away with total strangers, none of whom would expect anything of him except his presence? Would it have hurt him to tell Ceil he'd help out that poor woman? After all, he did know the pain she must be going through, knew it well.

She'd probably need her hand held.

Maybe more than her hand. He envisioned himself holding that long, lean, Nordic body, almost felt her thick golden hair soft against his cheek as she wept and he comforted her, wrapping her tightly in his arms, her large, firm breasts molded against his chest, warm and heavy, her long legs pressed to his thighs, her breath hot and steamy against his neck as her sobs finally eased and he lifted her face to his, looked into drenched blue eyes and . . .

Sank.

He came up spluttering, blinking into the unexpected brilliance of the floodlights that had just been switched on.

"Hi, Dad."

Shaking water out of his eyes, shoving his hair back, he hoisted himself onto the deck and grabbed the towel Ceil handed him, rubbing briskly.

"Thanks, honey," he said from under the towel, sitting hunched on the edge of the pool, grateful for the towel because it hung down over his lap and hid his face, a face in which he was afraid his daughter might read something that shouldn't be there: Longing. Desire. Lust for a woman he'd never met simply because she might be of the same physical type as the one he'd meant to grow old with.

"Listen," he went on when he felt more in control. "I've been thinking it over and, well, I've decided to—"

"Dad." She tugged impatiently at his towel. "Can it wait? There's someone here I want you to meet. Get up, will you?"

He lowered the towel. Another girl stood just behind Ceil, away from the splashes of water on the deck. A lamp backlighted her short hair, turning its ends to flames of dark red. He rose to his feet.

Ceil's friend was tiny, a head shorter than Ceil, and slight of build, wearing a pair of those painted-on pants, tighter than tattoos, that Ceil called leggings. He hated them. These were white, with pastel flowers splotched all over them, and she'd topped them with a huge gray sweatshirt that nipped in under her little butt and said something on the front about saving trees.

She smiled tentatively, took a step forward, and he realized she was not a girl. It didn't take Ceil's saying, "This is Karen Andersen," to tell him he had the kind of problems he hadn't even considered and was in deeper trouble than he'd ever thought possible.

The dream of the tall Nordic blonde faded as the woman took another step forward into brighter light, and was replaced by another dream accompanied by a rapidly hammering heart, clammy sweat on his palms, and a distinctly dizzy sensation of light-headedness. Who was this woman who affected him so strongly? Audrey Hepburn at thirty-five?

The thought slashed across his mind before he realized that she looked like a tired Audrey Hepburn, though the obvious weariness did nothing to distract from her singular beauty. Her triangular face was thin and pale, with smudgy blue circles under her large, sober eyes. It was those eyes that captured him, though he couldn't discern their color. They held him enthralled even as she swept her gaze over his all but naked form as if she might be considering buying him.

Then she smiled faintly and nodded. He could almost read her thought: *Yes, he'll do.*

Suddenly, to his shock, he knew if she was buying, he was for sale. Cheap. Hell, free! And the most striking thing about this whole encounter was that he could be so taken by a stranger, especially one whose type had never attracted him before. Yet something in him responded instantly, powerfully, to whatever it was in her that approved of him.

She did approve; he knew that as he stood very still under her scrutiny, glad he swam every day to keep his stomach hard and flat, glad he played tennis when he had the chance to keep his shoulders and arms and legs firm and muscular, glad his hair was still thick and rich and dark. Well, mostly.

Most of all, he was glad he had changed his mind.

"Ms. Andersen." He took the hand she offered. It was small and cool and silky smooth, as if she had just rubbed lotion into the skin.

"Mr. Cotts, I'm very glad to meet you. It would give me great pleasure if you'd join me this coming weekend on my trip to Montana." Her voice was low and musical, her speech oddly formal, considering his state of undress.

He smiled. "Jed," he said. "My name is Jedidiah, and nothing would make me happier than escorting you to Montana. Unless it would be your joining me in the pool?" *Naked.*

*Naked?* His eyes widened. Had he said that, or only thought it? She hadn't recoiled, so he must have kept the notion internalized.

"I—" She looked down at her baggy top, her print

pants, her flat sandals, and shook her head. Again, fire
danced in her dark auburn hair, turning its curls red, and
some kind of rueful amusement danced in her eyes, eras-
ing the impression of weariness. "I'm not exactly dressed
for swimming."

"Ceil can find you something, can't you . . ." As he
finally tore his eyes away from Karen Andersen, he realized Ceil had left them there alone.

"No, thank you. I'd rather not." She looked momentarily frantic as she, too, noticed Ceil's absence. Her
voice came out all jerky and breathless, as if she'd been
running.

"That's fine." He wanted to soothe her, to calm the
agitation that made her hands tremble. He clenched his
fists at his sides to prevent his reaching out to take her
hands in his. "Why . . . uh, why don't we have a drink
while we get acquainted? Would you like to sit inside or
out?" From inside, the heavy pound of rock music eased
as Ceil closed the door.

For the first time, she really smiled at him. "Out here
would be lovely," she said. "I'd prefer something nonal-
coholic."

"Coming right up. Have a seat while I get us something."

Jed steered her around the puddle where he'd dripped
and seated her under an umbrella no one had remembered to fold up. He dumped his towel in the middle of
the table. "Be right back."

He hurried through the patio door leading to his bedroom, dragged on a terry robe, and strode to the kitchen,
slamming glasses onto a tray, adding ice, and slopping
ginger ale into them, in a rush born of fear that when
he returned she might not be there. His hands, he noted
with a mental start, shook.

She jumped up as he approached and snatched the towel off the table to give him room to set down the tray. Their arms brushed and she jerked away, then reeled, staggered, slipped in the puddle, and went sideways into the pool before he so much as gasped out a warning or managed to reach for her.

She came up, as he had, spluttering, and groped for the edge. With one hand holding both of hers, he pulled her out.

"Yuck!" She dashed water out of her eyes, dropped the sodden towel that had gone in with her, and grimaced as it splashed the legs of her pants.

"Are you all right?" he asked. "What happened? One minute you were standing there, the next you were in the pool."

"I stood up too fast, got dizzy, and . . ." She shrugged. "I'm not hurt. Just feeling very undignified . . . and wet."

"You're that, all right." Jed let his gaze slide from her dripping hair, spiky wet eyelashes, and pink cheeks to where the once loose top molded the shape of her shoulders, stuck to her arms, conformed to the shape of her pointed breasts—and clung to a slightly protruding, indisputably pregnant belly.

Jed's eyes were drawn to it. Her eyes were drawn to it. Her hands encircled it. Then, slowly, both gazes lifted, met, meshed, and she sighed softly, still cradling the lump protectively.

Just as slowly, Jed took off his terry robe and handed it to her. "Get out of those wet things," he said, his voice thick with emotions he could scarcely begin to identify. Regret was high among them, and a sad sense of defeat, as if he'd finally reached the gate to an Eden he'd long sought, only to find it firmly locked.

# TWO

In the cabana, Karen struggled to peel herself out of the wet clothing, but when it was done, she stood for another moment, her hands pressed to her belly, head hanging, hair dripping down in a steady, cool trickle until, with an impatient hiss, she snatched up a dry towel from a shelf and wound it around her head. She grabbed another and began rubbing herself briskly all over. Now he knew the truth he'd back out of accompanying her. She'd have to find a way to help him do it gracefully.

When she emerged, wrapped in his robe, Jed seated her in the chair again, carefully, gently. She remembered Ceil saying that her father treated women beautifully. She wished that she could be beautiful for this man.

Heaven help her, she hadn't expected to be this—what was the word? *Fascinated*. She watched avidly as Jed, his legs long and lean below the powder-blue Speedo, strode to the cabana. In seconds he returned, wearing the blue shirt she'd seen hanging in there with the gray raw-silk suit and paisley tie.

She tried to look away, tried to keep calm about this entire odd situation, but she was undeniably drawn to him.

He took a chair opposite her, swinging it out from the table so he sat facing her, their knees almost touching. He leaned forward, his forearms on his thighs. "Is it his?

Your husband's? Is that why you don't want to go to his wedding alone?"

"Ex-husband." Her swift correction carried a hint of asperity. Her eyes held a challenge as she turned to him, daring him to make something of it. "Yes, it is his. The wedding—" She shrugged. "This isn't why I don't want to go alone. I don't intend for anyone to know about the baby."

It seemed perfectly normal for him to ask, "When is it due?"

It was just as natural for her to answer. "The eighth of November. She moved today. At least, I think she did. It was just the faintest little flutter, but I felt it."

Jed felt a vicarious thrill at the joy and excitement reflected in her eyes. For a moment he envied her the delights she had awaiting her, the magic of watching her child grow, and wished he could be a part of all that again, just once more.

"I just started showing in the last week or two," Karen said, almost shyly. "If I'd managed to stay dry, you'd never have guessed, would you?"

Jed heard the plea in her voice and smiled as he shook his head. "Never." He thought her soft sigh held relief. It was very quiet by the pool for several moments. An owl hooted; a cat yowled high and eerie, like a woman screaming in torment. Then silence.

Jed's question burst into the silence, rough, indignant. "You're carrying his baby and he's marrying someone else? You're *letting* him?"

She nodded her towel-rumpled head. "Of course. I'm sure he and Candice are very much in love."

"But, holy—what about you?"

She shrugged. "What about me? I don't want to be

with him anymore. If he knew about the baby, it would just cloud the issue."

He nearly groaned aloud. "You haven't even told him?" The intensity and variety of his feelings shocked him. "Why the hell not?" The passion in his voice shocked him, too; it was just short of an enraged bellow. Since he'd learned how years before, he had made a point of maintaining an even temper at all times, yet now he was getting agitated about a strange woman and her even stranger doings. It made no sense. But, damn it, he had to know. "How can you let him marry someone else when you're carrying his child?"

She smiled again. The faint, poignant curving of her lips brought a sudden sharp pain to Jed's chest. "Because," she said, "as I told you, he's in love with the woman he's planning to marry, and I wouldn't want to be married to him again myself even if he weren't involved with Candice. It didn't work the first time, so there's no reason to believe it would work a second time. Besides, by the time I knew I was pregnant, he was officially engaged and Candice was pregnant, too."

Jed shook his head. "What the hell is the man, promiscuous?"

*"No."* Indignation flared in her eyes and she half rose to her feet, then flopped back down. "All right, on the face of it, I suppose this does make Barry look bad, but he's not promiscuous at all. At least two months went by between his—between my getting pregnant and Candice's conceiving. More like three, I believe. Maybe his going to bed with me was part of his resistance to admitting how he felt about her. He said he had doubts. She's ten years younger and . . ." She shrugged. "Maybe he was trying to fend her off emotionally. Maybe—oh, what does it matter, anyway? His motivations are not my concern."

*Nor are they yours.* She didn't say it, but he read the message in her tone as clearly as if she had. He ran his gaze over her and shook his head ruefully. "Yeah. Okay, okay, I know you're right, but . . ." He shook his head again, then blurted, "What were yours?"

To his surprise, she didn't slap him down, either verbally or physically, though the moment the words were out he knew he deserved it.

"Motives?" she said with an almost puzzled expression on her face. "I don't know. Our divorce had been final for several months. Barry came out here to Seattle for a conference, called me, we had dinner, went back to my place for coffee, and, well, one thing led to another and we went to bed together."

Oddly enough, Karen reflected, he'd called her because he wanted to talk about Candice, and had done so—interminably, expressing his doubts about the depth of her feelings for him, his for her, his capacity to form a lasting relationship, and his inability to father children.

She'd reminded him that no one knew whose ability was at fault in his and her lack of children. It was just the way it was. She had never conceived, though his sperm count was adequate and her capacity appeared unhampered. Maybe, she'd told him, he'd have a family with Candice. That brought out more concerns. What if he didn't? Couldn't? Would Candice leave him, too?

It was the first time she'd realized that Barry blamed that lack in their lives for her decision to leave. It hurt that he thought her so shallow, and she'd wept. He'd held her. The rest was, as they said, history. Like most history, it had exerted considerable force on the future—hers, anyway.

She shrugged, glancing into Jed's watchful eyes. "It was a mistake. We both knew it as soon as it was over.

I'm not even sure why we let it happen. Sentiment, maybe. Maybe a last-ditch effort to recapture something that had once been very good, but which no longer was. Or, as I said, maybe it was an effort on his part to resist whatever was happening between him and Candice. I don't know."

"And he didn't think to take precautions."

Karen treated his condemnatory statement as a question.

"I suppose neither of us did a lot of thinking that evening at all."

Jed was silent. Karen stood and walked to the breast-high stone wall farther along the patio and stood looking down on the lights of houses below and of ferries wending their way to and from Bremerton.

Jed stood beside her, silent, a faraway look in his eyes. She wondered dimly why she'd bothered explaining. She had so far told no one of her pregnancy but her friend and colleague Esther Eldridge, who had guessed last week, the third morning in a row she'd caught Karen throwing up in the staff ladies' room.

Soon, nobody who saw her would be guessing. The whole thing would become self-evident, which was why it was important that she go home for a few days soon. She'd tell her parents, of course, but the fewer people back in Soda Creek who knew, the easier it would be for Barry and Candice to get a good start for their marriage, especially considering those doubts Barry had discussed with her over dinner the night she got pregnant. It had been, she reflected, almost as if he wanted Karen to come back to save him from a fate he didn't feel ready to face. Yet he'd claimed to love Candice.

"I understand how something like that can happen," Jed said, startling her so she looked up just as he swallowed hard. She watched his Adam's apple bounce, saw a couple of dark whiskers he'd missed when shaving. It was silly, the way those few bits of stubble brought an ache to her throat. Her lips tingled as if they had just grazed the skin where the whiskers grew.

"The last time I saw Crystal, my ex-wife," he went on, "if I could have talked her into bed with me, I would have." He cleared his throat.

"I, um, well . . . tried to." His mouth twisted in what Karen took to be an attempt at a smile, but which failed to hide his pain. "But she was already involved with someone else."

He laughed harshly into the silence that followed his revelation and covered his eyes with his hand for a second, elbow propped on the wall, then groaned softly. "Oh, hell, I can't believe I told you that!"

"It's all right. It won't go any farther. You loved her. It was only natural for you to fight to keep her. And she must have loved you once. I'm sure she didn't like hurting you."

He sighed and leaned his arms on the wall, gazing out over his favorite nighttime scene. Karen was right. Crystal had loved him once, or thought she did. And she was right about its not having been easy for Crystal to break up the family, to do what she did. She hadn't wanted to fall out of love with him, hadn't wanted to fall in love with Richard. He knew that. He'd always known it and never really blamed her. It had simply . . . happened.

*Because of my neglect.* Try as he might, he could never completely keep that feeling at bay.

He took Karen's arm and led her back to the table, seating her carefully as he wondered what had happened to break up Karen Andersen's marriage. Had her husband neglected her? Who had left whom, and why? It struck him just how badly he wanted to know, though it was certainly none of his business. He opened his mouth to change the subject to less personal and emotional matters.

"Do you still love Barry?" The words came from nowhere and everywhere within him. He clamped his jaw shut and stared at her, appalled at his own lack of tact.

"No." She smiled and took a sip from her scarcely touched glass of ginger ale. "You're thinking that's why I went to bed with him?"

Jed wasn't sure he liked the idea of being so easily read. He didn't reply. He knew he didn't have to.

"What happened had nothing to do with our still loving each other," she said, as if he had responded. "As I told you, it was a mistake, a grave error in judgment, and that's why I haven't yet told him about the baby."

"But you will?"

Her eyes widened in surprise. "Yes. Of course. I'll have to, won't I? I mean, he's her father. He has a right to know. But I don't need anything from him—not financially, not emotionally—so why should I risk damaging his chances of being happy with his new wife? I'll tell him later."

*How much later?* He didn't feel it was his place to ask and wondered why he wanted so badly to know. But damn it, he did. He wanted to understand what made Karen Andersen tick.

"And you were sure you could get through this entire weekend with no one guessing?"

She nodded as she stood, smoothing the robe down over her front. It came almost to her ankles. "Do I look pregnant now?"

He had to admit she did not. "But you won't be wearing a terrycloth robe to the wedding."

She smiled. "No, though I have something that I'm sure will be just as concealing. But now that I'm on my feet, I should be going." She extended a hand to him. "Thank you for the drink, Jed."

Belatedly, Jed unfolded himself from his chair. A lady was standing. What was he doing, still sitting on his rear end? He could almost feel his grandmother's cane prodding him in the rump. Then, as he shot to his feet, clearly startling Karen, he heard an echo of Crystal's derisive laughter. *We don't want men's seats on the bus. We want their seats on the board of directors.*

He took Karen's hand and held it while she shuffled her lightly tanned bare feet into her wet sandals and picked up her rolled clothing under one arm. "May I wear this home?" she asked, pulling free the hand he'd continued to hold, and brushing the backs of her fingers over the lapel of the robe. "I can have it washed and dried and ready to send back to you tomorrow if you need it to pack for the trip."

He looked at Karen's slender body enveloped in the robe, envisioning her naked within the folds of cloth, considered what would happen if her rickety little yellow four-by-four broke down on the road or if a cop pulled her over for a seatbelt check or if a trucker looked down at her at a stoplight just as the robe slid open or . . .

There were too many possibilities. He bristled like an old dog whose territory was being threatened, surprising himself again. "No," he said curtly, then realized he'd sounded like a jerk. "I mean, I'm sure Ceil could find you something more . . . comfortable."

Her eyes widened, filled with silent humor. "More comfortable than a bathrobe?"

"All right, fine, wear it if you like. Nothing of Ceil's would fit you any better than that does, anyway."

"Thank you." She turned to go.

Jed caught her elbow. "Wait. I'll follow you home to make sure you get there safely."

She looked startled. "That's kind of you, but not necessary. I live on Mercer Island."

"I'll still see you home."

"No, really! Mercer Island isn't exactly next door."

He continued to hold her gaze, wishing he knew her well enough to read her expressions. "It doesn't matter where you live, Karen. I'll follow you. I'll need to know your address anyway, won't I, so I can pick you up . . . when? Friday morning?"

She blinked as if her mind had wandered during those brief moments their gazes had met and locked. "Pick me up?"

"To travel to Montana."

"Oh! No. No, of course not." She laughed. "How stupid of me to forget to tell you. We'll meet at SeaTac. I have tickets. We'll fly to Helena, then I'll rent a car for the drive to Soda Creek." She smiled. "The wedding's not till two o'clock Saturday afternoon."

He stepped back and shot her a questioning stare. "Tickets? Plural? You were that sure of me?"

At once, her musical laughter rang out, echoing off the water of the pool before losing itself in the thick branches of the fir trees at the back. "Heavens, no! My friend Esther's brother was going to accompany me, but just a few days ago, he came down with, of all things, chicken pox! I still have his ticket, which you will use." She smiled as she skirted the now half-dried puddle, moving away from him. "Our flight leaves at eight-thirty Friday evening." She told him the flight number and airline.

He thought she sounded faintly wistful when she

asked, "Will you be there, Jed?" It was as if she were adding silently, *Really be there for me?* He was struck by the strength of his impulse, fortunately squelched, to swear to her that he would always be there for her, always look out for her, always fight her battles for her and . . . Lord almighty! He had to control these weird thoughts.

Besides, modern women didn't want their battles fought for them. They wanted sensitivity to their needs and issues and equal pay for their work. If that meant they had to give up a lot of useless courtesies, they were willing to make the trade to gain other advantages. He knew that. He might not like it, but Crystal had advised him long ago to get used to it, because it wasn't going to change.

He hesitated only a moment, then slid open the patio doors to let her into the sunken family room. "I'll be there," he said, raising his voice to be heard over the racket Ceil and Wes required while they studied. "Don't forget to say good night to Ceil on your way out."

She looked as if she didn't know whether to be miffed or amused by this reminder of basic good manners, but nodded, and he quickly shut the door, then raced to the cabana. He tugged on his pants over his damp swim trunks and shoved his bare feet into his shoes, not taking time to tie the laces. He was outside and in his car before she emerged and climbed into her yellow pickup. She didn't notice him, but he noticed her rubbing the small of her back as if it ached.

That made him feel strangely tender. He wanted to take her from that little truck of hers, lead her back into the house, and sit down with her on his lap while her rubbed her back. She was such a little bit of a thing. She'd fit perfectly on his lap. She made him feel . . . what? *Tender. Protective.* Yes.

Of course. That was it. She made him feel paternal, much the way Willi had when she was expecting Timmy.

Though he hadn't thought of holding Willi on his lap for probably ten years, it still came as a distinct relief to finally get a handle on his feelings toward Karen Andersen. Paternal and protective because she was alone and pregnant.

He followed her taillights all the way to her small bungalow near the Mercer Island town center. As he drove home, he wondered at his insistence on making a completely unnecessary trip at the end of a long, hard day. What the hell was it she brought out in him? The best? Or the worst?

His grandmother would have called it one, his ex-wife the other. But it didn't matter, he told himself as he unlocked the door to his house and turned off the light Ceil had left on for him. It didn't matter, because after the coming weekend, his and Karen Andersen's lives would never converge again.

Oddly, that made him more sad than happy.


Karen sensed Jed's presence before she looked up. Even at that, she wasn't prepared for the impact he had on her as he lounged in the doorway of her empty classroom. He filled up most of the space. Slowly, she stood and walked toward him. What in the world was he doing here at the college? It was only four-thirty. Their flight didn't leave for another four hours. "I thought we'd meet at the airport." Surely she'd told him that?

"The airport's closed," he said.

She stared at him. She had thought his eyes were hazel. Now, with the sun shining through the window, they were mostly green. "Closed? How can an airport close?"

"The baggage handlers are staging a wildcat strike. They've got pickets up that pilots and cabin crew and firefighters won't cross. Until the airport gets an injunction against them, nothing's moving. It might take as much as twenty-four hours, more if they can't get a judge because it's a weekend. I wanted to save you the trip down there."

Karen frowned, then nodded and managed to say thanks. The depth of her disappointment shocked her. She should be dancing with joy over the fact that she was off the hook as far as Barry's wedding went.

"Look at it this way," Jed said. "Now no one will think anything except that you couldn't make it because the airport was shut down. No feelings will be hurt, no noses out of joint, and you won't lose face. End of story."

Again, she nodded. He was right. So why was she standing there with her heart hanging down somewhere around her navel? "But what about you?" She jumped on that. "You need some place to go and—"

"No, no. That's okay."

"It's not okay. This trip was as much for you as it was for me, Ceil said," she added, as if that justified her arguing.

"You're worrying about me?"

"Of course I am," she said tartly, stiffening her spine. "Why not? You were concerned enough about me to come and tell me about the strike, and to follow me home the other night."

He laughed softly, indulgently, she thought, as if her worrying about him amused him as the antics of one of his children might. She wished he didn't have such a nice laugh, wished it didn't make her feel so good to hear it. He had a wonderful warm voice, too, that made her want to listen to it on and on. "That was different," he said.

"Different?" What a typically male thing to say! She tried to feel angry, tried to look angry. The man was patronizing her, for heaven's sake. She narrowed her eyes. "Different how?"

"I'm a man."

Well, that was certainly true. And a very masculine one at that—a bit domineering, a little stubborn. She had told him not to follow her home, but he'd done it anyway. Was that what Ceil had meant by courtly? Whatever. It had made her go to sleep smiling, feeling cherished.

Swiftly, she drew herself up. It was not Jed Cotts's place to cherish her.

"So you're a man. I still don't see how that changes anything."

Jed frowned. Couldn't she see for herself how different the situations were? She needed someone to worry about her. He, on the other hand, did not. "You're pregnant, for one thing."

She gave him a look that said clearly, *So?* and shrugged. "Well, thanks for taking the time to come and let me know. I'll call my folks and explain."

Something in her tone made him look at her sharply. "You didn't really *want* to go, did you?"

He saw her hesitate, then watched her chin come up an inch. "Yes," she said. "I guess I did. I don't want to disappoint anyone. My parents, in particular. I haven't seen them for—" She shrugged. "It doesn't matter."

But he could see that it did. He drew a deep breath and let it out in a loud gust. "You want to go. So we will," he said.

Her eyes widened in—what? Eagerness? Surprise?

"We will?" Then her face fell. "No. My truck will never make the pull through the mountains."

"No problem," he interrupted. "My car's right outside."

"I was about to say it's something like a twelve-hour trip."

He shrugged. "I've made longer ones. And I'm rarin' to go."

"Really?"

"Really." As he spoke, an unexpected, long unfamiliar sensation coursed through him, leaving him feeling triumphant and powerful and in charge. Decisive. Manly. He wanted to laugh aloud. He wondered if this was what the drum beaters felt like after they'd gone out to the woods together to reclaim their masculinity. By the Lord Harry, it felt good.

It made him want to thumb his nose at Crystal and her ultrafeminist ilk.

That thought reined him in fast. Karen was a woman, exactly like Crystal. What the hell must she think of him? He caught his breath, waiting for her disdain, her anger, braced for it. He'd earned it. He'd only come here to *suggest* that if Karen really wanted to go to the damned wedding, he'd be willing to drive her there. But the decision, of course, would be hers. That was the way a sensitive, modern man would handle things. He'd ask. He'd offer. He'd defer to her wishes because she was, after all, an adult, fully able to make her own decisions.

Maybe, he'd thought upon hearing the news about the strike, she'd see this as an easy way out of a difficult situation. Learning that she really wanted to go had pushed him momentarily off balance. Learning that she was worried about him and what the news had meant to him had all but blown him away.

"I have no more classes for the day," Karen said. Excitement flickered in her eyes. It turned her ivory cheeks pink, curved her wide mouth in a smile of pure delight. Her eyes held not a hint of the serenity gray eyes should. The smoke in their depths suggested a potential for fiery passion that challenged and emboldened him.

Or maybe it simply awoke something in him that had long been dormant. Whatever feelings she engendered, they were not paternal.

"Then let's go." He held out his hand.

She gazed at him for another moment, the color deepening in her cheeks, then took it.

"I should stop at home and pack some sandwiches and cookies and fruit and pick up a blanket and a pillow so whoever's not driving can get a bit of sleep." She snatched her hand free.

*What am I doing?* Karen asked herself, biting off the rest of her sentence. *What the hell is happening to me? Why am I organizing this trip like a Girl Scout leader determined to enter the forest despite the threat of bears? He's right. I don't have to go to the wedding. I don't have to keep up appearances now. I can stay home and sleep in my own bed, get sick in my own bathroom.*

"I'm way ahead of you," he said, draping an arm across her shoulders as he scooped up the suitcase sitting on a chair near her desk. "I have a pillow for you, as well as a blanket and a thermos of coffee. Food we can pick up along the way. Right?"

She looked up at him, aware of the weight of his arm across her shoulders. "Oh. You came here already planning to drive to Soda Creek?"

"I came prepared for any eventuality," he said, turning her through the doorway.

Karen nodded, feeling slightly detached, like a doll

without stuffing. "Oh," she said. Some small part of her thought she should assert herself, but in the end, she simply smiled back at Jedidiah Cotts and said again, "Oh."

Faintly, she heard hoofbeats, and out of the corner of her eye, was that a glint of shining armor?

She pushed the thought away. Pregnant women were often fanciful, she'd read. Maybe this, for her, replaced the spinach-with-chocolate-sauce thing.

She wondered which would be preferable, had she been offered a choice.

# THREE

"You know, when Ceil first mentioned this weekend to me, I refused to even consider it," Jed said two hours later as he deftly navigated the twists and grades of a mountain pass through the Cascades. "I told her that as a forty-five-year-old grandfather, I didn't do blind dates." He smiled. "I'm glad I changed my mind—not that this is a date, of course."

Karen half turned on the seat, staring at him. "You're a grandfather? But how? I mean . . . who? Not Cecelia, surely?" Ceil Cotts was one of the *youngest* nineteen year olds she knew.

"Good God, no!" Jed laughed as if he shared her views of Ceil's immaturity. "My oldest daughter, Willi— she's twenty-four—has a little boy." His broad grin told her how proud he was of his grandson. "Timmy's a great little kid. Really special to me."

"I can tell," she said, then added, "It never occurred to me that you could be a grandfather. You're *much* too good-look—I mean, you don't look like one."

"I don't?" Twisting the mirror down, he preened with exaggerated pleasure for a moment. "How should a grandfather look? Old and shriveled and stooped?"

Karen shook her head as she let her gaze travel slowly over his wide shoulders and the strong column of his neck rising from his shirt. She grinned. "Mine does."

He laughed. "I don't suppose he did when you were a one year old."

She laughed with him. "No, I guess not, but still . . ."

*Damn!* His half-mocking glance told her as clearly as words that he had caught the faint tinge of embarrassment in her tone. Why it should embarrass her for him to know she found him attractive, she didn't know. After all, he was a handsome, obviously virile man whom other women doubtless fell all over.

Cecelia had to be wrong in saying he didn't have a wide circle of friends. She'd bet he had far more women friends that his daughter ever surmised. She sighed. *She* was a woman.

Right. A *pregnant* woman who was probably having some kind of hormonal reaction, along with a bad case of wishful thinking.

Esther had explained about all that when Karen had asked, the day after she'd met Jed Cotts, how pregnancy had affected *her* libido. Following a night of erotic dreams starring Jed, she'd gone to work hollow-eyed and pale, prompting Esther to ask teasingly about her active evening.

Without thinking, Karen had blurted, "Don't I wish!" then been so embarrassed she'd wanted to teleport herself to the north pole.

Esther had said she'd spent much of her five pregnancies lying in wait for her husband, hoping to trip him and fall on his body before he reached the floor, and that her husband had loved every minute of it. Which was why, Esther insisted, she'd been pregnant so often and would likely be that way again before the year was out— maybe even twice.

Esther was given to exaggeration and flights of fancy, pregnant or not.

Karen knew no man in his right mind would be interested in a woman who carried a football in her abdomen—a football that in a couple of months would look like an overinflated beach ball. She could forget about men for the duration of her pregnancy and, once it was over, she'd probably go right back to having the libido of a stuffed toy, as she'd had for the last five years of her marriage.

She sighed and turned her gaze out the side window at the passing scenery. Waterfalls and rock faces were less dangerous to look at than Jed Cotts's rough-hewn profile. They wouldn't upset her equilibrium.

"You must have been young when your first child was born," she said.

"Yeah. Brother, was I young! Twenty-one going on twelve when we had Willi. I still hadn't learned a lot about parenting by the time we had Ceil five years later. Hell, when my first two kids were little, the word parenting didn't even exist. The bottom line was I was too immature to be a good father and too dumb to know it."

"How old was your wife?"

"Twenty-one, as well. We were both twenty when we married. But she knew what she was doing. She knew how to think right. Crystal was—is—one very smart lady. She always had all the answers before I even knew there were questions. She's a research psychologist."

Karen said nothing, just looked at him encouragingly. He'd said his first two kids, suggesting he had more. Before she could ask, he went on.

"There's a lot to be said about being a youthful parent, I guess." He smiled. "Believe me, as much as I love Tim and enjoy having him around, I'm sure glad when Willi and Kevin take him home. He's an exhausting little guy." His rich chuckle rose between them, his mood clearly lightening. "People should have their kids when they're young, even if they are young and stupid. When you're over forty, you tire easier."

His words sent Karen's mood plummeting. "Plenty of women have babies at my age," she said crossly.

At once, contrition creased his brow. "Oh, hell, I'm sorry," he said. "I didn't mean it like that." Clearly embarrassed, he gave her a weak smile. "And you're nowhere near forty."

"I'm thirty-eight."

A flattering degree of surprise dropped his jaw. "You are? Right at first, I figured you for about Ceil's age, then upgraded that to thirty-five for a few minutes. But I lowered the estimate again after you fell in the pool."

She shrugged. "You don't need to apologize. I know what I see in the mirror, and I'm not twenty."

Music from the CD player filled her meditative silence.

Until Jed had mentioned his grandson, and subsequently the raising of his children, she'd been savoring her time with him, enjoying the prospect of many more hours of the good companionship and pleasant conversation they'd enjoyed during the first stage of the trip. Now, watching snow-capped mountains, deep river gorges, and splashing waterfalls, she sighed quietly, replaying his words in her mind, wishing they hadn't made her feel so blue. Lord, she hated these mood swings!

It was odd how one short sentence could send her from deep melancholy to high elation and another send her back again. As a result of his comment, everything looked bleak to her. Even the sparkling mountain air had taken on a darker tone.

In another two years, she'd be forty herself. Was she going to find child rearing exhausting? Was she going to wish she had someone to send the child home with, especially since she was going to be doing all the rearing alone? No, damn it! She wanted this baby! She'd wanted a baby for a long time. She loved little children, their eagerness to learn, their active, inquiring minds soaking up everything she offered, like dry sponges requiring water.

She was also a member of the Big Sisters organization and spent several hours a week with Penny, an eight year old who'd tire out even the strongest adult. Yes, she did get tired, but she bounced back. She'd do the same in raising her own child.

"Hey, are you okay?" Jed's voice startled her. She'd felt completely alone with the road, the mountains, and her thoughts. "You've been quiet a long time. Are you tired, or are you sulking? I did apologize, if you remember."

She snapped, "I'm not tired and I never sulk! I wasn't aware you expected me to chatter constantly."

His eyes darkened as if he might take offense. Then, after a couple of deep, even breaths, he smiled coolly. "No. You're not expected to do anything you don't feel like doing. But you are getting tired, aren't you? I know pregnant ladies can't sit in one position too long."

*Pregnant ladies of a certain age?* she wanted to ask, but refrained. She stiffened her spine and squared her jaw. She was tired, but not because she was thirty-eight years old and pregnant, and she wasn't going to be worn out by raising her child. She was going to love it, enjoy every moment of her time with it, grow with it, learn with it, let it keep her young and active and happy. Heavens, lots of women her age had babies, and all the tests showed everything was fine, the baby healthy, the pregnancy progressing perfectly.

Damn it, she was strong and she'd survive.

Stretching her arms out before her, fingers linked inside out, she arched her spine and repeated her words a trifle more pleasantly. "I'm not tired in the least. But you must be. You've been behind that wheel for hours. I'll drive for a while."

The look he fixed on her might have been funny under other circumstances. "What?" He was aghast. "You're not going to drive!"

Her brows drew together. "Why not? As you suggested, I could use a change of position."

Suddenly, he was all sympathetic solicitude, his sweeping glance lingering for a moment on her slightly protruding tummy. With him, she made no attempt to hide it by adapting her posture.

"Would you like me to pull over so you can stretch your legs for a few minutes?" he asked.

"No." Oh, for the love of heaven, she sounded like a petulant ten year old! Too bad. She felt like an insulted woman. "I just want to drive."

"No." His tone was as flat as hers had been. Something had happened to his jawline. It jutted stubbornly and a hard knot had formed just forward of and below his ear.

She recognized rising testosterone levels when she saw them. He wasn't going to get away with it. "Why the hell not?"

He managed a taut smile. "It would be too hard on you. You're tired."

"I just told you I'm not!"

He cocked an eyebrow at her. "Then why are you so crabby?"

His unfailing but fake pleasantness further infuriated

her. "I'm not crabby! I just want to drive the damned car!"

He gripped the wheel as if she might wrest it from him. Indignation rose in his face, flared in his eyes, rang in his voice. "You're *not* driving the damned car, Karen! It's my car, and you're pregnant. I'm in charge here!"

She planted her fists on her hips. "Don't you bellow at me, Jedidiah Cotts!"

"I'll bellow at you if you need to be bellowed at, you stubborn, argumentative, bad-tempered . . . *woman.*"

The last word was an out-and-out insult.

Fine. She'd show him stubborn. Flouncing around, she turned and stared out the side window, pretending he wasn't even there. He spoke, said something polite. She ignored him. Minutes passed. He spoke again. Once more, she said nothing. He turned up the volume on the music and hummed along with the Eagles. He seemed to like golden oldies. Damn it, so did she. But that didn't mean she liked *him.*

She couldn't stand it. Twisting around, she glared at him. "Give me one good reason why you're behind that wheel and I'm sitting over here, stewing," she demanded.

"Oh, are you stewing?" He grinned mockingly. "Sorry. I thought you were resting. I knew you weren't sulking. You never do that."

Karen glowered. "One reason, Cotts."

"This is my car?"

She blew out an angry breath in a sound approaching a raspberry as she flopped back against the seat. *Damn him.* How could she argue with such an out and out fact?

He ignored her irritation and flashed her a quick smile. "We'll stop for dinner in about half an hour," he said, taking on that decisive manner again, the one that had gotten her into his car in the first place. "But before we eat, we'll have a brisk fifteen-minute walk."

He reached behind him with one long arm and snared a pillow off the backseat. "Shove that into the small of your back," he said, handing it to her. "Rest until we get there."

Karen scowled for a moment as she contemplated telling *him* where to shove his damned pillow, then astounded herself by complying. Damn it, but it felt good there. How had he known precisely what would help? Dumb question. He knew because, with a wife and a daughter who'd both had children, he'd had plenty of experience when it came to pregnant women. He'd brought the lousy cushion along especially for her because she was pregnant.

She leaned back and closed her eyes in order not to keep gazing at his profile. What was the matter with her, acting like a submissive ninny? She really did want to get behind the wheel and drive like a bat out of hell, trying to leave behind all the crazy emotions he had set churning within her.

What in the world was she doing there with him—a man she didn't know, a man she shouldn't even want to know? A man who, somehow, in a way she couldn't comprehend, had simply appeared at the college and whisked her away. Once more, she heard hoofbeats. This time an image formed behind her closed lids of a tall black steed with a flowing mane. Jed held the reins, instead of the wheel of a burgundy Buick with dark red leather seats.

He was no knight, damn it. He was an ordinary man— a grandfather, for heaven's sake. He'd also taken great pains to make sure she knew his status, his preferred lifestyle.

He was through raising children. He hadn't even *liked*

raising them. He was glad when his grandson went home. Arggh! Why were her thoughts arrowing down that particular alley? Why was she so frustrated? Had she been harboring some wild and futile hope that maybe, in spite of her pregnancy, the attraction so evident between them in the very first moments of their meeting might go farther?

No. Of course not.

Her tummy rumbled.

She was hungry, that was all. That dinner he'd promised would put her right back in form. Then she'd perk up, take the wheel, and show him she was made of better stuff than he thought—that, man or not, grandfather or not, he didn't know all there was to know about pregnant women and he didn't get to make all the decisions all the time.

He also didn't know damn-all about Karen Andersen. She was a strong, mature woman, every bit his equal in every way. It was high time he realized it.


As they walked outside into a crisp, high-country night following a delicious dinner in a roadside restaurant, Karen held out a hand for the keys. "My turn to drive," she said briskly, in a tone that left no room for debate.

Jed clenched the keys in his fist. "Absolutely not."

He opened the passenger door and seated her quickly, then shut the door just as quickly. For a moment he'd felt caught by an invisible hand pressing on his shoulder, urging him to bend down and place his mouth over the indignant parting of her lips.

He bit off a curse and snatched open the door, bent down, and did what he'd wanted to do almost from the first moment he'd seen her. He took her face between his hands, cradled it tenderly, and pressed his mouth to hers.

It was incredible.

His lips threatened to harden in response to her softness. With vast effort he kept his mouth gentle.

Her scent flooded him, and the sound of her swift breath nearly tipped him over the edge of rationality. By a powerful force of will, he released her, looked into her stunned eyes for another moment, then closed the door softly but firmly, making sure it was secure.

He walked around the front of the car, placing one foot before the other with great care, wondering at the need to concentrate, confused by the sensation that he could, if he took the slightest misstep, tumble into an abyss right there on the flat pavement. He watched his hand open the driver's door. He bent his knees, flexed at the waist, slid behind the wheel and shut the door, extinguishing the dome light.

He put the key in the ignition, then sat gripping it between finger and thumb, the metal warm from being in his pocket against his thigh.

He pulled in a deep breath and let it out in a long, silent whoosh, trying to release his tension. When he thought he could do it, he spoke, staring out the windshield. "I'm sorry. I had no right to do that."

"It's all right." He saw out of the corner of his eye that she was facing him, studying him. He couldn't meet her gaze, not even when she said lightly, "I've been wondering what it would be like, too."

He looked fully at her then. Those big, deep eyes of hers, wide-set and steady, were fixed on his face. "And?" he said.

She blinked. "And what?"

"How . . . how was it?" Hell, he felt like a total yutz!

*Was it good for you, too, honey?* The stereotypical inse-
cure male. He hadn't felt this way for at least twenty-five
years, which should tell him he'd be better off not steal-
ing kisses like a greedy teenager. It was too long since
he'd been one. He'd forgotten all the rules.

"You kiss very . . . politely," she said presently, having taken her time, clearly needing several moments to
assess his performance.

"Politely?" Hurt stabbed him. Not sweetly? Not tenderly? Not charmingly? And did she sound just a bit disappointed? Of course not. What the hell did he think?
That she'd have liked an *impolite* kiss? Hell, if he hadn't
held back, she'd have clocked him and he'd have deserved it.

"Yes," she said. "Very politely. But if you think for a
minute that a little kiss is going to confuse me and turn
me all wishy-washy, think again. I still demand my turn
behind the wheel."

She was going to debate the issue of driving, not kissing? Well, hell, why not? Maybe she was right. Maybe
it had been a polite kiss. A little kiss. Maybe it hadn't
stirred up a damned thing in her.

"Demand away," he said, settling himself comfortably
behind the wheel.

"I hope you don't intend to be stubborn about this all
night long, Jed, because I can be pretty stubborn, too.
But I feel too good and relaxed to fight about it at the
moment. Just bear in mind that I have a child to raise
and have no intention of doing it from a wheelchair just
because some macho male can't admit he's too sleepy to
drive safely."

Before he could come up with a suitable reply, she
shoved the pillow between her head and the window,
snuggled into the blanket and went to sleep. He couldn't

believe how fast she'd dropped off. He'd have thought she was faking it in order to avoid an argument she sensibly knew she couldn't win, except for the faint snores emanating from her. Would any woman ever *fake* snoring? He doubted it. Crystal had been more than insulted when he'd mentioned liking the sound of her soft little snores.

He glanced at Karen. He doubted she was the kind of woman who'd ever fake anything, including an almost hidden response to a polite *little* kiss.

Grimly, he drove on into the night. The next time he kissed her, she was going to know, without having to pause and consider it, how to accurately describe a kiss from Jed Cotts. The next time he kissed her, she wasn't going to call it polite, nor would the word little occur to her. The next time she'd know exactly how she made him feel, and she'd feel something damned similar or his name wasn't Jedidiah Cotts.

The way she made him feel? He released a breath he hadn't been aware of holding. How did she make him feel?

Desperately, he tried to sort through different emotions. Most of them had no names, but some he could pinpoint, and they made him ashamed.

For a moment, he'd felt wild when she argued with him over the issue of taking the wheel. Angry. He'd yelled at her, and she'd yelled back. To his shock, he'd liked that, enjoyed it. It had stirred up not only his blood, but an almost barbaric need to conquer her, to make her admit he was right and she was wrong and he had a mandate to look after her. He'd wanted to do something to make her admit he was bigger, stronger, smarter . . . a man. He'd wanted her to admit she wanted him as badly as he wanted her.

Hey! Hold it! He *didn't* want her. He was suffering some kind of brainstorm. Too much coffee and a couple of disturbed nights—thanks to Karen Andersen—were affecting his normally clear and logical judgment.

He made a serious attempt to channel his thoughts into different tracks, to keep his attention on the road and not let his gaze stray to the dim shape of the woman sleeping quietly at his side. Only—she was there. His head knew she was there. His body knew she was there. His mouth could still taste that one small kiss he'd stolen, feel the surprised parting of her lips, the response she hadn't masked quite quickly enough.

"Polite," he muttered. "Someday, lady, I'll show you *polite.*" Someday he'd show her passion. Someday he'd show her need. His need. Her need. The heat they could generate together. Lava running through his veins, through hers, merging in an explosion that would burn them like a volcano erupting.

Lord help him, it would be good. *Different.* Never before had he thought he'd want to make love to a woman who was not as self-possessed and controlled as he was. To make love to a woman who might like him to lose his restraint. Just once . . .

He hauled himself up short. Those were dangerous thoughts, stupid thoughts. Adults didn't make love because it was different or novel or an impulse they couldn't control. Adults made love to express love, and he was certainly not in love with Karen Andersen. Further, he had no intention of seeing her again after this weekend, so any sexual urges he might feel would have to be curbed. Besides, she was pregnant.

All the rationality in the world couldn't change one basic fact, though. Raw, aching desire pulsed inside him. The urge to pull the car over, to drag her against him and teach her unequivocally that he was a *man* and far from polite, ground into his gut. He forced the feeling down. It was crazy. Completely out of character.

He knew full well how women hated being dominated, resisted being overpowered. They found unrefined passion at worst threatening; at best childish and boring, a complete turnoff. A mature woman needed to be brought along slowly, tempted, gentled into accepting what he wanted, seduced in to wanting the same things. Women weren't animals. They didn't . . . rut.

He had learned early in his relationship with Crystal that he had to curb his own animalistic tendencies. Their lovemaking had been sweet and spiritual and beautiful, superbly controlled, and never, after he'd realized how it turned her off, wild, stormy, impetuous or . . .

*Passionate?* The word came to his mind as a stab of pain shot through his chest.

*Passionate.* The way he sensed lovemaking would be with a woman like Karen Andersen.

Guilt filled his throat like bile. What the hell was he doing, making comparisons? There was nothing wrong with self-control. His sex life with Crystal had been wonderful. How often had he lain suffused with joy, watching her serene blue eyes close in quivering ecstasy, listening to her contented purrs? Once he'd learned the joy of loving the way Crystal liked it, he hadn't often longed for the wild, mad passion of his youth. He had been content. He and Crystal had been perfect mates. Nothing had been missing. *Nothing!*

So why weren't they still together?

He glanced at Karen again as if she might hold the answer. A faint smile curved her mouth.

A smile, he thought as he drove on, that needed his kiss to cover it.

* * *

Karen woke with the cessation of motion, momentarily confused and disoriented, but the caress of warm fingers against her cheek soothed her. She turned into the cupped palm, knowing at once without knowing exactly how that it was Jed who touched her, Jed who spoke her name. She recognized the scent of his skin. It reminded her of the terrycloth bathrobe she'd worn home and, with a reluctance that disturbed her, laundered before packing it in her suitcase to return to him.

She opened her eyes to bright lights that hurt, making her squeeze her lids shut. "Where are we?"

"A truck stop. Want some orange juice?"

Her second attempt at getting her eyes open was more successful. She thirstily gulped the juice. It was icy, full of pulp, and, like a magic elixir, put strength back into sleep-loosened muscles. She sat up and shoved her messy hair from her face. Jed looked pale and weary in the harsh glare of sodium vapor lights. "Why did we stop? Are you tired?"

He smiled. "Of course not. Remember? I'm a macho male. We don't get tired."

Something compelled her to touch his bristly cheek with the tips of two fingers as she returned his smile. "I remember." There was an odd kind of intimacy in their hushed conversation, as if both were afraid to waken a world that might intrude on their cocoon of privacy.

"I remembered, too, as I was driving along fighting to stay awake, your saying you didn't want to raise your child from a wheelchair." He took a container of coffee from the dash, where it had made a ghost of steam on the windshield. His grin was crooked. "It was a low, sneaky thing to do, Ms. Andersen, planting such graphic images in my brain. Still, it made me think."

"Made you think maybe I should drive for a while?"

She could see he didn't like it, but he nodded. "Yeah. Two hours, Karen. No more." His steady gaze permitted no argument. Then he grinned. "I figure that's about how much gas we have left. When you stop to fill up, I take over again. Deal?"

Karen snorted, a sound that was half disgust, half laughing acceptance. "Deal." She slipped out of the car and headed for the rest room.

A quick brushing of her teeth—why did the combination of toothpaste and orange juice taste so terrible?—a few splashes of cold water, and a brisk rub over her face with industrial-grade paper towels finished waking her. She emerged to find Jed waiting. He escorted her back to the car as if she were carrying a sack of diamonds and the truck drivers wandering between their rigs and the restaurant were gun-toting desperadoes.

Again, his shepherding made her feel cherished, and put a taut, achy sensation in her throat. She'd never wanted to be cosseted. Never! So why now?

"Jed," Karen said, twenty minutes after she'd taken the wheel, ten minutes after he'd finally stopped issuing instructions and advice and out-and-out orders, "that has to be the phoniest snoring I've ever heard. You're going to hurt your throat."

He rolled his head toward her, the alertness of his eyes confirming at a glance her estimate of the true depth of his sleep. *"You* snored."

She jerked her eyes off the road and stared at him in disbelief. "I did not!"

He grinned. "Did too. Soft, whispery little sounds, more a purr than a real snore, but once in awhile you'd cut loose with a loud one and almost wake yourself up. I enjoyed watching you."

She glared. "So happy to have entertained you. Now sleep. And quit faking it. The clock on those two hours starts counting from the time you actually go to sleep."

As an answer, he flung the pillow into the back seat with the blanket he'd disdained earlier, poured himself a cup of coffee from the thermos and shook his head. "I tried to," he said. "I really did, but I can't."

"Don't trust me with your car?"

"I don't sleep in planes, either."

"Now that," she said, "was a nonanswer if I've ever heard one."

His eyes gleamed in the faint dashboard lights. "But tactful, wouldn't you say?"

"Oh, very. Why didn't you enjoy raising your family?"

He laughed. "What is this? I be tactful, you be blunt?"

"Sorry, but what you said earlier got me thinking. What if I *am* too old? I'll be around sixty when my child graduates from college. *Sixty!* I haven't even thought much about forty until the last few months."

"Forty's not fatal."

She gave him a dirty look. "I know that. I also know if I'm to prepare myself properly as a parent, I have to start picking brains. What was it about having kids that you didn't enjoy?"

"I didn't say that."

"But you implied it."

"Did I?" He went silent for a few seconds. "While I was doing it, I thought I was having a fine time. It's only in retrospect that I see how differently I should have done things—spent more time with them, given them more of . . . myself. And not just the girls. Crystal, too."

Karen discovered a strong aversion to discussing Crystal. "What was it like when your girls were babies?"

"Different with each one." He leaned back in the seat, stretching his legs out as far as they'd go—which was nowhere near their full length, with her needing the seat so close to the dash. "From the time Willi was a month old until she was nearly three, I took her to work with me every day."

Karen flicked a glance at him. "You did? Were you self-employed?"

"Nope. Days, I was a meter reader for the gas company. She rode along in her car bed and I took diaper and bottle breaks whenever required." She heard a smile in his voice. "It was a lot of fun."

"What—what was your wife doing while you did that?"

"Earning her doctorate in psychology."

"At twenty-one?"

"I told you she's a very smart lady. A genius, really. Finished high school when she was fifteen, and a few college courses, as well, just to keep her edges honed." He was silent for a few moments, then said, "I sometimes think she only married me because she wanted to do one normal thing in her life, and getting pregnant at twenty seemed like a good move to her."

Karen read something in his tone that prompted her to say, "But not to you."

He shrugged. "I had my heart set on a career in medicine, but it probably wouldn't have been right for me." Then, in a manner that told her he'd talked all he intended to about himself, he asked, "What about you? You must have a few secret dreams. Everyone does."

"I wanted to be on the national figure-skating team."

He turned toward her, folding his left leg and draping an arm over the seat. "What happened?"

Ordinarily, she cited the broken leg she'd suffered at the age of thirteen. Not this time, though. Something compelled her to give Jed the truth. "I simply wasn't good enough. Or dedicated enough. I guess I lacked the necessary drive."

"I understand it takes a lot of both, and a willingness to give up a normal life. I don't blame you for quitting. Do you still skate?"

"Recreationally. It's still one of my favorite activities. I like roller-blading as well, though, and I'm enjoying teaching my Little Sister."

"You have a sister?"

"I belong to the Big Sisters organization. My Little Sister, Penny, is an eight-year-old who's proving to be more adventuresome than I would have believed possible six months ago."

He flicked at the hair curling on her nape, and his smile caused a seismic disturbance in her heart. "I can tell you love her. What else do you enjoy?"

Karen rolled her shoulders to loosen them. Jed rubbed the tops of them with his fingers and thumb. "Books," she said, her voice thick, rusty-sounding. She cleared her throat.

"What books?"

She tried hard to pretend the massage was nothing more than an attempt to make driving easier for her. The trouble was, it was driving her toward the edge of self-control. With difficulty, she concentrated on the conversation, listing titles in literature, popular fiction, and biographies. To her delight, they had several special favorites in common.

When the gas gauge started reading dangerously low—almost exactly two hours after she'd taken the wheel—she pulled into a station and slipped out from behind the wheel, leaving him to deal with the self-serve hose. After returning from the rest room, she snuggled down, turned half away from him, and closed her eyes.

Jed sighed. He'd wanted her to talk. He liked her voice. When she slept, he missed its warmth. Or was it merely the illusion of warmth he missed?

One thing he did know was that he was glad he was with her—and not *just* because he'd needed a reason to get out of his own home while his ex-wife and her new husband were spending the weekend with Ceil to celebrate her engagement. Was it vain or stupid of him not to want Crystal and Richard to think he was so lame he couldn't get a date, didn't have any friends with whom he wanted to spend a weekend or who wanted to spend one with him? Thanks to Karen Andersen having needed an escort, he wouldn't have to meet the question head-on.

There was a lot to be said for denial . . .

# FOUR

Awakened by dawn poking over the dashboard and slicing across her face, Karen yawned and sat erect, blinking and rubbing her eyes as she licked her teeth with distaste. Blearily, she searched the prairie for some familiar landmark to tell her where they were, but gave up. One stretch of alfalfa almost ready to be cut, one sagging barbed wire fence, one scrubby little poplar grove looked pretty much the same as another. "Where are we?" she asked.

"Somewhere on Highway Twelve. I'll stop at the next place and get you some coffee," Jed offered.

"Are you okay? Would you like me to take the wheel?" she asked. "I wish you'd been able to sleep while I drove."

"I'm fine," he said. "It won't be long until we're there. There'll be plenty of time to get booked into a motel and grab a few hours' sleep before the wedding. Do you have reservations anywhere?"

Karen laughed. "Of course not. We'll be staying with my parents. The farm is just the other side of Soda Creek."

Jed stiffened. Stay with her parents? Not likely! She was pregnant. He was with her. There was a distinct possibility her father might shoot first and ask questions over his corpse. He knew that's how he'd feel if he thought someone had knocked up one of his daughters.

"That's fine for you," he said, "but I'll stay somewhere else. Your parents won't want an outsider intruding on what will essentially be a family reunion. Didn't you say you hadn't seen them for over a year?"

"Yes, but they'll want you to stay, and it won't be an intrusion. Honestly. They have the big farmhouse where my grandparents raised seven kids, and where my parents raised me and a whole series of foster children, not to mention entertaining all the aunts and uncles and cousins and friends who bunked with us whenever the mood struck. There's plenty of room, and you probably won't find a motel vacancy, not with a wedding in the community."

Jed was about to argue further when she swept on as if it were all settled. "Really, my parents are expecting you. They'll welcome you. When I phoned last night at dinnertime, I told Mom to expect us early this morning. She said she'd have breakfast ready within ten minutes of our arrival. The homemade sausages are probably simmering on the back of the stove now; she'll brown them while she cooks the potatoes and eggs. Mom is a fantastic cook. Wait till you taste her bread."

A big farmhouse breakfast sounded damned good, but Jed's focus was more on what Karen's father would say the minute he learned of her pregnancy. It was enough to curl his guts like a tangle of spaghetti. Once for that kind of horror was enough for any man to live through. Sure, he'd loved Crystal, but that metaphorical shotgun aimed at him had made his back burn until he'd done the right thing by her.

Karen's belief she could fool all her friends and relatives for the entire weekend likely meant she had a big surprise in store. If Crystal's mother was anything to go by, a woman could tell something like thirty minutes after conception that her daughter was pregnant. Even if her father didn't point a shotgun at Jed, if he took the time to listen, there'd still be the kind of fan-hitting crap that should be kept private.

"I, for one, don't want to be anywhere near your house if the truth comes out."

Her stare stabbed into him. "What does that mean?"

"Exactly what I said." He shot her a sideways glance. "I always hated it if one of my kids screwed up when there were witnesses around. And your father is going to see an unwed pregnancy, even though you're thirty-eight years old, as a major screwup on the part of his only daughter."

"Maybe you consider it a major screwup, but my dad is not like you."

"Don't bet the farm. He's male."

"He's my dad! I think I can predict his reactions better than you can."

"I doubt it." He flicked another quick glance at her and grinned. Her gray eyes had flared into animation. A tingling sensation began somewhere deep inside him, and he welcomed it. It helped him stay wide awake. "Anyway, I can certainly afford a motel room. I don't have to freeload on your family."

"Damn it, Jed, will you quit being so stiff-necked and . . . male?"

"But, Karen, I am male. And I am going to a motel after I drop you at your parents' house."

Angrily, she smacked the seat between them. Her cheeks turned pink. "Do you have to have everything your own way all the time? I gave in on the issue of your doing most of the driving. We managed a compromise on who was going to buy the gas. Once." Her fists clenched on her lap as she faced him; he could see she was trying hard not to let her temper get the better of her. "I dragged you here for my purposes. The least you can do is see it my way on the matter of accommodations!"

"But your way is the wrong way," he said evenly, his gaze resting momentarily on her rapidly rising and falling breasts. "Don't waste your breath arguing with me, Karen. I'm right, you're wrong, and that's that."

Her hands flew out in a wild gesture of fury. "Can it, Cotts!" Her eyes blazed and her face colored alluringly. "I hate it when you get that smug, superior look on your face!"

"I can't help that," he said, fascinated by the little shafts of green in the stormy gray of her eyes. He'd never seen those before. They were beautiful. "I don't necessarily see myself as superior, just *right.*"

"You are not right!" She slapped the seat between them again and he jumped. "You are *wrong!* You have never been more wrong in your life and—"

The rest of her words were lost in the loud, prolonged blare of an airhorn as an eighteen-wheeler bore down on them. With a curse, Jed wrenched the car back into his own lane. The semi careered by in a blur of sound and color. Jed felt the car lurch once as it left the road. It bucked hard as he fought the wheel. A sound from far away might have been a scream of terror from Karen. He saw tall plants at a strange angle, a fence post streaking past, and then . . . nothing.

His chest ached when he breathed, his left ear felt as if it were on fire, and his chin hurt. He tried to lift a hand, but it was too heavy. Then Karen was there, her face pale, her eyes huge, her mouth trembling, her dark hair haloed by the hospital lights.

"Jed? Oh, dear Lord, Jed you look terrible! I'm sorry! I'm so sorry. It was all my fault."

He tried to prop himself up on an elbow and fell back, staring at her. *"You're* sorry? Why? I piled the car up." His mouth felt full of cotton. "Water?"

With one hand behind his head, she gave him a tiny sip of water through a bent straw, then snatched the cup away before he was done. "I distracted you by losing my temper."

He managed to get one hand up to shove her hair back from her face, feeling it silky under his palm, warm. He'd never felt such warm hair before. It was as if she'd been sitting in sunlight—or maybe as if the sun was right there inside her, shining out from within, giving her hair those deep red glints.

"Not your fault," he said again as she sat back down, putting herself out of his reach. "Mine. Looking at your breasts."

Her eyes widened. "What?"

"Pretty . . . breasts. Pretty eyes. I like your temper, like you . . . mad."

Rearing back in her chair, she glared. "Well, of all the despicable things to say, Jed Cotts, that takes the—do you know how sexist that is? How completely it shows you for what you are? A hard-bitten, dyed-in-the-wool, sexist—"

"Repeating . . . self." Those green rays shot through the stormy gray of her eyes again. So it hadn't been a fluke after all. He smiled, closed his eyes, and listened to her rapid, angry breathing.

Karen stared at Jed, astounded and madly irritated to realize that he'd fallen asleep in midargument.

She stood as a nurse came through the yellow curtains surrounding the bed, lowered the rail, and checked Jed's vital signs. He didn't so much as stir. Karen felt dizzy. Maybe he hadn't fallen asleep. Maybe he'd fallen unconscious. What if he was even now slipping deeper and deeper into a coma? What was she going to tell his daughter? How would she be able to explain?

"You okay?" the nurse asked her. Karen nodded, not taking her gaze off Jed's face.

"Is he going to be all right?" Her voice wobbled.

"Sure." The nurse smiled and stepped back, gesturing for Karen to resume her seat. "He'll do. The doctor said he has a very mild concussion, but the worst of his problems is a lack of sleep. Let him get it and he'll be just great in a few hours. Then you can take him home. Doctor's already signed the release. She has a wedding to go to. Are you here for the wedding, too?"

"The wedding. Yes."

The nurse swept Karen with a professional glance. "You don't look up to any kind of celebrating, girl. Why don't you go get some rest yourself and come back for this fella here in three or four hours? I understand you're a local girl. Let me call your family to come for you. Your car's a write-off."

The nurse was about the fifth person to ask if Karen wanted to call her family. Most of those were old friends or, at the very least, acquaintances. When she'd refused to have her parents called, they'd understood her desire to stay with Jed. When she was sure he was all right, she'd call her folks herself, but she wasn't about to leave him to strangers when she was the one who'd gotten him into this mess in the first place. It wouldn't be fair.

"No. I'll stay here." The nurse continued to look doubtful, but left her there.

Karen was dozing, her head tilted over onto the edge of Jed's bed, when she was jolted awake by an excited squeal.

"Karen! Karen Andersen!" A blue-uniformed blonde rushed in, speaking excitedly but softly, in deference to the sleeping patient. "I can't believe it's really you, and with a brand new husband, too!"

Karen snatched her hand out of the grip Jed had kept on it even while he slept. "Cissy." She jumped to her feet and, to her horror, burst into tears.

"There, there, it's all right. One of the other nurses just called your mom and dad and they're on the way."

"Oh, no!" Karen moaned. "I wanted to call them myself when I knew Jed was okay."

The nurse patted her back. "We all understand your desire to protect your parents, but they're tough. They'd want to be with you. Lucie did the right thing. She said you looked ready to collapse. Don't cry, sweetie."

"It's just because she's pregnant," Jed said, and Karen tore herself loose from her old schoolmate to glare at him.

"Jed! Damn it, that's supposed to be a secret!" she wailed.

"A little late for secrets, I'd say," Cissy laughed. "Especially after the fuss this guy put up about you being looked after before him because you were pregnant. The rest of the hospital will have heard within the next thirty minutes. But Lucie didn't say a word about it to your folks, just that you'd been in an accident and were un-injured, but needed to go home and rest. How come your mom and dad don't know about this?" She patted Karen's belly.

"I—" Karen broke off, having no real explanation. Instinctively, she turned to Jed.

"They don't know about me, either," he said. "We'd planned a double surprise."

Cissy laughed. "I guess you're going to succeed."

Karen grabbed a fistful of tissues from the box on the bedside table. It was high time she got a grip on her wild emotions. She wiped her eyes and blew her nose before saying, "Cissy, Jed's not—"

She broke off as the curtains swished aside and her mother rushed in to sweep Karen into her arms. "Darling, are you all right? We came as fast as we could."

Again Karen burst into tears, burrowing against her mother's familiar shoulder, weeping as if she would never stop, but May Andersen didn't intend to listen to a bunch of blubbering for the rest of the morning, or so she said sternly. Karen stepped back, sniffing, fighting for control. Her mother continued to hold her shoulders, searching her face, her eyes traveling slowly over her body as if needing reassurance that Karen had suffered no injuries. They narrowed slightly as they focused on the limp, rumpled fabric of her blouse where it clung to her belly, and then widened in shock.

"My God! What's this? You're *expecting?*" Her hollow, disbelieving tone held outrage. "And you didn't tell me?"

She glared at Karen, glared at Jed, and then looked over her shoulder at her husband, who stood at the edge of the curtained emergency room cubicle, his gray-and-white denim work hat twisted between his hands, his face a mask of disbelief mingled with joy and not a little shock.

But it was neither her father nor mother Karen was concerned with just then. She stared in horror at the man beside her father, the man who now strode forward, white lab coat flapping around his knees, his eyes stunned, his face ashen, his blond hair standing on end as if he'd just rammed a hand through it. She knew he had; he always did that when he was upset. Right now he looked as if someone had walloped him in the solar plexus with a baseball bat.

"Barry," she breathed. "What in the world are you doing at the hospital on your wedding day?"

Barry whipped her around, out of her mother's grasp. His eyes blazed as he raked them over her before he shoved her down into the chair. He crouched before her, holding her hands. "Karen. Is this true? It's all over the hospital that you're here with a man and—" He broke off, shaking his head. "Pregnant?" Despite his question, she could see that he knew, that there'd be no use in denying it. She nodded, then gulped, fighting down the strong desire to throw up.

"Barry, back off a bit, dear. Can't you see she's—"

Gently, he thrust her mother aside. "May, let me talk to her. This is important."

His eyes bored into Karen's. "How far along?" he demanded.

From somewhere, she managed to call up a smile, one she hoped was jaunty and devil-may-care. "Not far, Barry. As you can see, I'm hardly showing. Quite a surprise, isn't it?"

"Surprise? That's not the term I'd use! Who the hell is this guy and what is he doing here with you?"

She laughed again. "He's attending your wedding with me. The invitation said *and escort*." She swung her head to the right. "Mom, Dad, Barry, I'd like you to meet Jedidiah Cotts."

Karen's parents exchanged a look, then both nodded at him. Jed stuck out a hand and shook Barry's, extremely briefly. "Doctor—" He pushed himself up with his elbows and read Barry's name tag. "Dr. Renton. Nice to meet you." His tone and facial expression belied the words.

"Yes. You, too." Barry rose to his feet, his manner distracted and about as friendly as Jed's had been. Karen wrestled down hysterical laughter.

Poor Barry. Confusion mingled with concern and consternation on his face. His gaze raked over Jed, taking in the bandaged ear, the sutured chin, the lump on the side of his head . . . and the hand that had released his own and ended up holding one of Karen's.

Again Barry's sharp hazel eyes burned into hers, searching, demanding the truth. Again she had to fight her gag reflex. "What I want to know," he said, his voice dangerously quiet, "is your due date."

"I . . . why, uh . . ." Karen gulped again and lurched to her feet. "The uh . . ." She put a hand over her mouth and looked wildly for escape.

"Twenty-first of December," Jed said as her mother all but dragged her across the emergency room and into a bathroom, where Karen succumbed to a violent bout of morning sickness. "Damn it, Renton! She's my concern now! Get my wife a bed!" he bellowed. "She's the one who needs to be hospitalized, not me! Move it!"

"Wife?" Barry lunged for Karen as she returned and snatched up her left hand. "I don't see a ring, Cotts."

Jed dragged her hand free of Barry's as if he had every right to do so, tucking it out of sight. "Fingers have been swelling overnight." His look was a direct challenge, a dare to Barry to call him a liar. "You're a doctor, Renton. You should know about that." He kept a hard, uncompromising glare fixed on Barry's face. Both men breathed hard.

Barry's eyes went cold. "If the baby's not due till December, it's a bit early for her to be eclampsic."

"She's not. Our ob-gyn says it's nothing more than a bit of fluid retention. If it means anything to you, she's had a long, tiring night of traveling, and has just been involved in a car accident. She needs to lie down."

"I think I know enough about Karen to see what she needs. Her parents have come to take her home. I suggest you let them do so."

"I want her thoroughly checked out."

Karen struggled in Jed's hold. "I've *been*—"

He ignored her. *"Now,* Renton."

Karen wrenched herself free. "Damn it, Jed, will you quit acting as if I'm incapable of thinking or speaking for myself?"

Barry caught her shoulders. "Are you happy with this man?" His attitude showed considerable doubt—as if he thought he was the only man capable of making her happy and that, upcoming wedding or not, he might not relinquish the right to try.

"Of course I'm happy!" Karen shouted. For the third time in fifteen minutes, she burst into tears.

"Would somebody please get her to bed?" Jed roared.

Karen wheeled back to him. "I don't need a damned bed, Jedidiah Cotts! I simply need to go home. Mom, Dad, *please.* Let's go."

"Sure, baby, come on." Her father's arm encircled her shoulders. "Your husband's right. You need to lie down."

"If she's leaving, I'm leaving. Get me my clothes." No one moved and Jed lunged for the first suitcase he saw, which happened to be Karen's. He opened it and snatched his robe off the top of her clothes, leaving a trail of lingerie behind.

Karen tried to stuff it back in the suitcase as he tugged on his robe. "Jed, you're injured. You have to stay here."

He leaned forward, cupped her chin, and bent to shut her up with a warm kiss. "Hey, quit arguing with me, woman. Where you go, I go."

Beside her, Barry ran a hand into his hair and released a loud breath.

Karen ignored him and continued to glare at Jed. She wiped her face dry with the crumpled, disintegrating tissue in her hand. "If I lie down, will you lie down?"

Jed met her gaze. "Yes. As long as we do it at your parents' house."

She wanted to laugh in triumph. "I thought you didn't want to impose."

He looked at her mother. "Will I be imposing?"

May smiled. "Not at all, if you can get this girl to go to bed."

"Never had any trouble along that line before," he said with a broad smile. "Why should today be any different?"

Karen tried to glare him down, with no luck at all. His irrepressible grin brought an answering one to her lips. The laughter that bubbled up in her throat was one degree short of hysterical.

"Come on, honey," he said, swinging an arm over her shoulders as her dad scooped up the suitcases the ambulance attendants had salvaged from the car. "If we're going to attend a wedding at two, we need a little rest."

He glanced over his shoulder with a curt nod as they entered the hospital corridor. "Renton."

Karen's backward glance might have lingered on

Barry's scowling, doubt-filled countenance, but Jed turned her forward to follow her parents toward the exit.

Between her mother and Jed, Karen didn't stand a chance. She was home and in bed within twenty minutes of leaving the hospital, and asleep within another three.

It was getting close to noon when Jed came in, bearing a tray before him.

"For heaven's sake," she said, sitting up as he set it on the bedside table. "You're supposed to be in bed, too. You have a concussion, and we had a deal."

"Your mom is one take-charge lady, isn't she? I have been lying down, but fine, if you insist. Shove over. I'll join you."

She didn't shove over. She stuffed three pillows behind her and reached eagerly for the glass of milk on the tray, taking several healthy swallows before breathing again.

"The whole town's buzzing about us, you know," Jed said with a grin, "and your poor mother's hardly had two minutes off the phone since we got here. I think she's planning a barbecue-cum-belated wedding reception for tomorrow."

Karen stared at him over the rim of her glass. "What? You mean you haven't told them the truth?"

He shook his head. "No. That's up to you." He grinned. "Wife," he added.

Suddenly, her glaring muscles gave out. This time, her laughter wasn't in the least hysterical.

"You didn't have to do it, you know," she said. "Make believe we were married, I mean. But it sure helped me through a bad few moments with Barry. Thank you, Jed."

He lifted the tray and set it on her legs, then nearly upended it by sitting beside her. He caught it as she caught her sliding soup bowl. Together, they steadied things down.

He glanced at her. "Do you really mean that?"

"Of course I mean it." Karen took a triangle of toast and dunked one corner into her chicken noodle soup. She swallowed the soggy bite, realizing how hungry she was. "Why wouldn't I?"

She watched his gaze dart around the room, from the pink and green bedspread to the curtains blowing in the window and the rose-dotted wallpaper she and her mother had hung so many years ago she couldn't remember exactly when it had been.

At length, he looked back at her, troubled. "If I screwed things up for you by making a wrong assumption, I'm sorry. I mean, if you'd had any intention of getting back together with Barry, my letting on we're married must look like as big an obstacle as his engagement. When I said that, I guess it was in response to a gut instinct I had about the guy. He's all wrong for you."

Karen stared at him. "Jed, I know he's all wrong for me. *He* knows he's all wrong for me. That's why we're divorced. For goodness sake, this is his wedding day! Even if I wanted him back—which I absolutely do not— he doesn't want me."

His eyes narrowed. "Oh, no? I'm not so sure of that. His ill-disguised interest in the details of your pregnancy was a dead giveaway."

"His interest in the details of my pregnancy stemmed solely from his fear that I was about to wreck everything for him. Trust me. He has no personal interest in me."

He snorted. "Then he's so full of sour grapes he's about to turn into vinegar. The man acted like a jealous baboon."

"Maybe he did at first," she conceded. "Just a little.

But put yourself in his place. My pregnancy must have left him feeling as if the rug had just been jerked out from under him. I mean, though he doesn't love me, though he's completely eager to get on with his life with Candice and raise a family with her, my showing up pregnant must have been an appalling shock for him, especially considering the circumstances of our last meeting. He had to wonder. He had to ask."

Jed grunted. "When I intimated your baby was mine, he didn't have to look at me as if I'd debauched the vestal virgin."

"Well, you didn't even want to be in the same city as your ex-wife, did you?" she demanded, a trace of annoyance sharpening her tone. "How do you think you'd feel if you'd thought, even for a few minutes, that she was carrying your baby and then learned it was someone else's, especially if she hadn't been able to conceive with you for ten years?"

"Hell, how can you expect me to relate to that kind of dog-in-the-manger jealousy?" he asked disgustedly, relating all too well. "Crystal conceived if I took off my pants in the same room."

"Then you don't know the frustration of wondering why you can't make babies with your wife."

"No, and I have no intention of wasting time sympathizing with a guy who's got his ass in a knot because he believes his ex-wife is carrying someone else's kid."

The truth was, he didn't want to think of Karen's pregnancy at all or of how it had come about. It was more bothersome to him personally than it should be, and that was just plain dumb. She wasn't his wife, in spite of what all her friends in Soda Creek believed, to say nothing of her parents.

"When are you going to tell your parents the—"

He broke off in response to a knock on the door he'd left ajar. Karen looked up and gave her parents the kind of smile he'd seen on her face only a time or two before: once when she'd mentioned Penny, her Little Sister, and again when she'd said how much her baby meant to her. Love radiated from her.

He stood, envy ripping into him. "I'll leave you folks alone. I'm sure you have lots to talk about."

# FIVE

"No!" The sharpness of Karen's tone brought Jed back around. She held out a hand to him. "Stay, Jed, please."

He let her tug him back to the bedside. Her mother took a chair near the window; her father gripped its back.

In Jed's clasp, Karen's fingers trembled. As much as he felt he had no place in the scene about to follow, he could no more have walked away from Karen, ignored her plea and her need, than he could have let her drive up and over the Rocky Mountains by herself.

"Mom, Dad," she said, "I have something to tell you." She took a deep breath and let go of Jed's hand, swinging her feet over the side of the bed so she sat facing her parents. Jed, beside her, experienced sympathetic tension to match what he saw in her neck and shoulders. He wished he could help her. She straightened her spine, lifted her chin, and he knew she had the strength to face whatever she must.

"I know this isn't the kind of news you want to hear, or expected to hear, from me at my age, but Jed and I are not married." She spread her hands and gave a deprecating shrug. "You've got every parent's nightmare, an unwed, pregnant daughter, and I'm sorry for any pain and embarrassment this will cause you."

"What?" Felix lunged forward, halting only inches

from Jed. "What the hell is this? Are you married to someone else? If you think you're going to get—"

"Felix!" Karen's mother shot to her feet, grabbed her husband's arm and tried to tug him back.

He shook her off. "Stay out of this, May! This is between me and this . . . this—"

"Dad!" Karen bounced up, then swayed and caught at the headboard. Jed's hand on the middle of her back helped steady her. "Damn it, I can't believe this! Jed told me you'd . . . I didn't believe him." She plunked back down on the bed. "The baby is *Barry's*, Dad."

That left her father speechless.

Into the heavy silence, she went on quickly. "However, under the circumstances, I'm sure you can understand why I've chosen not to tell him at this point."

Her father exploded. "Barry's? You *and* Candice? That little shithead knocked up both of you in—" He broke off and rubbed a hand over his weather-beaten face. "Karen! How in the hell did—why did you—I'll throttle him! I'll—"

This time, she stood more slowly. "Dad, for heaven's sake, listen to yourself. My God! You're acting positively Victorian! I'm thirty—"

He shoved his face into hers. "Don't you take that tone with me, young lady! I want to know how this happened. I want to know why, and if I can't get the answers from you, then, by God, I'll get them from Barry, wedding day or not. He has to take respons—"

"Now, Felix," May said in a calming tone, sliding her arm around his waist and pulling him back a step or two. "The hows and wherefores are none of our affair. Karen needs our support now, our help and understanding."

Though her voice was calm, her face had paled visibly. Jed admired her strength and recognized it as the source of Karen's, just as her temper had clearly been inherited from her father.

"Your not being married will cause us no hurt or embarrassment, Karen," May continued. "We know what a fine woman you are, and so does everyone else in this community. Any who don't, don't matter to us. We're proud of you. We love you and will love your baby as well. What can we do, darling?" she asked her daughter. "How can we best help you?"

"Damn it, May, Karen knows she has our love and support in this, as in everything. I want to know why the hell we're going to Barry's and *Candice's* wedding in a couple of hours when our daughter is pregnant with his child! That's what's important! Not Candice, not Barry, no one but Karen and her baby and what's best for *them*."

As if suddenly remembering there was another person involved, Felix took another step toward Jed. "I also want to know where the hell *you* fit in, mister. That bathrobe you hauled out of my daughter's suitcase sure as hell wouldn't fit her, and I don't suppose it got there by accident."

"Dad!" Karen stepped between the two men. "Jed is my friend, the father of one of my students. He was kind enough to act as my escort for the weekend. That is the *only* way he fits in. His bathrobe in my suitcase is a fluke, which I'll explain when you've calmed down."

Felix was not convinced. His eyes gray, like Karen's but steelier than Jed thought hers could ever be, continued to bore into Jed's. "Then why the bogus marriage?"

"It was an impulse, sir. I could see Karen was distressed by her ex-husband's questions. Since several of the hospital staff had already made the assumption we were married, I simply let it stand, because I'd already blabbed the news about her pregnancy. When Barry started giving her a hard time, it seemed the best way to get him off her case."

Felix subsided. "I guess it was, at that." He dragged his hand over his face again. "I suppose you know, young lady, that your mother has planned a welcome-home party for you and your new husband?"

"We'll worry about that later." May's decisiveness showed in her swift rising. "Right now, we have a wedding to get ready for. Jed, Felix, you can use the downstairs shower. Karen and I will take turns up here. You first, Karo. Jed, unpack your suitcase and I'll press whatever needs it while you shower. Be sure to keep those stitches dry," she added on the way out of the room. Her husband followed her, like someone accustomed to being towed along in the wake of a tornado.

Jed gave Karen his hankie. "This is the way the ex-wife saves face? Weeping copiously at the wedding?"

She sniffed. "I'm not weeping copiously. I'm shedding a few, sentimental tears. I always do at weddings."

"Why?" he whispered, leaning closer to her.

She drew in a deep breath of his aftershave scent. "I'm a woman."

"I noticed." His eyes clung here and there appreciatively.

Karen swallowed hard, tears forgotten, her gaze lost in his for much too long.

She, unfortunately, had been noticing that she was a woman and he a man from the moment she emerged from her bedroom dressed in a two-piece, fine-pleated dress of flaming silk crepe to find Jed stepping through a doorway across the hall. His shoulders looked broader, his hips narrower, and his height greater in his light gray suit with a dark pinstripe. His sutured chin and bandaged ear gave him a rakish look, emphasizing his masculinity.

She found herself noticing it more and more as the evening progressed. They sat at a round table with her parents and several other couples. "You stay here," he said, bending for the benefit of anyone who might be watching and brushing his lips across her cheek. "I'll get your dinner."

She sat feeling pampered, watching him as he moved through the buffet line with two plates held easily in one large hand, serving food with the other.

She skipped the wine, except for one sip to toast the bride—and so did he, keeping a supply of ice water topped up for both of them. When the flower girl and the ring bearer brought around the doily-wrapped, silver-ribboned slivers of wedding cake, it was his long fingers that flipped open her beaded clutch purse and slid both pieces inside. "To dream on," he said, patting her bag closed. His gaze, warm and intimate, held hers. "Don't forget to give me mine when we get home. I have a great dream planned."

Karen didn't dare catch her father's eye, though she felt his stare boring into her. To her chagrin, she blushed, and hoped he'd recognize that Jed was maintaining the pretense of being her husband purely because of the others present.

Martina, sister of the bride and Karen's friend since diaper days, dragged her into the rest room the minute she got a chance. "Karen! Why didn't I hear about Jed before today? The man is gorgeous, and so much in love with you it's enough to make me sick. Was Ed ever that besotted with me?"

Karen managed to laugh off the questions, assisted by Martina's mother bursting into the room, needing her eldest daughter to deal with an impending disaster involving the caterers. But Martina's pointed look over her shoulder told Karen she was due to be subjected to a lot more questions the first chance Marti got.

It would be an interesting discussion, because she'd have to make up every answer as she went along.

Still, she had never spent an evening with a man quite so attentive, so focused on her and her needs. He did act besotted, she had to admit. The man was earning an Oscar right before her eyes.

Despite that, though, he found time to charm her parents and the other couples at the table, sharing interesting, informative tidbits about his experiences. He'd traveled widely in the Orient and Europe, and she listened, fascinated, to his humorous tales, experiencing a misplaced sense of pride in this new husband of hers.

But it wasn't pride that flooded her when he stood and slid her chair back the minute the band began to play a slow, dreamy melody. "Do you feel up to dancing?"

Her voice wobbled so slightly she was certain no one else noticed. But she did. She felt distinctly wobbly all over. Nevertheless, she tilted her chin and said, "I always feel up to dancing."

His hand, large and warm, enfolded hers as they walked to the edge of the floor. There he swung her into his arms and Karen was immediately lost in a kind of magic she had never before encountered.

When she remembered to breathe, each breath she drew was laden with his scent. When she remembered to look up to try to find something intelligent to say rather than merely staring mutely at his chest, his gaze penetrated her. When she parted her lips in an attempt at speech, he lifted their linked hands and brushed her mouth closed with the back of his knuckles. Then, tucking their hands up against his chest, he drew her into a deeper embrace, and Karen closed her eyes.

Despite his being nearly a foot taller, they fit together as if they'd been designed for each other by some celestial engineer. He danced smoothly, led masterfully, and Karen let him and the music carry her around the room on a cloud of delight.

She wanted to protest when the first of several old friends cut in. As she danced away, trying to make polite conversation with someone she'd grown up with, her gaze followed Jed as he walked back across the room to their table. Moments later, her mother smiled up at him as he swung her into a fox-trot.

Throughout the rest of the evening, Jed danced only with Karen or, rarely, her mother, though there were many other choices he could have made, especially considering the number of different partners Karen had, up to and including the bridegroom.

"You look a little better than you did this morning, Karo," Barry said.

She laughed. "I feel a lot better. But as Jed said at the time, I'd had a long night on the road and just survived a car crash."

He cut his glance toward Jed, who danced past with May. "He seems popular with your parents."

"Why wouldn't he be? He's a very nice man, Barry."

"And the father of your baby." He sounded, she thought, just a tad rancorous. For a moment, he held her back from him, his gaze sweeping over her dress. Its peplum top concealed her pregnancy. "Your folks must be delighted."

"Yes." She paused for only a beat before changing the subject. "Candice is a beautiful bride. You're a lucky man, Barry."

After a tense moment, Barry turned so he could see his new wife. "Yes." Candice, dancing with Barry's brother Ross, looked radiant. Barry's strained face belied his words. "Very lucky."

She smiled. He was beginning to show the ragged edges of a man who'd just put in an emotional day. Even happiness, she knew, could be wearing in excess. On the day of their wedding, she'd been an emotional basket case.

"I'm sure you and Candice are going to live a long and charmed life together."

"Are you." His tone was flat.

She frowned and looked at him sharply. "Hey, what's with you?"

"I—" Suddenly, he seemed to realize where he was and who he was talking to. He shook his shoulders as if to shed a load and cleared his throat. "Sorry. Don't mind me. It's been a long day for me, too, after a long and difficult night. I lost a patient at five this morning."

"Barry, I'm sorry." She knew of old how he suffered when a patient died. Out of habit, she said, "Need to talk about it?" before she realized it really wasn't her place to ask that question any longer. "Sorry." She laughed. "I'm sure if you do, when you do, you won't have to go far."

Under her hand, she felt his shoulder lift in a seemingly uncaring shrug that matched the smile he turned toward her, but not the bleak expression in his eyes. "Actually, Candice doesn't like me to talk about hospital events. She'd like me to get into something clean like research, preferably far from Soda Creek. Or even Montana."

"I . . . see."

His lips twisted in a bitter half smile. "Yeah, you probably do, where thousands wouldn't. Hey, can I say something?"

"Of course. We agreed to stay friends, Barry. You can always say anything to me."

They hadn't had a lot of choice but to stay friends, considering the closeness of their families. He'd been her friend forever, and she suspected she'd feel that way about him till the day she died.

"I'm not sure if I ever made this clear," he said, "but I know our marriage failing was mostly my fault. I was never there when you needed me, even though you were always there for me. I hope I can do better this time around. So if you have any advice for me, go ahead. Shoot." His mouth quirked up on one side. "I'm ready to listen. I don't want to make the same mistakes all over again."

"I don't suppose you will." She smiled. "You'll make different ones. And so will I. But we'll live through them just the way we've lived through the others."

"Our marriage didn't live through them, though. Part of me will always regret that, Karen, just as part of me will always love you."

"I feel the same way. That will never change, Barry. I loved you, too. I still do. Just not . . . that way . . . anymore."

"No," he said. "Now there's Jed."

She looked up and met his gaze. "And Candice."

"Right." He glanced over to where his bride swayed in a slow dance with his brother. "And Candice."

Something was wrong, but Karen didn't have the right to ask him what. They were mostly silent until the music ended and she broke from his loose hold. "I think you need to get back to your bride."

"And you to your husband." Had there been, she wondered, a slight edge to the way he said *husband* and a hint of despair in his eyes? When she glanced at him again, though, his brow was clear, and his eyes held a calm smile.

She was being overly imaginative. There was nothing wrong with Barry. How could there be? This was his wedding day, and he was perfectly happy in his choice of a bride. Of course he was. She'd be crazy to worry about him. Yet old habits died hard.

Her concerns fell from her under the warmth of Jed's smile as he stood at her return. He had impeccable manners. Each time she returned to their table, he was there waiting for her. He'd either stand at once and see her comfortably seated, or sweep her away into another dance. He did the latter this time.

"You two seemed to be having a serious conversation out there."

Karen tilted her head back and looked up at Jed. His eyes held a fathomless expression. His mouth was taut, with curved lines bracketing it. "Not really," she said. "More light social patter."

"You sure?" He scowled. "I hate the idea of your being unhappy, Karen."

"Jed, I'm not unhappy, I promise you. But if I were," she added, smiling, "it wouldn't be your responsibility to fix it."

He drew her closer, increasing her sensation of being cherished. "Yeah. I know."

His cheek rested on top of her head as he enfolded her in his arms, swaying with the music, making her feel dainty and feminine. The heat of his breath in her hair, as he murmured the words of the love song, made her heart pound and her brain go muzzy. She drew in a deep breath and released it slowly, but it did nothing to reduce the tension winding tighter and tighter in her.

Pregnancy hormones, she reminded herself firmly, and wondered how long the anomaly would last.

"Damn it, Jed! It's just not right!" Karen exploded the long silence following their argument—Jed had called it a discussion—over who should pay for the rental car. He and her dad had sneaked off that morning, returning to present her with a *fait accompli*. She was not pleased.

"What's not?" His innocence put him in grave danger of being brained, but he was driving, so she kept her hands to herself.

"You know perfectly well what I mean," she snapped. *"I* planned to rent the car for the drive back. This entire trip, I remind you, was for my benefit."

"The trip, I remind you," he retorted, settling his shoulders back against the seat as they gained highway speed, "was as much to get me out of town for the weekend as to provide escort service for you. Besides, we're not driving all the way back to Seattle, only to the airport in Helena. Quit making a fuss."

"I'm not making a fuss. I'm trying to do the right thing."

He gave her a quick grin. "I'm the one who wrecked the car, not you, so quit arguing with me. You know I'm right—as usual."

If he'd hoped to provoke her further with that, he was destined for disappointment. She knew better now than to distract him with her temper when he was behind the wheel. Instead of cutting loose with some of the things she'd have liked to tell him, she shrugged, letting the subject go.

She pulled out an emery board and began shaping her nails, glad to be on the road again, glad to be alone with Jed leaving Soda Creek, even if it was a day late.

Though her confession of not being married to him had forestalled the belated wedding reception her mother wanted to throw for them, the barbecue had gone on from noon on Sunday till the small hours of Monday. Whether from physical exhaustion or emotional strain, she'd awakened Monday morning too sick to leave as planned.

Jed had changed his morning flight out of Seattle for an afternoon one. He'd also rebooked both their flights back home at the same time. Then he and her dad had disappeared early this morning in the truck and returned later with Jed driving this very comfortable rental job.

And he called her mother a take-charge kind of person!

It was, though, she was forced to admit, pleasant to be looked after. She blew the nail dust off her fingers, brushed her lap, and zipped her emery board back into a side pocket of her bag. Squirming back deeper into the plush seat, she pulled up one knee and wrapped her arms around it, turning her head to smile at Jed as he slid a quick glance at her.

Jed found himself more aware of Karen's every move than he'd ever been with any woman. He even liked watching her file her nails. He liked the way she wore them, not long talons, but short and neatly rounded on the tips, only lightly coated with pale pink enamel. She had, all in all, the prettiest pair of hands he'd ever seen. Now, with her knee lifted and her arms around it as she stared out at the scenery, her right hand was closest to him, curved around her left elbow. He wished he could reach out and touch it. The texture of soft, silky skin over firm strength tempted him. She had hands that could caress a man's body with as much sureness as gentleness, with authority blended with sweetly shy exploration and—

"Would it really have been so hard," she asked, "seeing your ex-wife again? With Richard?"

It took him a moment to make the transition to an entirely different train of thought. He cleared his throat. "I, um, don't really know, I guess. I thought it would be uncomfortable all around, and I wasn't willing to take the chance."

He *had* thought it would be difficult; he'd thought it would be impossible. Now, though, he wondered, because he realized with a jolt he'd scarcely even thought of Crystal during the past few days. It was as if she had suddenly become several degrees less important to him.

Before, he'd spent too much of his time worrying about her, wondering if she were really happy, if she would have the courage to come to him and tell him if she ever realized she had made a mistake. He'd spent even more time fantasizing about their possible reunion, thinking of the kind, forgiving, understanding words he'd use to welcome her back.

Crystal, however, was not a subject he intended to discuss with Karen.

"Your mom filled the thermos before we left," he said. "Will you pour me some coffee, please?"

She handed him a cup. "Are you still in love with her?"

He lifted his eyebrows. "Your mother? I liked her fine, Karen, but I wouldn't say I was in—"

Her mock-threatening fist and the dangerous glint in her eyes brought a grin to his face and a laugh rumbling from his chest, but her question drew him back on track.

*Was* he still in love with Crystal? No. Would he take her back? Odd how the idea had suddenly lost much of its appeal, even if it meant having his family reunited the way he'd dreamed of.

He thought about it, then surprised himself by saying, "No, I guess maybe I'm not."

It was an odd admission to make and left him feeling vaguely uncomfortable, as if he'd left something behind, but couldn't put his finger on exactly what or where or even when.

"How could I still love her?" he continued, speaking more to himself than to Karen now. "She left me, discarded me and our marriage, made a mockery of everything we, as a couple, ever were and ever did. How can you love someone who rejects not only you, but your entire life together, even when it's your own fault?"

She hitched one knee up on the seat as she half turned to face him. Her eyebrows drew together. "You honestly think it was your fault she . . . changed toward you?"

He disliked his own harsh bark of laughter. "I know it was."

"She said so?"

Jed shot a glance at her, expecting to see derision in her expression, but all he read was concern, caring that made him look away quickly. Sympathy, but not pity. He didn't think he'd been aware of the distinction before. It took several minutes to rid his throat and chest of the heavy thickness that settled there.

"She never said so," he replied finally. "Not in so many words. She didn't have to. Her actions said it all, didn't they?" The words tasted as bitter as they'd sounded. "You know, when I think how hard I worked at changing my attitudes, burying beliefs I grew up with, reevaluating things I'd long taken as givens, and then realize it was an exercise in futility, I get so frustrated I could choke. I've tried and tried to figure out what more I could have done, should have done, but I've run out of answers."

"I don't see how you can blame yourself. It takes two to make a marriage work and two to make it fail."

"How profound," he said, and her hurt expression brought a quick apology to his lips. "You're right, of course, but I was still the one most responsible for the things that went wrong."

"How do you figure that?"

"I've spent a lot of time thinking about it, remembering the way it was, what I did do, what I didn't do. Mostly the latter."

When he failed to continue, she murmured a small, female sound that let him know she was listening, was receptive to what he might say. It was a long time since he'd heard a woman make that little sound to encourage him to talk about anything.

"You know, until Crystal left, I wasn't much for thinking about feelings, for trying to figure out why I felt one way and not another, why I liked one thing and disliked something else. In fact, throughout our marriage, she was forever trying to analyze stuff like that and get me in on the process. I resisted. Maybe—" He broke off with an impatient puff of breath. He was tired to death of *maybes* and *what ifs*.

"After Willi was born and Crystal went back to school, she tried to share with me all the things she was learning, the insights into human behavior, but I couldn't seem to get a real handle on it.

"Yet, when she left, I was forced to think about it, to try to figure out where and when our marriage started to fail."

"I know what you mean."

He smiled to himself. She did, didn't she? "Did you ever come up with an answer?"

She laughed ruefully. "Nothing concrete. Did you?"

He glanced at her, saw a half smile on her lips and a quiet, waiting, sensitive expression in her eyes.

"Yeah," he said with a laugh. "I concluded I'd been a jerk all my life. I had learned to talk like a liberated man, but most of the time she saw right through me and accused me of merely paying lip service to the concept. She was right. I still believe in keeping women barefoot and pregnant, I guess."

"Oh, Jed." Karen laughed, too. "Be serious."

He didn't bother to tell her he was being serious. Maybe not about the barefoot business, but he thought there was nothing more inspiring than a pregnant woman.

"Once I started thinking about it," he said quickly, before he let that thought carry him too far off the subject, "thinking, reading, learning as much as possible what it is women want made it easier to see that it was my weaknesses as a husband, a lover, even as a father—I guess just my way of being a man, the *kind* of man I am—that drove my wife away."

*"What?"* He didn't have to look to know she stared at him in disbelief. "Jed, that's just plain nuts! How can you say you drove her away?"

"Because it's true. We had a perfectly normal, perfectly happy life until a couple of years after Bunny was born."

Well, maybe happy wasn't quite the word; it hadn't been that for a long time. Maybe for Crystal it never had been and he'd simply been too insensitive, too wrapped up in getting his own satisfaction, to realize. He frowned. There was a possibility that she didn't get satisfaction because he was the wrong man, but if that had been the case, why hadn't she admitted it to herself, to say nothing of him, long before Simone, Richard's wife, died? Or could it be that, as she'd claimed, she simply had not known?

All she'd known, she'd confessed, was that something was missing in her life, and as she and Richard grew emotionally closer, she began to see what it had been. Richard answered some very basic needs for her. But why had *he* been unable to fill them in the twenty years of their marriage? Damn it, why?

He wished his mind would quit throwing that question at him. He had no answer to it.

"I knew Richard and Crystal were spending a lot of time together after Simone's death," he continued, and, at her questioning look, explained. "Richard was my business partner. Simone was his wife."

"I see."

He doubted she did. "I thought she was helping Richard through his grieving period—as I suppose she was, given her training and expertise. Simone took her own life, so Richard experienced a lot of guilt as well as grief. And he was very much alone, because they'd never had children."

"Suicide because she'd learned her husband was having an affair with his business partner's wife?"

Jed started. "No. Absolutely not." Something compelled him to deny it, and swiftly, probably as much to himself as to Karen. "The affair started after she died. I'm almost positive of that. Simone didn't so much as hint at anything like that in her note."

"What did she say?"

"Just that she couldn't go on. She was tired. And she was sorry." Jed shrugged unhappily. "She'd had a history of severe depression, but we thought it was under control. Then *bang!* She was gone."

"You were friends, the four of you? I mean, you socialized a lot, as well as being in business together?"

"Yes."

"I imagine your partner's wife's death put a lot of pressure on you at work."

"Yes, but—" He didn't finish the thought, still vaguely ashamed of admitting the truth—that in a way, Richard's lack of focus on the business had been a blessing to Jed. All he'd known was that every time he had to take one of the foreign buying trips that had formerly been Richard's domain, he'd experienced a sense of guilty relief that, for the duration of the trip, he didn't have to deal with Crystal's patent unhappiness.

He hesitated for a minute as he passed an eighteen-wheeler, wondering why he was pouring all this out to Karen. Maybe it was easy because they were isolated in the car, insulated from outside interference. Or possibly it was just what Karen had said: as the survivor of a broken marriage herself, she understood much of what he'd been through.

He remembered his mother suggesting he join a group of people recovering from divorce, remembered he'd rejected the idea completely.

"When Richard came back to work," he continued, "he seemed almost to hate me, sniping, disagreeing with everything I said, did, or suggested. I thought at first he resented me for still having a living wife while his was gone. Then, because I knew Crystal was helping him deal with his emotions, I figured maybe she was griping about me to him, and it was affecting his opinion of me."

He laughed harshly. "I was on the verge of suggesting that I buy out his shares just to get him off my back when he and Crystal hit me with the news that they were moving to Portland. Together. That they were in love and wanted to get married."

He wondered how long it would have taken them to admit the truth had he not found them in bed together on his return from a business trip.

"At first, I didn't believe it. I wanted to think they were pulling a practical joke on me. I . . . laughed." His balled fist pounded rhythmically on his right thigh, and he forced it to stop.

"When I finally had to accept it, I offered them what I'd planned, to buy Richard out, but he refused. He would need the income from his shares so he and *my wife* could set up housekeeping together. In other words, I was supposed to keep on working like a dog, doing the jobs of two men, to support the pair of them."

His deep sense of outrage returned, thickening his voice. "I drew the line right there. Either he worked with me in the business, carrying his end of the load, or the partnership would be dissolved. Those were his only two choices, and if he wanted the matter to go to court, with all the publicity that would entail, I was willing."

He hadn't been willing, of course. He'd have died rather than expose his family and himself so publicly. Yes, of course, lots of marriages failed. Lots of partnerships, too. But he hadn't wanted his business contacts to know the extent of the betrayal he'd suffered. He'd been ashamed.

"Was he? Did it come to a court battle?."

"Of course not." He laughed mirthlessly. "After consultation with Crystal, Richard was quite ready to get out of the partnership as quietly and gracefully as possible. Crystal seemed to care almost as much as I did about what the neighbors would think."

"Crystal had children to think of."

"Yeah. The kids." He sighed raggedly. "God, it was tough on them! I guess they felt the same sense of abandonment I did—at least the two older ones. They refused to go with their mother, but Crystal took Bunny, our little one. She was seven at the time." To his horror, his voice cracked.

Karen reached across the width of the front seat and curled her fingers over his fist, which had resumed the rhythmic pounding on his thigh. "I'm sorry. It must have been terribly hard, losing both of them like that."

"Yeah." Jed unclenched his fist and slid his fingers between hers as he linked their hands on the seat, nearer his thigh than hers, but at least in a safer position.

Idly, he stroked his thumb over the backs of her knuckles, reveling again in the smoothness of her skin, the satin warmth of it. It felt so alive. She made him feel alive in ways he hadn't for a long time.

Quickly, he resumed the correct driving position of two and ten, silently berating himself for being so physically, so *sexually* aware of her while spilling his guts about his failed marriage. Trouble was, he couldn't find a way to make the feelings go away.

"Do you see Bunny often?"

"No." He saw her when Crystal decided he could, mostly when it was inconvenient for her to have Bunny with her or when she wanted something from him and used Bunny as a bargaining chip. He hated that, but there was nothing he could do about it.

He thought Karen might commiserate. Most people did. Not her, though. She looked angry. At him. "Don't you *want* to spend time with her?"

"Yes." Again, his voice came out harsh and taut. "I'd prefer to have her with me all the time."

"So fight for custody, or at least more liberal visiting rights," she said, in a how-can-you-be-so-stupid? tone.

"I can't."

"Can't or won't?"

"All right, won't."

She didn't ask why. She merely looked as if she were deeply disappointed in him, and then stared through the windshield, watching the long, straight road unfold before them. Before long, she slumped down, and he saw she was asleep.

He wished she had stayed awake. Now, for reasons he chose not to explore, he wanted to explain his decision about Bunny.

# SIX

When Karen woke in half an hour, he could see her nap hadn't improved her opinion of him. After pouring herself some juice from the cooler her mother had packed for them, she stared straight ahead, the same shuttered expression on her face as before she nodded off.

Into the silence, Jed said, "Karen, please don't judge and condemn me for something you don't understand."

After a moment, she turned to look at him again. She heaved a sigh, and her shoulders slumped. "I was, wasn't I? Sorry, Jed."

Her failure to come up with a swift, indignant denial surprised him, pleased him.

"It's none of my business, and I was wrong to make a judgment. I'm sure if you'd thought it in Bunny's best interests you'd have fought to the death to keep her with you and her sisters."

"Thank you." He swallowed. "She was so young when we split. With my work schedule, my traveling, I'd have been putting too big a burden on the other two girls if I'd insisted on bringing her home as often as I wanted. I get down to Portland to see her whenever I can, and she spends some vacations with me."

Again, her hand touched the back of his. "Oh, Jed! I know how much you must love her and miss her. I'm truly sorry."

Then, swiftly, before he could reply, she changed the subject.

Suddenly weary, he wished the drive was over, wished to be far from Karen so he could think things through and maybe start to understand himself for once in his life.

Mercifully, they didn't have adjoining seats on the plane from Helena to SeaTac. He sat near the front, she in a row halfway back. That, Jed told himself, suited him just fine. He needed the time apart from her to get a grip on his wildly fluctuating emotions. For a man whose wife had accused him of not having any, he sure as hell had begun to develop them over the past few days.

It was anything but comfortable.


"Good-bye, Jed." Karen held out her hand while the airport crowd swirled and bumped around them. Jed took it, held it for just a moment, and nodded to her, coolly, politely.

"So long."

*Damn!* He was as taciturn in his farewell as he'd been over the last several miles of the drive. All during the lonely flight back from Montana, she'd wracked her brain trying to recall what she might have said to offend him, but nothing specific came to her. She'd apologized for judging him, then gone on to talk about the barbecue her parents had thrown on her—their—behalf the day following Barry and Candice's wedding.

He'd smiled and laughed and reminisced with her, so she was sure no part of that conversation had ticked him off. Eventually, it had just petered out, and she'd stared out the side window until they were entering the airport area.

Maybe he'd simply gotten tired of trying to maintain

a conversation that they both knew was going to be their last one.

"Thank you for everything," she added. "You were very, um, helpful."

"You're welcome." His voice was as stiff as his manner. "Good-bye, Karen. Take care, okay?" It sounded as if he hated good-byes as much as she did.

"Of course." She managed to smile. "I always take care."

Damn it, why didn't they call his flight? Or, failing that, why didn't she simply walk away, call a cab or catch a shuttle, and go home? He'd said good-bye. She'd said good-bye. She'd said thanks in several ways and probably too many times. She'd risk embarrassing him if she said either again. If only she could leave—but something held her there. If she wasn't careful, in another minute she'd start blubbering. Those damned hormones were acting up again.

They both stood silent for several minutes, listening intently to the crackly voices from the loudspeakers, their gazes clashing now and then. Mostly he stared at the wall behind her head, and she stared at the eighteen inches of tiled floor between his toes and hers.

She looked up. "Jed—"

"Karen—"

"You first," she said.

"I just wanted to say that I, uh, enjoyed our time together."

"Even with its being a day longer than it should have been?"

He smiled. "I could probably take maybe as much as another two or three hours of this relationship before we call it quits. Or even longer. Say another thirty or forty minutes if my flight wasn't due to leave right about now."

She smiled at his attempt at humor. "Are you kidding?

My life is much too full of complications to consider taking on a relationship, even short term."

Before he could comment, she went on. "Besides, what would a nice, contented grandpa like you want with a pregnant lady like me for longer than a weekend interlude?"

"Yeah," he said, "you have a point, but what you should be saying is what would a nice young woman like you, with your life and your child's life ahead of you, want with a man who has grown-up children as well as a grandchild?"

"Is that what I should be saying?"

"Yes." His tone was curt. "You'd better go now. Find a cab and get yourself home. You don't have to wait till my flight goes."

"I know." Karen tried to move, but couldn't.

He frowned. "See that you get more rest than you've been getting." Lifting a hand, with one finger he traced an arc high on her cheek. "These circles under your eyes shouldn't be there. And exercise. That's important, too, and the right food." His frown deepened. "Are you taking prenatal vitamins?"

She had to laugh. It felt good to laugh. For a terrible moment, she'd been on the verge of tears. "Jed! You sound exactly like my mother!"

His face reddened. "I'm sorry. I don't mean to. I mean, I know it's none of my business, but, well, I was thinking. Out here on the Coast, far from friends and family, you have nobody to look out for you, no one to keep you on the straight and narrow and . . . hell, I'm sorry." The call came for his flight to Omaha.

"That's okay," she said, having to fight an absurd impulse to fling herself into his arms and cling to him, beg him not to leave.

If he was so concerned, why didn't *he* volunteer to look out for her, to keep her on the straight and narrow and make sure she took her vitamins? He obviously knew more about pregnancy than she did—maybe more than her mother did.

Her mother had been not at all helpful. "Maybe it means nothing more than you're attracted to Jed, possibly even falling in love with him."

"Mom! I can't be! I met the man for the first time last week, for heaven's sake."

Her mother had shrugged negligently and continued shelling peas. "So? That has no bearing on anything. Look, just because you knew Barry all your life and took your time falling in love with him doesn't mean that's the way it has to happen. I fell in love with your dad in the space of an hour.

"All I can suggest," May continued, "is that you wait and see. If you still feel the same way toward Jed once the baby comes, then I figure you can safely assume your emotions had nothing to do with pregnancy hormones."

Jed, she had wanted to weep, wouldn't be around after the baby's birth, or even before it, following this weekend, but her father and Jed returned with the rental car at that moment, and she'd said no more.

Now she wanted even more intensely to weep, her loneliness increasing as Jed's fellow passengers shuffled past them on their way to board the plane. Soon he'd have to join them and she'd have to stand here and wave, though suddenly she felt too weak to lift a hand. She wanted him to hold her, make her feel safe, protected.

Oh, hell, what was she thinking? She didn't need a man to take care of things for her, to remind her to take her vitamins and get plenty of exercise.

"I do so have people to look out for me, to advise

me," she assured him. "My friend Esther; my obstetrician." She managed a smile. "And my mother certainly knows how to use a telephone."

"Yeah. Yeah, I know, but . . ." He didn't look comforted.

"And you take care, too, okay? Don't forget to have those stitches out on Friday." She lifted a hand and gently ran one finger just at the edge of the flesh-colored bandage on the point of his chin. "Any emergency department will do it."

"Yeah. I know," he said again. "Okay, gotta go." He bent, grabbed his bag. "Bye, Karen."

He strode away, then spun back, dropped his suitcase, groaned her name, and jerked her into his arms. He tilted her head back with one balled-up fist against the underside of her chin and fastened his mouth over hers, kissing her until her head roared and her knees turned to jelly.

Karen could no more resist than she could voluntarily stop her heartbeat. Vitally aware of the feel of his skin, she cradled his jaw in one hand; the other clung to his neck. She parted her lips in willing acquiescence to his invasion and stroked her tongue over his.

The taste of him was something she would never forget. She had known that with the first kiss he'd taken from her, relearned with each successive one, as warm and gentle and sweet as they'd been. This one, though . . . this was like nothing she'd ever dreamed of. At the same time, it was everything she'd ever wanted. It filled her even as it increased her hunger for him.

A soft growl issued from him as he held her tighter, enfolding her. "Oh, God," he groaned against her throat. "I want to drag you away somewhere we can be alone!"

He took her mouth again, deepened their kiss, and in moments, she'd all but forgotten they weren't alone.

He tangled his hand in her hair, spread the other one across the small of her back, his fingers pressing her spine until she felt the hard lump of her pregnancy against the hard rod of his sex. She knew the instant he became aware of how tight he held her, because with a gasp of shocked realization, set her away from him.

His throat worked as he looked long into her eyes. "Oh, Lord!" he said. He dragged his hand from her hair, peeled the other one from her back and stepped back from her. "I'm sorry!"

She stared at him as, with an oath, he reeled away from her, joining the other late-comers in a stampede for the aircraft.

He was sorry? Did that mean she was never going to see him again? Of course it did. Karen forced herself not to care, not to cry, not to give in to the dictates of female hormones. Instead, she kicked her carry-on bag so hard her toes still ached an hour later.

The flowers came on Friday afternoon. At first, Karen thought they were from her parents. When she saw they were from Jed, she sat down quickly and discovered, to her chagrin, that she was clutching the card to her breast as if it were a magic talisman and smiling like a lunatic. She read it again.

*Hope everything's fine with you. Why not give me a call when you have a few free minutes?*

*Yours,*
*Jedidiah Cotts*

*Yours, Jedidiah Cotts . . . ?*

Hah! She dropped the card onto the table near the flowers and shrugged. On second reading, it sounded like a message he might have dictated to accompany flowers going to a casual acquaintance. She sighed gustily.

Moments later, she sat up straight. What was she complaining about? She *was* a casual acquaintance, despite the weekend they had shared and the extraordinarily sexy kiss they'd indulged in at its end.

It was very nice of him to have sent the flowers, she told herself, getting to her feet and rubbing the small of her back. She must remember to drop a thank-you card into the mail. First, though, she'd have to buy one.

Unfortunately, she kept forgetting to pick up a card. As she lay in bed Sunday morning, the scent of the freesias in her floral arrangement wafted to her on the breeze flowing from one open window to another. Darn it, she was going to have to call him. With any luck, he'd be out somewhere at nine o'clock on a Sunday morning. He'd said he often went in to work when it was quiet and no one was around to distract him. He'd also said he was an early riser. She'd leave a message on his answering machine. Then it would be up to him to make contact again if he wanted.

He answered on the second ring, his voice rich and husky and a tad grouchy in just that one word of greeting.

"Jed." Her voice cracked slightly. "Hello. It's Karen. Uh, Karen Andersen?" After all, maybe he *had* forgotten, put her out of his mind after sending the floral arrangement. "I'm calling to thank you for the flowers. They're lovely. It was so, so . . . nice of you."

"Flowers?" He sounded bewildered, as if he hadn't

the faintest idea what she was talking about. He also sounded, she thought, as if he had a headache and it hurt him to talk. Oh, good grief, he'd forgotten having sent them! That's how much it had meant to him. Of course he hadn't gone to the florist and chosen them himself. He'd had his secretary phone and order them.

"I got them Friday afternoon," she said. "A lovely arrangement of scarlet glads, cream freesias, asparagus fern, and baby's breath. It was so very thoughtful of you and I want you to know how much I appreciate it." Oh, hell, she was babbling. What would he care about the flowers and greens that comprised the bouquet? Men didn't care about those things. He'd probably forgotten entirely her saying how much she liked the scent of freesias.

His silence lasted several seconds too long, then he said, a touch hollowly, "Oh, yes. Those flowers. Sorry, I'm a bit . . . distracted today."

"Oh. Then this is a bad time. My apologies. I just wanted to say thanks, anyway. I'll let you go."

"No!" His tone was sharp. "Since you're on the phone, and I've been wondering, how—how are you feeling? All recovered from the accident?"

"Oh, sure. I'm fine. Fine. Thank you. And you?"

"Can't complain." He sounded very distant. Nearly two weeks since she had last seen him, last touched him, last breathed in the scent of his skin. Her throat ached.

"Good."

There was a long silence during which she painfully remembered the look of stunned disbelief on his face when he'd lifted his head from having kissed her at the airport. She'd thought him as deeply affected as she had been. Had he been appalled at the way she'd kissed him back, like the sex-starved divorcée he must consider her?

Had she misinterpreted what he had meant to be a nice little so-long peck? Had it escalated in only seconds because she hadn't been able to control the impulse to cling to him, to touch his face, to open her mouth and demand that he deepen the kiss?

"Well," she said, and then didn't know what else to say, how to end this stupid phone call gracefully.

"Well," he said at the same time, and she burned with embarrassment.

They both laughed awkwardly and she was about to cut short the conversation, if it could be called that, by means of simply hanging up, when he asked quickly, as if he had known her thoughts and wanted to be kind, "How goes your work? Was it hard to get back to the routine after being away?"

"It was fine. I had no trouble settling back down." Oh, what a lie! "Did you have a good trip? Did your business survive without you?"

"I guess it did. They still call me boss there, anyway."

"You sound tired," she said.

He sighed audibly. "No. Not really. Just a little . . . well, maybe fed up is the term."

"Your meetings weren't productive?"

"No. No, they went well enough. I have federal go-ahead to link up with that log-cabin company I mentioned and begin exporting the prefab kits to Japan."

"That's good." She remembered Jed and her father discussing his import-export brokerage business at great length one morning over breakfast. "I'm glad for you. I know you wanted that contract."

"Yes." He said nothing more.

She should simply thank him again and hang up. He didn't want to talk to her, for heaven's sake, to tell her why he was fed up. He had better, more important things

on his mind. But, oh, having his voice on the other end
of the phone line did wonders for the aching loneliness
she'd been experiencing.

It wasn't simply that it was Jed Cotts's voice. Any
voice would have done. Unfortunately, she knew very
few people in the Seattle area well enough to call and
say, "Hey, I'm lonely. May I come over?" Esther was
away with her family on a three-week vacation. She'd
spent most of the previous day with Penny, her aunt, and
little brothers, but couldn't intrude on them and expect
them to fill all her companionship needs.

"What are you fed up with?" she asked, as if his silence had given her permission to probe. At least he
hadn't rushed on, changing the subject.

His laughter was strained. "I know this is going to
sound really stupid, a trifling reason for feeling out of
sorts, but I can't find my copy of *Atlas Shrugged,* and I
was in the mood to reread it. It keeps my mind occupied
when it tends to wander into . . . areas where I'd rather
it didn't. Somebody must have borrowed it and not returned it. I have to confess, I was feeling grouchy about
that when you called. Sorry if it showed."

"Oh. No. No, it didn't show. I do crossword puzzles
when my mind wants to wander into avenues it's better
kept out of." She'd gone through three entire crossword
books in the past week and a half and had started on a
fourth. "I have a copy of *Atlas Shrugged,* if you'd like
to borrow it."

She could hear his breathing.

"I could bring it to school tomorrow and give it to
Cecelia."

"No, no. I wouldn't want to impose on you that way."

She took a solid gulp of air. "It wouldn't be an im-
position. If you'd prefer not to wait, of course, you could

come over here and get it now. Now that the sun's shining again I was thinking of going for a hike, but that can wait."

There was a silence that again went on too long, as if he were considering her invitation, before he said, "No, that's okay. I was just planning a lazy hour reading by the pool. I have a tennis game later today."

"Right." With a woman, of course. A slim, vibrant, unpregnant woman. A hot date that would cool off in his pool, then heat up again in his bedroom, no doubt. She knew the way single men lived, especially single men who looked like Jedidiah Cotts. And kissed like him.

"Thank you again for the flowers, Jed. It was thoughtful of you." Oh, damn, she was repeating herself now! "Good-bye."

His breath against the phone sounded like a long sigh, but then he said quietly, "Sure. Bye, Karen."

She hung up.

"And that," Karen told herself, dusting her hands together briskly, "is that." She picked up her crossword book, opened it to the challenger section, placed several letters, then flung it and her pen across the room.

Jed sat staring at the phone as it rested in its cradle. Flowers?

It was obvious who had sent them and signed his name to the card. Damn Ceil. He had a good mind to call her on it, but if he did, Ceil would know he and Karen had been in touch. She'd want to know what Karen had said, what he had said, if they were going to see each other again, and the answer to that was an unequivocal no.

He should have sent Karen flowers, not left it to his interfering daughter to do behind his back. After all, he'd endangered her life, limb, and baby by wrecking the car. If he'd been thinking, he'd have ordered an arrangement for her. But where Karen Andersen—for that matter, any woman—was concerned, he wasn't very good at thinking of the right thing to do and the right time to do it.

Maybe instead of berating Cecelia, he should thank her. He snorted. He couldn't do that, either, for the same reason he couldn't yell at her.

Damn, but a man's life got complicated fast when a woman entered it. It was tough enough being a father to three daughters without his even contemplating letting another woman in. But . . .

For just a moment he let himself remember Karen's flattering disbelief when he told her he was a grandfather. Some women could boost a guy's ego without even trying. Slowly, he withdrew his hand from the phone and stood, sending his swivel chair rolling back. He looked at it in surprise as it bashed into a bookcase. Carefully, he set it back where it belonged by his desk and strode outside.

Suddenly, his energy level was higher than it had been in weeks. He'd work in the garden until time for his tennis game.

# SEVEN

A sudden spurt of restlessness sent Karen on a bath-room-scrubbing spree, but it wasn't enough. She needed more activity. She needed . . . a hike. Right, she'd told Jed she was considering one. And she had thought about it before calling him, but had decided against it.

That didn't mean she hadn't *planned* one. So she hadn't lied to him. Better to say she had things to do than let him think she was just sitting around hoping he'd call.

So a hike it was. That was what exactly what she needed. Good physical activity. Her doctor had told her to get plenty of exercise.

So, she remembered, had Jed.

She'd call Penny's aunt and see if the little girl could go with her. She often took Penny on impromptu outings. Up in the mountains it would be deliciously cool, and she might even find a quiet little pool in one of the froth-ing streams where she could soak her feet.

Unfortunately, no one answered the phone at Penny's house. Karen frowned and took her time making sand-wiches, then walked briskly to the corner store, where she selected fruit for herself and her small friend. Maybe Penny and Gloria had taken the younger kids to the park to feed the ducks, as they often did on a Sunday. She'd keep trying.

Ten minutes later, there was still no reply. She pulled on a pair of hiking shorts, thick socks, and her sturdiest high-tops, then tried again. No luck. She dragged all the standard survival contents from her backpack and checked to make sure everything was there. When nearly an hour had passed since her first phone call to Penny, she tried one last time, then gave up.

All right, fine. She'd go alone. It wouldn't be the first time. She knew only that she had to get out of the house, out of the neighborhood completely, or go nuts from claustrophobia.

She was just about to back out of her drive when a dark blue car with smoked windows coming a tad too fast along the street made her stop and wait. It pulled into the driveway beside her, the sun glinting off the glass and obscuring her vision. Nevertheless, something inside her responded wildly, crazily, to some indefinable quality pulsing in the air, and she turned off the key, bracing herself for the impact of seeing Jed again.

No amount of preparation would have been enough. Gripping the wheel, she clung to it as she waited for him to reach her side. It would have been pure folly to alight. Her knees never would have supported her weight. He looked stupendous, dressed for tennis—the match he had either passed up in order to come to see her or to which he was on his way. He wore white shorts, white socks, white shoes, and a white shirt with bright blue patches for pockets, closed with brass buttons. His dark hair looked wind-tossed. His legs and arms and face were firm and tanned a healthy, virile brown. His hazel eyes reflected the green of the trees overhead.

His smile reflected heaven.

A stabbing shot through Karen's abdomen, nearly making her gasp, followed by a moist heat that suffused her and made her forget there was such a thing as pain, such an emotion as loneliness. He was there!

He bent at the waist, his hands clasped over the window opening, his brown arms straight, his eyes smiling. His chin had healed nicely. A pink scar remained, but it would fade. Still, she wanted to kiss it better—and his ear, too, where a small scab showed.

*Just practicing,* she could say. *You know, for when I'm a mommy.* She gripped the wheel tighter to keep her hands under control.

"Hi." His voice slid right under her skin.

"Hi." Lord, couldn't she do better than a faint little whisper?

His smile faded. "You're on your way out somewhere?" he asked. "Or have you just arrived home?" Was that hope she heard in his tone, accompanying the last question? "I called, but didn't get an answer."

"But you came anyway?"

He shrugged. "I was in the car and it was pointed this direction. I was heading for my game when someone called me from the warehouse with a problem. Before I could get there, the problem got solved without me, so I tried to get hold of you, and when I couldn't . . ." He shrugged again. "I just . . . came." He broke off, looking charmingly, boyishly abashed, as if realizing his explanation was too long, too involved.

Karen struggled against joy. It was joy she was not entitled to feel, joy she'd be insane to pursue. "I went to the store for apples. I was about to drive up to Mt. Rainier Park to go for a hike."

"Mt. Rainier?" He might have been saying *the River Styx?*

"Yes. One of my favorite hiking trails skirts the edge of the park up there."

"No. No, really, you can't."

"Why not?"

"Why?" He blinked. "Well, because Mt. Rainier is a volcano!"

She felt her jaw go slack. "But it's been dormant for hundreds of years!"

"Then it's likely due to go up again anytime. It's not safe, Karen."

"Of course it's safe. I go there frequently. I was going to take Penny, but she's not home."

His eyes glittered as his jaw squared. "You're planning to go alone?"

She swallowed hard. He was too close. She wanted to get out of the truck, take a few steps away from him, give herself breathing room, but with his hands on the door, she couldn't. Scuttling across to the other door seemed too undignified. "Yes, I'm planning to go alone," she said. "But there's no big rush. I have time to get you that book, at least, before I go."

*Or I could stay home, if you really came to see me, if you wanted my company for, say, another hour or two, or even thirty minutes . . .*

He palmed her chin with a none-too-gentle hand and turned her face around to his. "You are not going hiking by yourself."

"Certainly I am. Why not? I often hike alone." *I do most things alone,* she wanted to add, but knew it would sound like self-pity. To distract herself, she asked quickly, "Did you . . . did you buy a new car?"

"It's a loaner until my replacement car arrives, and you're changing the subject, Karen Andersen."

He swung her door open and planted one foot just below her seat, folding his arms across his chest as he looked down his nose at her. It put him so much closer she could smell the citrus scent of his aftershave.

"Jed, please excuse me, but I really do want to get on my way."

Stubbornly, he repeated, "You can't go hiking alone!"

"I need to get out of the house," she retorted, gripping the wheel tighter, pressing her knees together to keep them from knocking. "I'm going stir-crazy, and I'm not heading alone into back country where no one ever goes."

"That's right, you're not," he said. "And you're not going up to Rainier alone, either, even on one of the most popular and well-used trails." He reached around her and undid her seatbelt. "Shove over."

Anger became a matter of necessity, a form of self-defense. "I beg your pardon?"

"You heard me. I'm going with you. Move over."

"Move *over?* I thought you came to borrow a book."

"Book?" He looked mystified, sounded vague. "Oh, yes. That book. Right, I did, but it can wait. If you're absolutely determined to go for a hike and I can't talk you out of it, then I guess I have to go with you."

"What about your tennis game?" *What about your partner? What happens if she finds out your emergency at work was also canceled, and you could have played tennis with her after all?*

She didn't ask out loud; she didn't want to hear the answer.

His brows crunched together. "Ten—? Ah, yes. I thought I told you. It's been canceled."

"When I go for a hike, I go for the whole day," she said huffily, not knowing why she had to argue with him, knowing only that it was necessary. "I pack a lunch, get away where I can enjoy some solitude."

"Do you mean you hike for the entire day? You can't do that, not now."

She glanced at her watch. "It's barely eleven o'clock. I can certainly go for what's left of it. If you get out of my way, that is, and let me leave."

"I mean you can't go for the entire day because it would wear you out. You're not thinking clearly, Karen. You're pregnant."

"Excuse me? Pregnancy prevents clear thought?"

"In you, something certainly does. You're not being sensible." He gave an impatient snort. "What if you fall? What if you get too tired to walk out of wherever it is you go to find this solitude you crave? What if any one of a wide variety of things go wrong? Have you thought about any of that?"

"Of course I have."

"And so have I. It's only a good idea for me to go with you."

It sounded as if he were trying to convince himself, as well as her, as if he had to talk himself into spending time with her. Karen clenched her teeth until her jaws ached. Her suppressed emotion—fury, that's what it was, outright rage—pressed against her throat and tongue, demanding she cut loose with her opinion of him and his good idea.

He'd decided to go with her not because he wanted her company, but because he didn't trust her not to get into trouble? That hurt. It hurt bad. She counted to ten. To twenty. To thirty. Then, drawing in a deep breath, she let it out slowly. "I see," she said, her voice sounding hoarse and taut. "Having found a woman perfectly happy and about to do something for herself, by herself, your great masculine ego insists you take charge?"

"Karen, I'm not trying to take charge," he protested,

his tone even, possibly even a tad condescending. Damn him! How could she justify getting mad if he continued to be so calmly reasonable? And if she couldn't get mad, she was going to fall all over him like an eager puppy, begging him to go with her.

"All I'm doing is suggesting that it's not a great idea for you to go off into the woods alone in your condition," he continued.

There it was again. Her condition! That was obviously all he cared about, his only reason for showing concern. Shoving him out of the way and grabbing for the side of the door to close it, she said, "This is my life. I live it as I see fit, and I don't need you to tell me how to do it!"

He crowded back in, put his foot up again. She pushed him again with as little effect. "Damn it, get out of my way or you'll get run over!"

"Karen . . ." A faint flush of color rose up under his tan and a peculiar light flickered in his eyes that she thought at first was amusement. As he continued to stand there, one foot inside her truck, the other planted firmly on the driveway, she saw a pulse hammering in his throat, heard his breath rasp as he sucked it in. Her heart flopped over like a doodlebug as she recognized the signs, remembered where she'd seen that strange, simmering quality in his eyes before, and when.

She couldn't speak, couldn't breathe, couldn't think.

But she could want. Need.

Suddenly, the same kind of urgent warning rushed through her as in the seconds before the driver of the semi had blared his horn, and she responded to it with defiance, possibly even welcome. Swinging one foot around, she stomped it down on top of his pretty white tennis shoe and said, "Move it or lose it, Cotts."

His excitement erupted along with hers as he dragged in a deep, ragged breath and hauled her out of the truck into his arms.

His head came down and his mouth covered hers in a wild, impetuous kiss.

She didn't struggle, not even for form. She thought about it, then the taste of him got through, the scent, the feel, the memory of that kiss in the airport, and it was game, set, and match.

Her lips parted. Her tongue sought, found, and was rewarded. She slid her arms around his big torso, feeling the hard prickle of his hair against the backs of her legs as he picked her up and sat her on his uplifted thigh. He smelled of freshly ironed cotton, male musk, and something that was uniquely Jedidiah Cotts. She hung on for the ride.

It was as she'd remembered it, a heady, thought-destroying delight, being properly kissed by this man. It made her want to burrow into him, become part of him, meld her skin with his, fuse her body with his, her soul. And it wasn't enough. Nothing would ever be enough. She clung, straining him to her, hands in his hair, on his neck, his shoulders, testing the power of the muscles that held her, stroking over the hollows of his cheeks, then gliding back into his hair again, her head spinning, her blood roaring, her body aching with need.

His breath came swiftly, rasping in and out as he dragged his mouth from hers, trailed it down her throat to the vee at the top of her blouse, whiskers whispering against her skin. His hand cradled a breast gently, a breast newly full and hard and round, and she was glad they had grown in the past months. She didn't want gentle any more than she had ever wanted polite, and thrust herself into his palm. She felt totally female, voluptuous, giving of all that was good. He murmured his delight, dragged his thumb over her nipple again and again until she ached with the need to have his mouth there instead. She arched against him, whispering his name, a soft plea.

"Karen." His voice was hoarse. "Oh, Lord, Karen, I want . . ." He pressed his hand down her front, under her breast, to her waist, to the bulge of her belly—and then snatched it away. He straightened his leg, lowered her to the pavement and let her go, staggering away from her.

Leaning both hands on the box of her truck as if he were trying to push it sideways, gripping tightly, arms and legs rigid, feet braced apart, head hanging between hunched shoulders, he sucked in a hard breath, let it out in a rush, then took another and another for several minutes before standing straight, still blowing like a whale. He wiped one forearm over his brow, drew a hand down over his too-pale face, then turned and looked at her, his dark eyes filled with . . . guilt? Remorse? Shame?

*Disgust?*

"I'm sorry," he said. "Oh, hell, Karen, I'm more sorry than I can tell you. I shouldn't have done that, but—" He shook his head, not quite meeting her gaze. "No. There is no excuse. I just shouldn't have." He stepped back a pace or two. "I'll go now."

He said it, but he didn't move.

She drew in another deep breath and blurted out, "Jed, please. Come with me."

"I—" He sucked in a deep breath then let it escape in a rush. "Karen, I—" He puffed out another breath, shaking his head, his gaze never leaving her face. "Damn it, woman, you've done it again."

"Done what?"

"Left me not knowing what to say."

"Then say you'll go on that hike with me because you'd enjoy being with me, not because you think I'm some kind of incompetent who can't look after herself," she said, her gaze holding his. She smiled. "After all, aren't you the one who said I should get plenty of exercise?"

"You *want* me with you?" Jed asked, his tone incredulous.

"Yes. Yes, I do." Karen knew as she said it that it was one of the most basic truths of her life. It was The Truth. She wanted Jed with her wherever she went. There was a futility behind that wanting, but that didn't make it stop.

Her mother had been absolutely right. She was in grave danger of falling in love with him. It might, she realized, already be too late.

"Why?" he asked. "Why, after all your objections, do you now want me to go with you?"

Of course she couldn't tell him. But that didn't mean she had to lie. There were Truths, and there were truths.

"Because I . . . like you," she said, thinking what a pale word *like* was, though she meant it wholeheartedly. It didn't do justice to the sweeping, glorious feeling of being with him, but it would have to suffice. "I enjoy your company." Oh, Lord! Ditto the word *enjoy.* "And, well, I must confess, I'd rather not hike alone. Not now, with the baby and all. You were right about that. Although I'm strong and healthy and everything's going fine, I know that could change without much warning. I *could* fall or something with no one around to offer immediate help, so I don't want to take chances."

He looked completely bewildered. "Then why did you get so mad at me for asking to go with you?"

She shook her head. "Jed, you didn't ask. You ordered.

You told me to move over. You acted as if you thought I didn't have a brain."

He ran a hand over the top of his head. "Yeah. All right, I guess I did. Damn! You know, I've been taught bet—I know better than that, too, so I can't understand why I did it. There's something about you that turns me into an unthinking primitive. I'll try to curb it."

She hoped he wouldn't. Not entirely. There was, after all, something to be said for the alpha male, no matter how much feminists decried him. But being decisive and determined was one thing. Being a bully was quite another. There was a fine line between the two. It would take a strong woman to keep herself from being overwhelmed by such a man, to keep him from overstepping that boundary.

Was she that kind of woman? She'd never thought much about it, but now she wondered. She wanted to be. She wanted . . . a lot of things. First among them right this minute was to get going, to get out of town and into the countryside where she could breathe and see something besides houses and cars, where if Jed's car phone rang he'd be nowhere around to answer a call to business. Today, she wanted him all to herself.

"If you really want to join me, I'd like to have you along."

Jed continued to regard her silently, as if warring with something inside him. She knew if she didn't act, he would get back into his car and drive away.

Slipping past him, she headed up the front steps to the house. "I'll just make another couple of sandwiches. I made peanut butter and jelly for myself," she said over her shoulder. "Is that okay for you?" The sandwiches she'd made would fill about a fourth of Jed's masculine appetite. She'd need plenty more.

Jed stared at her, bemused. Though he knew she'd said something, he hadn't heard her. He was still suffering acutely from the aftereffects of that kiss, from her touch, from hearing her say that she liked him, that she enjoyed his company. Damn it, every time he saw her, she managed to get him spinning like a wonky top until he didn't know which way he faced—or wanted to face.

She was a hell of a lot more thought-provoking than Ayn Rand's *Atlas Shrugged,* and for the first time since he'd found himself in his car headed toward her house, he admitted it wasn't the book he'd come for.

He'd come for exactly what he'd gotten . . . and more. He hadn't realized until only moments before exactly how much more he wanted.

However badly he wanted it, though, it wasn't something he was going to get, going to *take,* even if she was offering, and he wasn't exactly certain she was. But if she wasn't, why would she kiss him like that, come to his arms so willingly, so warmly, so eagerly?

She was lonely. He recognized it because he knew loneliness intimately himself. And the father of her baby had just married another woman. Inside, however much she might deny it, her heart had to be breaking.

He watched her walk up the steps, her slim brown legs bared by a pair of the shortest shorts he'd ever seen a pregnant lady wear. From the back she didn't look the least bit like someone in the family way. Hell, she hardly looked pregnant from the front, for that matter, but her rear view showed a slender girl. Hah! *He* knew she was a perfectly formed woman, with round, firm, heavy breasts that filled his hands to perfection. And she was inviting him to go out into the woods with her all alone, with nobody else around.

Was the woman completely out of her mind?

After he'd dragged her into his arms and kissed the living hell out of her, she still wanted to be with him?

Going out with him was not sensible, especially considering the way he reacted to her. He swallowed again. "Karen?"

But the screen door had slammed behind her, leaving him standing in the driveway and feeling as if a truck had run over him.

An eighteen-wheeler, like the one they had missed on that Montana highway. Only he knew now he'd escaped nothing at all. That eighteen-wheeler was still bearing down on him, and this time it was going to connect. It was going to squash him flat.

So why wasn't he steering the hell out of its way?

As if she had no idea of the danger Jed felt pressing in around him, Karen kept up a light, inconsequential conversation. By the time they'd reached the highway leading to the foot of the mountain, Jed had himself back under control.

*Whew!* he thought, mentally wiping sweat off his face again. *Okay, so I had a few bad minutes. There's no such thing as fate. A man controls his own destiny, and mine does not include a pregnant woman who explodes at the slightest provocation—and unleashes something ferocious in me.*

All he had to do to remain safe and keep her safe was not to make her mad. If he didn't have to see her eyes catch fire, her face flame with anger, her chest heave, or her nipples jut out as her level of agitation rose, he'd be perfectly all right.

Jed groaned as he stretched his cramped legs upon alighting from the truck. Karen had to have the seat close to the front to reach the pedals, and he'd felt like a pretzel crammed under the dash. "How did a woman with a good, Nordic name like Karen Andersen and two tall, fair-haired parents end up a half-pint like you, with auburn hair and gray eyes and a wild Irish temper?" he asked.

She slammed her door and reached out to take the pack from him. Her eyes smoldered with a laughing warning. "What Irish temper?"

He held the pack out of her reach while he lengthened the straps, deliberately avoiding her eyes. Even her smoldering could set things alight in him. "The Irish temper you cut loose with at least three times an hour."

"That, I'll have you know, is perfectly legitimate Danish volatility that I inherited from my grandmother Andersen. She was a Christiansen by birth. Dad says she continued waving wooden spoons at him and his six brothers and sisters and making violent threats long after her children towered over her. She berated them soundly for any misdemeanor right up to the day she died at the age of eighty-three.

"When she had, as he puts it, 'a mood on her,' they scattered, even as adults. He says he married Mom, who's cool and serene, because he wanted to spend his days with someone who wouldn't raise her voice."

She grinned. "And he got stuck with me as his only child." Her grin turned into an outright laugh. "He used to call me Seed of Hagar until my mother took offense." She paused for effect before adding, "Mildly and politely, of course."

Jed slipped the pack onto his back and turned so she could stuff the extra sandwiches and the jug of juice into it. She zipped it shut and patted it to show she was done. He turned, surprised she hadn't given him a battle over possession of it, and took her hand as she moved toward the beginning of the trail.

"Your dad seems pretty content with you."

"Yes." They fell silent, walking in step, loosely linked hands swinging between them.

Felix Andersen wasn't merely content with his daughter, Jed reflected. He was immensely proud. It had warmed Jed to see that. As a father, he could empathize with the older man, understand the glow of knowing he and his wife had done their job well.

"Why wasn't Barry?" Jed asked, startling Karen, who had been off in a dream world that did not include her ex-husband in any way at all.

She jerked her head around. "Why wasn't Barry what?"

"Content. With you."

She sighed. "He was, Jed. I was the one who wasn't content with our marriage."

"Oh. I see." He dropped her hand and fiddled with the pack straps. She recognized it as a excuse to let go of her. They both came to a halt.

She squinted up at him, the sun in her eyes. He moved to put a shadow across her face. "No, you don't see," she said. "You think I left him like Crystal left you. You're judging me, condemning me." Deliberately, she used the same words he'd said to her when he'd refused to discuss the custody issue of his youngest daughter.

He gave her a cool look, one she recognized as meant to quell her. "So now you're a mind reader?"

She didn't back down, but continued to stare into his eyes, challenging him to deny her statement. "Not a mind reader," she said. "A face reader."

He sighed. "I'm not condemning you. Hell, why

should I? I never condemned Crystal, either. I know why she left me. I didn't make her happy."

Karen turned and faced along the trail again, not wanting to see the torment in his eyes, torment put there by the woman he still loved, probably would always love to the exclusion of any other. They walked together, but he didn't take her hand again.

"Jed," she said presently, "I've always believed that one person can't make happiness for another. Each of us makes it for ourselves. That's why I left Barry. I was content, too, but I realized that contentment wasn't what I wanted out of life, out of marriage. We were in our thirties, married eleven years, and I felt as if we were in our seventies and had been married fifty years. Maybe it's because we've known each other since early childhood. By the time we'd been married eight or nine years, we'd all but stopped talking together, as if we'd said everything there was to say. We didn't do things together anymore. We didn't even have the same friends."

Jed glanced into her troubled eyes. "Why? You lived in the town you both grew up in. Your friends were his friends right through from childhood, surely."

"Many of them had moved away, farming being what it is," Karen said, "and we'd both made other friends through our work, not all of whom liked each other. I taught junior college in Helena. His work was at the hospital in Soda Creek. I had teaching colleagues. He had hospital colleagues. Our social lives had become almost polarized because I couldn't count on him as an escort to any function I wanted to attend. He was either working or on call. And hospital functions, with their politics and pecking order, bored me. Infuriated me.

"That might have been something we could have worked on, but when I realized all of it had ceased to matter to us, that it wasn't worth the effort, I knew we weren't husband and wife, but more like fond roommates who shared a bed part time."

"So you left him."

"I didn't run out on him. And I didn't find another partner," she added pointedly. "I told him how I felt. He treated my concerns as having no validity. I got mad and *he* walked out. He just brushed me off and went back to where he was happiest, the hospital. I'm stubborn when I want to be; for a while I tried to make things work. I got mad a lot, and it was like getting angry with a wall. I saw a position offered out here on the Coast, teaching English and creative thinking. I applied and was accepted."

She smiled and gave a small shrug. "It was harder telling our two sets of parents I was leaving than it was telling Barry. When I told him I was taking the position, he didn't put up much of an argument—at least not for very long. Maybe what he'd really wanted all along was what my dad did—someone who wouldn't raise her voice."

Jed reached out and linked his fingers with hers.

If Barry Renton didn't see what he saw when Karen raised her voice, then the man was as blind and as cold-blooded as a deep cavern fish.

It occurred to Jed after several hundred yards of walking hand in hand with her that until he met Karen, he might have been considered cold-blooded, too, instead of a man who made a practice of exercising the proper restraint. Funny. Crystal was the one who had encouraged him to become more controlled. Then, in the end, she had accused him of lacking real emotion. That was something to ponder.

Especially now, the way he was in danger of losing that proper restraint all too often around Karen. His blood grew perceptibly warmer merely thinking about it.

# EIGHT

"Getting hungry?" Karen asked as the trail came out onto a high, sunny bluff overlooking a lake that reflected the surrounding trees and a few puffy clouds. The view down a long valley ended in a swatch of misty blue that could have been cloud or sea. An eagle soared high overhead, then dipped out of sight behind a ridge. Here, this close to the mountain, the trees obscured the view of its ice-cream-cone shape.

"Sure," he said, shrugging out of the pack and stripping off his shirt. "Sun or shade?"

Karen opted for the shade of an old mountain hemlock that grew beside a stream bubbling down the bank toward the lake. She crouched and rinsed her face in the clear water, then wiped it dry with the tail of her shirt, and quickly prevented Jed from taking a drink from the creek.

"Ever hear of giardiasis—beaver fever?"

He had, but only vaguely, and she explained, then sat back, reaching for the pack. "Sorry. I didn't mean to lecture you. Here, have some lemonade."

They took turns drinking from the jug, then set it aside and dug into the sandwiches, discussing the variety of trees and shrubs that grew around them.

"You're very knowledgeable about the woods," he said presently, lying flat on his back on a slope of grass, hands folded under his head, letting the cool breeze glide over his bare chest. From this position, he could no longer see the terrain falling away to the lake and the valley below. He had a better picture before him.

Karen sprawled, half sitting, two or three feet away. The pack formed a pad at the small of her back, her head and shoulders rested against the trunk of the tree, and she'd folded her hands around her belly. Even in two weeks, she was showing much more than when he'd first met her. She looked entirely feminine, completely fetching, with the sun making red shafts on her dark hair, dappling her tanned legs with bright golden shapes.

"I love the forest," she said. "When I came out to the Coast a year and a half ago, I joined a hiking group, but it was too structured, so I started going out by myself. I could go were I chose, when I chose. There's something special about emerging from the forest into a place like this. I find a sort of peace within myself when I've reached a high point where the view goes on forever. Maybe it's because I grew up under wide skies, with a horizon a long way off. Being in a place like this lets me think more clearly."

"What do you think about?"

She shrugged and gazed away down the valley below. "All sorts of things."

Jed watched her for a moment before he rolled to his side, getting closer, facing her. He propped his head on one hand and trailed the fingertips of the other across the knuckles of her right hand, hoping to draw her focus in closer to home. He felt incredibly lonely when she stared into the distance, as if she were shutting him out. "World-saving things? The first time I saw you, you were wearing a tree-hugger shirt."

She sat up and crossed her legs tailor-fashion, shooting

him an irritated glance as she brushed her hair off her forehead. "I dislike that phrase."

"What? Tree hugger?" Well, she was focused, all right. And on him, her eyes snapping. A flicker of excitement ran through him like an electric current.

"Yes, tree hugger," she snapped. "It makes people who care about the environment sound superficial and trendy."

Her cheeks flamed. He tried to suppress the tumultuous emotions only she could elicit, but it was impossible. They licked through him hotly, tumbling over one another, tripping on his hang-ups and eroding them like water on the rocks in the creek bed.

*Stop now,* he told himself. *Don't let the heat build. What are you, a man in control, or an animal out to prove something?* "Isn't being a tree hugger trendy?" he asked. "Maybe even superficial? It's certainly politically correct."

Her eyes flared. "Do I look superficial to you?"

Jed shrugged, an irrepressible smile forming on his face, a wild, crazy exhilaration growing inside him. "Maybe you don't look that way," he said, "but some of your attitudes could do with a bit of adjustment."

She popped to her feet. Her fists clenched. "And you think you're just the guy to adjust them?"

He nodded. "As a matter of fact, I do," he said, and watched her explode before him.

She planted her fists on her hips. "My attitudes are mine, thank you very much, and I don't need you or anyone else taking it upon himself to reprogram me."

He cocked a brow in a manner that he knew made Willi and Ceil grind their teeth. His eagerness to see how it affected Karen almost shocked him. "Why not," he asked, "when you've so obviously been improperly programmed by all your preservationist friends? How much of your paycheck each month do you waste on politically correct causes, anyway?"

She took a deep breath that lifted her breasts, tautening the fabric of her shirt. "What the hell business is it of yours what I do with my paychecks?"

"I hate to see otherwise intelligent people taken in by self-righteous groups with secret agendas," he said. "Of course, if you give your support in a more physical manner, by actually hugging trees, that's a different thing. Not much smarter, but different. Although it would be hard on your soft little hands." He stroked her nearest fist with the tip of one finger.

She snatched her soft little hand out from under his. "Soft little hands be damned!" she snorted and flung her arms around the tree. "There! See? You now know a genuine tree hugger."

She released the tree and brushed down the front of her blouse, where little bits of moss and bark clung. "I belong to no *self-righteous* groups, and I don't believe any I've joined have secret agendas!"

He laughed. "Of course they do. Every one. It's a conspiracy that takes in well-meaning but innocent citizens."

"Damn it, Jed, are you one of those head-in-the-sand industry-first people who refuses to accept how serious this whole issue is?"

He sat up and grinned. "Serious? Come on, Karen. Look around you." He waved a lazy hand at the thousands of square miles of heavily wooded slopes marching away into purple infinity. "Can you honestly expect me to believe we're suffering from a shortage of trees?"

"Maybe not here. Maybe not yet. But the time will come! We're cutting them faster than they can grow."

He smiled up at her. "Don't you use paper? Don't you live in a house made of wood?"

Her gray eyes sparkled. Her chest rose and fell rapidly. Her mouth was tautly compressed. Those flags of color in her cheeks angled toward her ears, the pink reflected brightly in her lobes. That was an effect he'd never noticed before. It made him want to kiss those hot little tabs of flesh, suck them into his mouth, bathe them with his tongue. . . .

It made him want too many things. Hell, what was he doing, deliberately goading her like this, simply because she rose to the bait so well? He'd have brought the whole game to a halt, but she strode to within inches of him and glared down at him.

"Yes, damn it, I use both paper and wood products, but I make sure I use them judiciously. I recognize that we need lumber to build houses and furniture, that using trees is often less harmful to the planet in the long run than the manufacture of bricks or plastic or aluminum, but that doesn't mean I agree with slashing down everything standing in a watershed. There must be limits!"

"Don't you think the entire thing is a fashionable bandwagon to be on, a trivial excuse for city people to poke their noses into the lives and livelihoods of people who rely on the forests for their jobs?"

"Trivial?" Outrage echoed off the trees. "Are you calling me trivial? I have a genuine concern for the environment, Jed Cotts, and if you have a problem with that, too bad. I will not let you mock it!"

She poked him in the chest with the tip of her shoe and then planted her foot down again, well apart from its mate, as she went on, her eyes blazing, her face aglow.

He laughed again. He had to. She was wonderful.

"Why, you—"

As she took a swing at him, he caught her hand, eased

her down into his arms, into the cradle formed by his bent leg.

"The only thing I have a problem with is controlling myself around you," he said, his voice coming out in a low, tense growl. His hands trembled as he cupped her face and stared at her—at her parted lips, her glowing cheeks, her sparkling eyes with bright green shafts in the deep gray. "Oh, hell, Karen, you're—"

What, he didn't say, couldn't say. He wanted to kiss her until he quenched her fire, but if he did, what would quench his?

She went very still as he held her, her eyes wide, gazing into his, her right hand clenched on his shoulder, her left spread over his bent knee, her bottom pressed against his thigh. He felt the heat of her, the heaving of her chest against his, her breath on his face as he stared back at her, their mouths so close they were only a shadow away from touching. He slid one hand to the back of her head, the other to her side.

"What are you doing to me?" she whispered.

"Holding you," he whispered back. If he moved, he might unleash the beast within. Even her breathing threatened to kindle his passion beyond his control.

"Why?" She swallowed.

"Because I'm going to kiss you."

She licked her lips. They glistened. Her eyes danced. Her smile was one of anticipation. "Politely?" she challenged him.

He drew a deep, painful breath, and let it out all at once. *"No!"* he groaned as his control shattered and he grabbed a fistful of her hair, tilted her head back and kissed her in a way he hadn't kissed anybody for a long, long time.

He kissed her as he hadn't kissed anyone at *any* time.

Except her. Only her. Once in an airport, but mostly in his dreams. He'd kiss her until they risked making Mt. Rainier explode from its dormancy, and politeness would have no part in it.

He prodded with the tip of his tongue, wanting to master her, to force her mouth open . . . and found it parted eagerly. He plunged deep with his tongue, meaning to plunder. Her eagerness matched his. He cradled her tighter against him, trying to remind himself to be gentle, but her fingers raked at his back, demanding more.

Her scent enflamed him. Her taste engulfed him. Her body was hot and alive, moving in erotic rhythms that incinerated what little restraint he had left. Her hands roved over him, sliding inside the open front of his shirt, her fingers spreading across his shoulders, down to his chest, stroking his nipples, pinching lightly, flexing, digging into his muscles. Her breath came moist and rapid against his neck as he tore his mouth from hers and leaned his head back, gasping for air before lowering it again and nibbling at her lips with small, hot kisses that she returned one for one, nipping with teeth, soothing with tongue, then kissing again.

His hands trembled as he unbuttoned her shirt, shoved its sides apart and unhooked her bra. Laying her back on the grass, he stretched beside her, folding her close, groaning with the sensation of her hard, hot breasts against his bare chest.

She drew in a tremulous breath and breathed it out on his name, a plea.

Rising part way, he bent over her, tonguing her nipples, wetting them, reveling in their tautness, the small sounds of pleasure she made as she held his head in her two hands. He drew one hard bead into his mouth, sucking gently, then harder as she arched up, her cry of pleasure igniting him.

He murmured and gasped out his hopes, his wants, his needs, pressing the words against her flesh, branding her with them, a small, detached part of him hovering above and looking down, wondering at his total lack of inhibition. The sun shone in dappled streams across her face, caught in her hair, slid shadows over the curves of her breasts as she breathed. He followed those bars of light and dark, captured one atop a nipple, and drew it into his mouth. She tasted of sunshine. Her other breast, when he moved on to it, tasted just as good as its mate had, felt just as hot and silky to his tongue, and the damp one he'd left fit perfectly into his palm.

He could have feasted on her for hours, but slowly it came to his notice that she simply lay there in his arms. The soft little sounds of pleasure she'd been making had ceased. Her hands, instead of tangling in his hair with heated passion, now pressed against his chest, forcing him away. He lifted his head and stared down at her, appalled to see tears glistening in her lashes, and was struck by the worst guilt he had ever felt.

He rolled apart from her, then reached down and fastened her bra, drew the front of her shirt together and buttoned it, all without saying a word. He couldn't speak. What could he say? He had let the animal in him take over, and he had hurt her. Hurt her badly.

*Made her cry.*

She lay half turned from him, and he watched one tear trace a silver track over the bridge of her nose before it trickled out of sight. Finally, she sat up and wrapped her arms around her legs, leaning her cheek on her folded knees, facing away from him. Need ate at him to do something, say something, make amends in some way.

He uncapped the lemonade jug, poured a stream into the cup, and nudged the back of her arm with it.

"Here, honey. Have a drink." His voice rasped painfully.

She shook her head, still without looking at him. The silence went on. A squirrel chattered angrily. A circling eagle piped plaintively and was joined by its mate. Two canoes made leisurely tracks across the smooth lake, four paddles sending silver shafts of light like mirrors tilted into the sun. Somewhere, a seed popped with a sharp sound and something rustled in the underbrush as if trying to escape a trap.

He had taken Karen's special place and sullied it for her. She'd never be able to come here again without remembering what he had done to her, how he had defiled her, almost forced her to succumb to his passion—a passion she clearly did not share.

Lord almighty, he was ashamed.

"I'm so ashamed I could die of it," Karen said, lifting her head and facing him. "Jed, please forgive me. I can't tell you how sorry I am."

He felt as if she'd kicked him between the legs. Nothing could make a man's own guilt trip worse than a woman trying to take the blame onto herself.

"What the hell do you have to be sorry for?" He wanted to bang his head on that damned tree of hers, but if he did, she'd probably accuse him of harming it, too. "I'm the one who did wrong. I—"

"Didn't stand a chance," she interjected sadly. "Not a single, solitary chance."

He blinked. "What?" He stared at her. Her nose was red and shiny. Her eyes, pink-rimmed, stared back at him, big and dark and gleaming. She was the most beautiful

*Judy Gill*

thing in the world, but she didn't make any sense at all. The woman was obviously out of her mind.

"What did you say?" he croaked, knowing he couldn't have heard her right.

She sighed. "I said you didn't stand a chance. I set you up for that. It's my fault and, oh, damn, but I wanted it to be real!"

Jed shook his head chidingly. "Karen, you can't take the blame for that on yourself. That's patently the most . . . it isn't logical. It's—"

"The truth," she interrupted again. "I did it. On purpose. I didn't get mad at you, Jed, I got mad *for* you, because I know it turns you on."

He blinked again and got to his knees, facing her, taking her shoulders in his hands. "You do?"

She nodded. A couple of fresh tears welled up and splashed away. "I'd have to be pretty stupid not to have figured that out by now. Every time I pitch a fit, you kiss me."

He groaned and rubbed a hand down over his face. "I'm sorry. I was trying to tell you how—"

"Jed, please, it's my turn to grovel. Don't deny me that."

The idea of any woman groveling before him was novel, maybe even appealing, but he couldn't permit it. "You don't have anything to grovel over," he protested, but she placed a hand in the middle of his bare chest, thereby cutting off his air supply. It was the first time he'd known a soft, silky palm on his skin could immobilize his lungs.

"I wanted you to kiss me *im*politely. I wanted you to kiss me like you meant it because those kisses from you are addictive. I wanted more."

He shook his head and drew in a deep breath, head

swimming from oxygen deprivation. "No, you didn't, Karen. You stopped participating. You'd had enough and I kept right on."

"That's my fault, too," she said. "None of it should ever have happened. It's because I'm pregnant, you see. Esther—the friend I've mentioned—explained it to me, though you probably know all about it anyway."

He stared at her, trying to make sense of her words. "Know all about what?"

"About how pregnant women get . . . well . . ."

She broke off, her solemn gaze sliding away from his before she brought it back—bravely, he thought, judging the level of her embarrassment—and continued. "We have an excess of hormones that make us . . . that increases our . . . sexual desire."

"Let me get this straight. Are you saying that pregnancy makes you horny?"

She nodded. "And weepy and hungry and sleepy. Esther says it happens to all women."

Jed stared at her. "That's the first I've heard of it!"

It was as if she didn't hear him. "And since I have no one else in my life, like a husband or a boyfriend, I hit on you."

"You *hit* on me?" It wasn't even personal?

"Yes. Right. I mean, you saw what happened, didn't you? You even wrecked a car because I got mad, Jed. I knew how potent the results could be. And I wanted those results because of those damned hormones."

Jed traced a line from the point of her shoulder down to her elbow.

She wanted those results. She wanted *him*. Thinking about that made it difficult to breathe again.

He concentrated on drawing in one breath after another, evenly. He frowned thoughtfully. "Hormones or not, the responsibility was still mine," he said, more to himself than to her. "I didn't have to make you mad. I know how to disagree productively, even if you don't. Anger is never productive."

She grinned. "Isn't it?"

He almost grinned back, but stopped himself in time. This was serious, and she had to recognize it. A discussion that broke down into mirth—or worse, turned to sexual passion—never got anyone anywhere.

*Except laid,* a small voice whispered in his ear. He ignored it as best he could.

"I could have kept our discussion on a nice, even tenor, not goaded you. I used deliberately provocative terms, like tree hugger and preservationist. I chose to whip up your temper because it—you're quite right. It turns me on.

"But this time, it more than turned me on. It turned me *wild.* And then I got too rough with you. I manhandled you. I hurt you. I made you cry. And that's what I can't forgive myself for. I hurt a helpless, pregnant lady."

*"Helpless?"*

He read the warning in her eyes, and this time, he was determined to ignore its effect. "Karen," he said reasonably, his hand resting on her bent knee, on her warm, smooth skin, gliding, as if he was no longer in charge of it, toward—

He snatched it away and went on. "Face it. You couldn't stop me, couldn't prevent what I was doing. You're a lot smaller than I am. Hell, you could have begged and pleaded and said no a thousand times, but it wouldn't have done any good."

She snapped her legs straight and was back in a standing position so quickly, so smoothly, he was left gaping at the place where she'd been sitting, but which now only

held her feet. She could move awfully damned fast for a pregnant lady.

"Bull!" she snorted as he scrambled to regain his feet. "You quit the moment you realized I wasn't fully with you anymore."

She did have a point there. "Well, yes," he conceded, "but how could you know I would?"

"I didn't. No woman ever does, but I trust you, Jed. Don't forget, I spent several days in your company. I think I learned a few things about you. And one more thing. When I set out to get you to do what you did, I had no intention of trying to get you to stop."

He looked at her silently for a long moment before he said with infinite gentleness, "Karen, honey, no woman ever sets out to turn a man into an animal."

She stared at him. "Wow! And you called *me* politically correct!"

He ignored that. "I think maybe you were curious. Maybe you had some instinctive need to be held, to be reassured about your femininity, your attractiveness to a man, but you weren't looking for . . . sex."

Karen flared again. "Are you saying I don't know what I want when I want it? And how I want it, and with whom? Are you saying you think I can't look after myself in a tight situation? Are you saying you think I've got marshmallows for brains? That I'm such a bubblehead I'd have let you get within a hundred feet of me on a lonely trail if I didn't trust you implicitly?

"You, Jedidiah Cotts, spent too many years in a marriage with a manipulative, brainwashing woman who tried to turn you into her ideal mate, except she was destined to fail because her ideal mate just happened to be someone else. And you know what else? I'm *glad* she left you when she did. There might still be hope for you, if you'd just get over some of those dumb things you learned from her about what women want and need and expect from a man. Trust me, most of what she taught you is pure, unadulterated *crap!*"

Karen snatched up the pack, stuffed in their sandwich wrappings, crammed the juice jug down on top, and slung it over her shoulders. The straps, stretched out to fit him, let it bounce against her rear end as she marched away down the trail. He stood there, not knowing whether to laugh or bellow with rage.

His feet slipping on pine needles and tripping over roots, Jed thundered after Karen, his heart hammering, adrenaline sizzling through him. He caught her in less than thirty yards.

"Now, just hold on a minute there, lady!" He took her shoulder, spun her around. "You don't even know her, so you have no call to insult my wi—ex-wife."

She slipped her shoulder out of his grasp with ease, merely shrugging him off. "Why, Jed," she said, her eyes wide and mocking, "are you on the verge of losing *your* cool?" She poked him in the stomach with a knuckle and grinned impudently. "Bucking for an impolite kiss, Cotts?"

He threw up his hands in despair, wanting to curse, wanting to laugh, wanting to kiss her again. "Damn it, Karen!"

"Don't sweat it," she said, tapping him not particularly gently on the chin with a fist. "Just consider this one argument you lost." She strode off down the trail, legs and arms swinging easily, the pack still bouncing up and down on her butt.

Jed followed, keeping just close enough to have a chance of leaping forward to catch her if she fell but not

quite close enough to touch. It was safer that way, he thought. Safer if a man didn't mind torture.

Over and over, his mind echoed her words: *dumb things you learned from her about what women want and need and expect from a man. Trust me, most of what she taught you is pure, unadulterated crap!*

Why hadn't he ever thought of it like that?

It was such simple logic. All their married life, Crystal had tried to make him over. She had been angry with him for failing to become what she wanted, and he had been angry with her for trying. Their marriage had been doomed, whether he liked it or not.

Maybe, just maybe, he wasn't as inept a husband as he'd thought. Maybe he'd just been caught up in an impossible situation where he could never expect to win. Would he stand a chance in another relationship?

He closed his eyes for a second, felt a pebble roll under his foot, and nearly fell. Quickly, he forced himself to concentrate. If he fell, he'd knock Karen down, and the last thing he wanted in this world was to hurt her. From somewhere deep within him, a huge, unhappy sigh rose up. He let it out slowly, but it failed to bleed out his melancholy.

He was glad, he thought as he crunched himself into her truck, that Karen was pregnant. For that reason alone, their friendship could only be platonic. She was going to become a mother, begin raising a child just as he was finishing that phase of his life.

If he was going to reassess himself as a man, reassess his readiness for another relationship with a woman, it would have to be someone other than Karen, which meant, above all, that he'd have to stay away from her.

She had too strong an effect on him, could too easily

turn him into the kind of animal he didn't want to ever again be accused of being.

At his age, if he needed companionship at all, he'd be better off with a woman who would be soothing to come home to after a stressful day at work, someone who'd be as ready as he for early retirement in, say, ten years, not someone with a child in high school or college. He'd need a woman who'd enjoy his grandchildren and her own, not someone who, in a few months, was going to have her first baby. And not someone who, by the very fact of that baby, was going to be forced into an ongoing relationship with her ex-husband who, whether he knew it or not, whether *she* knew it or not, still had some deep and unresolved feelings for her.

He released a jagged breath, which brought a glance from Karen. She smiled ruefully and shook her head, slowed as she drove across the gravel parking lot, then stopped. She slid out of the truck. "You drive," she said. "You look like a grasshopper over there with your knees up around your ears."

# NINE

Jed thought of suggesting they stop somewhere for dinner, even for just a burger and fries, but a moment's thought told him that was as bad an idea as hiking with her had been.

He knew he couldn't afford to see her again. He was going to have a hell of a job staying away, because how could any man of good conscience let a woman go through an entire pregnancy all alone? For reasons that made no sense at all, he felt responsible for her.

Because she had no one of her own close by? Of course. That was all. Still, maybe a few days' cooling-off period would get his crazed libido back under control.

If he couldn't walk out of her life, however much sense it might make, he'd have to search for ways to be with her safely, for her sake as much as his own.

Aroused, he'd just discovered, he was a dangerous man.

They were silent for most of the trip back to her house. While she was inside getting her copy of *Atlas Shrugged*, which she insisted on lending him, Jed pulled the bench seat of her truck as far forward as he could so she wouldn't have to do it the next time she wanted to drive.

She handed him the book as he stood by the door of his car, the glow of the setting sun casting shadows over one side of her face, backlighting her hair like half a halo. "Just give it to Cecelia when you're done," she said, "and she can return it to me."

Jed nearly staggered under the weight of his disappointment. It appeared he was getting the brush-off. So much for his magnanimous decision that they'd have to see each other again so he could keep an eye on her.

He forced back his arguments. All right. So she didn't want to see him again. Could he blame her? Obviously, she'd done some serious thinking on the drive home and come to the conclusion any woman in her right mind would have reached after today's display: Jed Cotts was a man to avoid. "I understand."

She pierced him with a questioning look. "What do you understand?"

"That I'm not to come back." He shrugged. "I get the picture. It's no more than I deserve after hurting you."

Her bright laughter stung his ego. Then, sobering, she shook her head. Little shafts of light bounced off the ends of her hair. She reached up to touch his face in the briefest of caresses. "Jed, please listen to me. Please believe me. You did not hurt me. That's not why I think it would be best if we didn't see each other again."

Her touch caused him terrible pain this time, instead of easing it as it had before. "I made you cry, didn't I?"

"No." She was quietly—uncharacteristically quietly—adamant. "You did not, repeat, *not* make me cry. *I* made me cry. Shame made me cry. I was using you, and I wanted to go on and on using you because it was wonderful to be held, to be kissed, to be that close to another human being. A man."

She drew in a tremulous breath that he ached to catch and replace with his own. "When you kissed me," she went on, her wide-eyed, earnest gaze holding his, "when you stroked my breasts, warmed my skin with your hands, it felt so damned good that I didn't want it ever to stop."

Damn it, neither had he. Didn't she know that? He was tempted, sorely tempted, to drag her into his arms and do it all over again so she'd have not even a hint of doubt left, but her mouth quivered for just a second, staying his impulse.

"I wanted more," she went on, a faint tremor in her voice, "but I knew it was wrong, Jed. I knew it couldn't go on, that I couldn't take more from you. It wouldn't be fair. And that is why I cried. I didn't want to say stop and knew I must."

How could he believe her? Even when he wanted to believe as badly as he'd wanted to believe in Santa Claus when he was seven years old, he could not, not quite. Gruffly, he demanded reassurance. "Not because I hurt you?"

She shook her head. "You didn't hurt me. But . . . I see hurt ahead if we continue to see each other, because this isn't the real thing."

He forgot his earlier resolution to make his reassessment and conduct a sensible search for some quiet, calm woman to grow old with, enjoy grandchildren with—on a limited basis. His eyes narrowed. "It felt damned real to me, Karen."

Her tremulous, indrawn breath nearly undid him. "I know," she whispered. "I know. It felt that way to me, too, Jed, until I remembered that this isn't the real *me*. This is the pregnant me, the one with such mixed up biochemicals she hardly knows right from wrong. So it's better if I—we—don't get involved."

Momentarily, caution deserted him, along with the desire for a serene relationship. "I think we are involved, whether we like it or not."

"And we don't like it, do we? Neither of us. You because I'm going to have a baby and you're finished with that aspect of your life, and me because I know I won't feel like this after the baby's born. So it's a lost cause, Jed. We may as well end it now before it has a chance to go any farther."

He gazed at her for a long time. "You really mean that, don't you?"

She drew a deep breath, held it for a moment, then let it out. "I do. Good-bye, Jed."

Without waiting for a reply, she turned and walked back up the steps to her front door.

He stood staring after her, wanting to protest, wanting to follow her, wanting to tell her she was wrong. He couldn't.

She opened the door and went inside, not once looking back.

"Good-bye, Karen," he said softly as she turned off the porch light. He tucked her thick, heavy book under his arm. He wished it were thicker, wished it were heavier, wished it could keep his mind engrossed and occupied for seven hundred years.

He knew, though, it would take a lot more than Ayn Rand's fattest tome to do that.

July simmered along for another hot week, then for the entire weekend, it drizzled.

How long, Karen wondered, did it take to read *Atlas Shrugged?* Jed hadn't returned it. She'd thought he would, and in person, despite her instructions otherwise. It was true she didn't think they could have a relationship, but damn it, that didn't mean she didn't want to talk to him, see him, hear his voice. Couldn't they be friends?

Maybe she should call and subtly remind him about the book. At the end of the month, her short summer session on creative thinking would be over, and Cecelia would be gone from her class. She'd have to wait until the fall semester started before she could search the campus for the girl and ask her to get the book and bring it to her. The thing had cost thirty dollars in the college bookstore, even with her staff discount. Besides, she'd want to reread it, too, someday. Really, the man should have the consideration to return it, considering how upset he'd been at the loss of his own copy.

On the first Saturday of August, following another morning of showers, the lawn steamed under the heat of the sun. Karen went for a walk, but that wasn't enough exercise. She returned home for her roller blades and went to get Penny, who lived five blocks away. They skated until her muscles fairly sang.

Inside, though, she still felt something vital missing. When she skated with Penny into the driveway and found Jed's car there, she had to grab on to something in order not to fall. Unfortunately, that something was Jedidiah Cotts as he leapt forward, bellowing, "What in hell do you think you're doing, woman?"

"Skating," she snapped, attempting to heave his hands off her shoulders, responding to his irritation in kind. "It's Saturday. Penny and I skate on Saturdays. Why, what does it look like I'm doing?"

"Like you're endangering yourself and your baby. Damn it, Karen, does this make any more sense than hiking into the mountains alone?"

"I didn't hike alone," she reminded him, still trying to break free. As she struggled, one foot rolled out of control and she nearly went down. Jed scooped her against him just as Penny recovered from her shock and flew to Karen's rescue.

"Let her go! Let her *go!*" she shrieked. "Get your hands off her, mister! Let go!"

He made sure Karen stood steadily before he captured the girl's fists, laughing as he crouched before her, holding her firmly. He gave her a little shake. "Hey now, cut that out, young lady!"

At his touch, Penny went stiff. Her eyes went wild; her mouth opened in a silent scream. Her olive skin paled until it looked faintly green, and her obsidian eyes rolled back in her head.

"Jed!" Karen snatched Penny away from him. "Stop. Don't touch her." She lifted the child and skated with her to the steps, where she sat, somehow folding the stiff form to fit on her lap.

"Penny, sweetheart," she murmured. "It's all right, baby. He won't hurt you and he won't hurt me. He's my friend. His name is Jed. Remember I told you all about him?"

Penny's deep shudder shook her whole body, but Karen kept talking to her, reminding Penny about the trip to the wedding, about things she and Jed had done and seen, people they'd talked to along the way.

She wasn't sure the little girl even heard the soothing tones, but after perhaps five minutes, she noticed Penny's rigidity had eased and her eyes fell closed as if she were worn out. One fist clung to a handful of Karen's sleeve. Some color had returned to her face.

At length, Karen fell silent, all talked out. Her mouth was dry, her back ached. She couldn't think of one single thing more to say. Now and then, a shudder coursed through Penny's body. Karen stroked her hair, her face, her shoulders and back, willing calm to the child, peace, wishing she would fall asleep.

Gloria, Penny's aunt, said she often did sleep after one of these episodes. While not seizures in the true sense of the word, they were close, and were never triggered by anything other than violence. It could be violence Penny saw on TV when Gloria wasn't vigilant enough, violence witnessed accidentally on the street, or, as today, what she perceived as violence against someone she loved.

Penny continued to squeeze her eyes shut—to block out the sight of Jed, Karen suspected. He crouched beside them and caught Karen's eye. "Will she be all right?"

She nodded, whispering, as he had. "She'll be fine. You just startled her, grabbing me like that."

Regret dulled his eyes. "I didn't mean—"

"I know." His contrition brought an ache to her heart. "It's all right, Jed. It wasn't your fault." She smoothed Penny's straight black hair back from her brow, rocking her. "You had no way of knowing."

*Knowing what?* She saw the unspoken question leap into his eyes, but it wasn't one she could answer at the moment.

She tried to catch his eye again, to tell him he should go, but his gaze remained fixed on the tense child on her lap. As he sat beside her, Karen shook her head in warning, but if he saw, he chose to ignore it. He slid one arm around the small of her back, supporting her, cushioning her from the sharp edge of the step behind her.

It felt good. She was glad he hadn't left.

Then, to her astonishment, he began to sing softly in a rich and pleasant baritone. One right after another, he sang nonsense songs clearly written with children in mind. He never seemed to have to search his brain for another one; they tripped off his tongue as if he sang them every day. He was, she suddenly realized, making them up as he went along. Karen stared at him in awe.

It wasn't until Penny slumped into an obvious sleep that Jed stopped singing. Then, kneeling in front of her, he took off Karen's skates.

"I guess I'd better go before she wakes up."

Karen would have loved to say he was wrong, but she didn't think he was.

"Jed." She met his gaze as he got to his feet. His eyes were expressionless, and his mouth formed a taut line. "I'm sorry," she said.

"Don't be." He shrugged. "It wasn't your fault."

Wasn't it? Karen asked herself repeatedly over the next few days. If she hadn't been so shocked at seeing Jed literally on her doorstep, if she hadn't had to fight so hard to keep from flinging herself onto him and clinging, if she hadn't had to use anger to stiffen her spine and her suddenly wobbly legs, none of that would have happened.

Jed would have helped her steady herself, she'd have stepped away from him, and all would have been well. But oh, no. She couldn't respond to him like a normal woman, as if he were just any man. Obviously, he'd been startled to see a pregnant woman roller blading. He wasn't the first and he certainly wouldn't be the last. People often stopped and gaped at her. She knew they all thought she was crazy, that she was endangering her baby.

She knew she wasn't, but that didn't change other people's opinions. Jed's reaction had been normal. Her overreaction to it had not.

But since when had she ever responded normally to Jedidiah Cotts?

She hadn't so much as asked him why he'd come to see her. If it was to return her book, he'd obviously forgotten. He hadn't called in the five days since, and it was hardly likely he'd show up again.

It was her own fault, and she'd simply have to live with it. Besides, hadn't she told herself time and time again there was no future in any kind of relationship for the two of them? Of course she had.

And she'd been right.


The last rain had made the lawn sprout wildly, and it desperately needed mowing. Karen forced herself to the task after her Wednesday dinner with Penny. The following night, she did the front yard and looked sorrowfully at her poor pansies in the weed-choked beds bordering the driveway. The chickweed was taller than the blooms.

Then, though her back ached from having mowed the lawn and from too many hours sorting files and lesson plans in preparation for the fall semester, she admitted to herself that she couldn't put off weeding another day. With a sigh of self-pity, she crouched down and got at it.

Other pregnant women had husbands to mow the lawn, to weed the gardens, to rub their backs. Other pregnant women had fathers for their babies, someone to share the hopes, the worries, the fears. Her hand fell idle in the lush growth of chickweed as she stared at a purple and gold pansy close up. It looked angry. It scowled at her, as if she were doing everything wrong.

"And I am, aren't I?" she asked, easing herself down onto the cool grass beside the flower bed. She laid her head on her arm, still gazing at the colorful flowers whose faces swayed in the soft breeze, then blurred and wavered as her eyes lost focus and her lids fell shut.

*"No!* Oh, no. . . ." Jed shouted the words over the screech of his brakes as he came to an abrupt halt and flung open the door of his car. His head swam and a black cloud threatened to blank out the scene: the crumpled figure lying on the grass, the pale face, the closed eyes, the limp limbs.

"Karen! Karen!" He dropped to his knees beside her.

She opened her eyes, her startled gaze pinned to his face, a faint flush coming up under her skin. "Oh. Jed. What—"

"Hush," he said, placing an unsteady, tender finger over her lips. She was alive. She was conscious. He had never known such gratitude to whatever powers ran the world. "No, don't move, baby. It's all right. Don't try to talk, don't try to move. Just lie still, sweetheart. Tell me what happened."

"Jed!" She tried to shove his hands away. "For heaven's sake, if you don't want me to talk, how can I tell you what happened? Besides, what are you doing here?"

"Did you fall?" he demanded.

"No! Of course not. I . . . damn it, what are you doing?" He was running his hands up her legs, right to the bottoms of her very short shorts. His face was white to the lips, his eyes frantic, his brows drawn together.

His patrolling hands shook, then slowed as they traced her legs back toward her knees, and she quit trying to bat them away. "Were you dizzy?" he asked. "Are you in pain? Do you think you've broken anything?"

"What?" She sat up.

Quickly, he cupped a hand at the back of her head. "Where do you hurt?"

"I don't hurt. I'm not injured." Pushing him aside, she used one of his shoulders as a prop as she got to her feet.

He remained there, crouching on the ground, staring up at her. "Not hurt? Not sick? Not dizzy?" She shook her head. He shot to his feet, towering over her. "Then what the hell were you doing on the ground?"

She stared at him. "Stop yelling at me."

He drew in a deep breath, held it, then let it out slowly. Just as slowly, he sucked in another one and released it as he unclenched his fists. "I am not yelling," he said in a calm, pleasant tone that held only a faint quaver. "I'm simply asking what you were doing lying in the driveway if you aren't hurt or ill or in pain."

"I was lying *beside* the driveway," she corrected him smartly. "And I was weeding."

He wiped one shaking hand around the back of his neck. "Weeding?" It came out at just below a bellow, and Mrs. Harrison from next door gripped the top of the fence, staring.

Karen indicated the piles of wilted chickweed beside the neat bed. "The pansies."

He breathed again several times, deeply. "Pansies?"

He seemed, Karen thought, to be having difficulty swallowing. His face was growing redder and redder, his eyes wider and wider.

Good grief! Was he having a heart attack? She clutched his elbows. "Jed, are you all right?"

"Fine. I'm fine. Yes. Just fine. I was a little concerned, though." He let out a tremulous breath. "I thought you'd fainted or something. Pretty dumb, huh?" His voice rose again. "Who the hell lies down to weed pansies?"

"I do."

"I mean," he said with heavy patience, clearly struggling to control himself, "who in their right mind lies down to weed pansies?"

"Pregnant people whose backs ache if they squat or kneel."

"Then why in hell don't you let the pansies take care of their own damned weeds?" he roared as if at the end of his rope.

Karen stared. "Stop swearing at me. I don't want my baby to learn foul language *in utero.*"

"Then stop doing stupid things that scare me out of my mind, woman! Lying down to weed the garden! Of all the boneheaded, inconsiderate tricks to pull, that one—"

"Inconsiderate? Who do I have to consider except myself? *I* knew I hadn't fainted! Maybe I fell asleep for a minute or two, but I sure didn't faint."

He gaped. "Asleep? *Asleep!*"

"How was I supposed to know you were going to come roaring in here, shouting at me, grabbing me, putting your hands all over me, pretending to be afraid for my health and safety simply as an excuse to . . . to feel me up?"

The most magnificent sensation came over him as he shouted right back at her. "Feel you up? By the Lord Harry, Karen Andersen, if I ever feel you up, you'll know you're being felt up! When I start to feel you up, you'll know you've never been felt up before in your entire life!"

"Oh, yeah?" she said, and Jed knew he had come to a watershed moment in his life.

"Oh . . ." *Yeah,* he had been going to say, but his words died out into a shuddering sigh as he hauled her bodily up into his arms, feeling the lightness of her, the fragility, drawing in the scent of her, nearly passing out from the sweetness of it.

Ignoring the elderly voice that demanded to know who he was and what he was doing to Karen, he marched up the steps to her front door, pulled open the screen with one finger, then shouldered it wide as he crowded inside, where he dumped her feetfirst on the floor.

"Oh, yeah," he said, softly this time, but fervently. He cradled her face between his hands, bent his head and took her mouth in a deep, provocative kiss, one that had been building in him since the day he first saw her.

Karen swayed and clutched at his shoulders, prepared to ride out the storm, but it caught her in its vortex and whirled her away.

Eagerly, she spun with it.

She reveled in Jed's embrace, returned it. The feel of his body against hers, the taste of his mouth on hers, the scent of him in her nostrils combined to create a heady rush of desire. She parted her lips for his kisses. They allayed some needs even as they fueled others and added new ones. He held her and kissed her as if starved for her touch, but gently, softly, with a kind of tenderness that made her ache deep inside. She stroked one palm down his chest, loving the textures of his hard muscles under his shirt.

She wanted more. She wanted his skin, his heat, cradled against her. Nimbly, she popped his buttons free one by one until she'd exposed an expanse of sleek warm skin to her touch. Hair sprinkled its center line, created whorls around his pecs. He groaned as her lips skimmed his chest, then sucked in a harsh breath and tangled his hands in her hair when her mouth found and nuzzled a hard bead.

Raking her hands over his shoulders, she divested him of his shirt, then scraped her nails across his back. He plundered her mouth and she tore free, whipped off her blouse and bra, needing the joining of skin, his and hers, to ease some of the pain. It only deepened it.

"Jed, Jed," she murmured, as he arched her back toward the bed, lowered her, and knelt astride her, his gaze greedy as he held her arms above her shoulders.

She struggled to reach him. Her breasts burned. He moved his mouth from one to the other and she nearly heard her skin sizzle. With both hands full of his hair, she held him to her. She stroked his cheeks, tingling at the faint rasp of whiskers under her fingertips. When he lifted his head to gaze at her, she captured him and pulled his mouth to hers.

He held her tight, rolled over until she sprawled atop him, and ran his hands up under her shorts. Her back arched. She undid her waistband, opened her shorts and shimmied out of them, taking her panties with them, kicking them free. With a gasp, Jed rolled them over again, cradling her close. She parted her legs, welcomed him to her softness, scissored her thighs against the rough texture of his jeans and whispered his name again. In response, he thrust toward her. She clenched her hands on his waist, then struggled with the buckle on his belt.

"Jed, please, help me . . ."

He rolled apart from her, stood, and undid his belt, his gaze never leaving her body as she lay sprawled on the bed, shameless in her need of him. "Karen, sweetheart, are you sure?"

She groaned. "Yes! Please, Jed, I need you now!"

He popped the snap, undid the zipper, and started to slide his jeans over his hips.

*Wham! Wham! Wham!*

Jed and Karen both froze. He hopped on one foot as he turned toward the source of the noise. Through the bedroom door they stared down the short hall to the front door, which nearly bulged with the force of the hammering on it.

"Open up in there! This is the police! The house is surrounded. Ms. Andersen! Answer me if you can."

While Jed and Karen continued to stare at the door in disbelief, the amplified voice paused, then continued. "You in there, the man with Ms. Andersen. Come to the door with your hands clasped on top of your head."

Slowly, Jed backed away from the bed. He did up his jeans, strode to the front door and opened it slowly. Then, linking his hands atop his head, he stepped outside.


"Karen, cut it out! This isn't funny!"

Karen tried. She honestly tried. She closed her mouth, squeezed her eyes shut, clenched her fists, and breathed slowly until she felt calm. But when she opened one eye warily to peer at Jed, she was off again, laughing until she rolled on the sofa, clutching her middle with both arms. "You . . . have a grass stain on your . . . nose," she choked.

Jed muttered a curse, rubbed at his nose, and paced away, pounding one fist into his opposite hand. "What am I going to do with you?" he demanded, wheeling and striding back to where she had collapsed. Distractedly, he tugged down the hem of her short blue satin wrapper. It had hitched up to show a dangerous amount of the all too tantalizing mound of her pink bottom. "You're not taking this nearly seriously enough."

She sat up, sniffing, rubbing her eyes. "I'm sorry. Of course you're upset. I'd be, too, if I'd been attacked by a bunch of goons."

He frowned. "They weren't goons. They were perfectly reasonable police officers acting in response to a 911 call."

She made an indelicate, unladylike sound as she blew air out her lips. "They looked like goons to me—black pants and jackets, black watch caps pulled down over their foreheads, attacking you the way they did. I have never been more infuriated in my life!"

"But they were right, you know. They had no way of telling if they had a rape, a robbery with violence, or a hostage-taking on their hands. They couldn't take chances with your safety."

"Well, it took them too darned long to decide I wasn't lying when I said I was in no danger and neither needed nor wanted their help and that Mrs. Harrison was the one who'd called."

"You were pretty hard on them."

"I apologized in the end, didn't I?" She giggled again, a giggle that threatened to get out of hand until the expression on his face choked it off. He really was in a sweat about this whole situation. It was unkind to make fun of him.

"Yes," he said heavily, "you apologized, but you shouldn't have had to. None of that stuff should ever have happened. Don't you realize I came within a hairbreadth of . . . of taking you by force?"

That made her stare at him in shock. "Force?"

He crouched before her, taking her hands in his. "Yes, Karen. Sweetheart, please understand. I was out of control. I was so intent on what *I* was doing, what *I* wanted, what felt good to *me,* just like that day we went on the hike. If you had tried to stop me, you couldn't have done anything. Your clothes were off, if you'll remember. If you'd said no, I wouldn't have heard you. If the cops hadn't banged on the door, who knows what would have happened?"

Karen slid her hands out of his clasp and wrapped her fingers around his thick, masculine wrists. She loved the feel of them, bristly with hair, taut with bone and sinew and muscle. She smiled as she rubbed her hands up and down them, then released one and slid her hand up to his shoulder, where she straightened the collar of the shirt he had dragged on hurriedly after the police left. *"I* know what would have happened."

Jed scowled, as much at the way her touch affected him as at her irrepressible grin. "Of course you do. And I want you to think about that, think about the serious ramifications of it. What if I'd hurt you? Harmed your baby?"

She slipped a finger inside the neck of his shirt, trailed it down and around to where the buttons began, and flipped one open. Her eyes twinkled. "You big brute, you. You ought to be ashamed."

He captured her hand and held it flat on his chest. "Stop that. I am ashamed. And sorry." He closed his eyes for a moment, stroking his palm from the back of her hand toward her elbow, soaking up the sensation of her skin against his. "That's what I'm telling you."

"I don't want you to be ashamed," she said softly, and he opened his eyes again, discovering that she had several more of his buttons undone. Damn! The woman was more dexterous than an octopus!

"I don't want you to feel sorry for wanting to make

love with me." She leaned forward and pressed her lips to his throat. "I want you to do what you were doing before we were interrupted, before you were snatched from my arms and flung face first onto the lawn and I had to pile in to rescue you, wearing nothing but this." She fingered the satin of her short wrapper.

"It wasn't exactly like that," he said, unable to contain the beginnings of a grin.

Really, she had been something, tearing into the cops the way she had, and on his behalf. And her language! Assuming she was right about what infants picked up even before birth, her baby had been tainted *in utero* and was destined for a life of juvenile delinquency.

When she was done with them, the cops were the most chastened-looking bunch he'd ever run into. Not that he ever wanted to run into a SWAT team under those kinds of circumstances again. Damn it, what was he grinning about? He was as bad as she was.

It was not funny.

"If we hadn't been interrupted, we'd have made love, Jed, exactly the way I wanted us to do. If you remember, I wasn't saying no. I was saying now, and you were holding back, teasing me."

No, she was wrong, Jed thought. He hadn't been holding back nearly enough.

"I wasn't teasing you. I trying to contain the crazy, juvenile impulse I had to take you without restraint, and without restraint, whether you think so or not, isn't exactly the way you wanted to make love."

"It isn't? What makes you so sure?"

He had to laugh. Really, she was too much. "Karen, sweetheart, believe me. I know what women like. I know what they want. I was married to one for twenty years, remember? Intellectually, I know what's right and what's

not, and I've spent most of my adult life trying to remember it, trying not to let my baser side take over."

She wrinkled her nose. "Why? If you've had to work
at remembering it, seems to me your intellect is in conflict with your nature. I don't think that's good for you,
Jed."

"*I* don't think it's to any man's credit when he fails to
remember how different women are from men in their
needs and the way they like to have those needs met.
And with you, I forget it all too easily."

She shoved his hands away from her and pushed herself to her feet, turning away from him and putting half
the room between them. Her eyes snapped angrily. Her
face flared with flags of color. "I've said it before, and
I'll say it again: You don't know damn-all about me."

"You're a woman. I know a few basic facts."

She smiled and slumped to the bench in front of her
small electric organ. Shaking her head, she said, "I'd like
to explore those basic facts with you. Maybe you'd discover some of them are myths, or at the very least ex-
aggerations, misconceptions. Or perhaps simply not
applicable to all women."

She paused for a moment then met his gaze squarely.
"Jed, you make love, from the little experience I have
with your lovemaking, wonderfully well."

# TEN

Her words hit him in the chest like a hammer blow. Oh, Lord! What kind of woman said that to a man? As far as he could tell, since they hadn't really completed the act, *she* made love with a kind of fervor and intensity that, until her, he'd forgotten existed. He'd wanted, *hungered* to explore it, burned to complement it with equal enthusiasm. Only it wasn't—wouldn't have been—right to get so caught up in the flames she ignited that he forgot everything he'd ever learned about finesse. He'd wasn't even sure he'd been in any kind of control when the cops came.

He was glad he'd been stopped by the hammering on the door. When she had time to think about it, she'd be glad too.

"Karen, there's no need for you to be kind to me, to make excuses for my bad behavior. I—"

"Was not the naked one when the cops pounded on the door," she reminded him, rising with lithe grace to her feet and returning to the sofa where he now sat.

He went hot all over, remembering the sight of her nude body, the feel of it in his arms, under his hands, her breasts against his naked chest. "What—" He paused to stand, to clear his throat, to clear his mind. "What difference does that make? If anything, it simply helps to prove my point."

She put her hands on his chest again. He swayed and caught at her shoulders to steady himself. "Jed, I was undressed because I ripped my own clothes off. And I had started doing the same to yours when the law arrived."

She smiled as she parted the front of his shirt. She'd managed to free the last two buttons while he was distracted, and she raised her hands to shove it off his shoulders. When he stiffened, she stopped. "Do you mind if I continue?"

"Karen . . ."

"Jed." Her tone may have been faintly mocking, but her eyes were hot, her mouth parted, asking silently for his kisses. She left his shirt alone, kept one hand on his chest, and undid the knot in her sash.

His throat thickened so he could hardly force out, "Oh, Lord, woman."

She smiled. "Do I have to get mad at you?"

He could only stare at her, his heart pounding so heavily he wondered if it would go into overload and stop.

"I want to make love with you, Jed. But I'd prefer it to be because we both want it, because we're making an adult choice to share our bodies and emotions with each other, not because we're carried away by my temper and your peculiar response to it. If you want me that way, too, then stay. If you don't, then please go. Now."

He groaned and wrapped his hands around her, inside the satin robe, separating its front, filling his palms with warm silky skin, weighted globes, quivering, eager woman.

"How can I say no to you?"

"You can't. It wouldn't be"—she giggled like a girl—"polite."

With another groan, he lifted her up and carried her
back to her bedroom.

He tried to be gentle. He tried to take a long time
arousing her. He tried to show her how deeply he cared
by taking exquisite care of her, but the wildness of her
passion caught him again, stripped him of inhibitions as
easily as she stripped him of his clothing.

There was no finesse, no subtlety, no refined nuances,
no careful pacing of his performance. It wasn't a performance. It was just the hot, impetuous kisses they shared,
the gasping for breath, the sharp, agonized whispers of
two people who together bred a terrible, unslakable need,
coming together to complete each other, touching, stroking, dipping, encircling.

"Now, Jed! Please!" Karen cried out, arching into him,
fighting his damnable restraint, clutching his hard, narrow hips in her hands. He lifted over her, seeking. They
both fumbled in their eagerness, and then he took control,
arrowed into her hard, fast, hot, voicing a harsh cry of
triumph as he filled her to her depths.

She squeezed her muscles around him, felt herself going wild and frenzied, and bucked against him, but he
caught her hips in his hands, held her, controlled her, and
she willingly gave herself over to his powerful mastery.

He lifted her, moving her eager body in a rapid dance
that brought completion nearer, nearer. She cried out,
stroked him with her palms, with the soles of her feet,
raked his back with her nails as he encouraged her with
hoarse, short, gasped words.

She writhed in his arms while he held her, plunging
deep and hard, and it came closer and closer, that which
she sought. It was there, almost within reach, so tanta-
lizingly close that she cried out again and stretched for
it, higher, harder, clamping her legs around him, her

hands clinging to his back, her neck arched, body as taut as a strung bow. Then he plunged deeper than she'd thought possible, with a hoarse cry of climax, and she flew away and away and away.

"Sweetheart?"

Karen opened one eye and looked at him.

"Are you all right?" He stroked a hand down her side, curved it up and over the mound of her pregnancy, and then bent to touch his lips to hers with all the tenderness he'd forgotten to show her before. "Did I hurt you?"

"No." Her voice was a murmur, as soft and as lazy as the hand that traced the shape of his shoulder and upper arm. "Jed?"

"Hmm?"

"Is it politically incorrect for a woman to say thank you to a man?"

He swallowed hard and lifted up on one elbow to kiss her eyelids before dropping his head back to the pillow, then turned his face to the side so he could see her. She was smiling. "Not that I know of. Are you?"

She opened both eyes this time and her smile deepened. Her gray eyes shone. If the green rays had been there earlier, he hadn't taken the time to notice. He felt only mildly cheated. There had been so much more to treasure.

"Am I what, politically incorrect, or saying thank you? The latter. That was the best." Inexplicably, her eyes shimmered with tears. She shut them. "The best ever. In my entire life."

He felt like hell, hearing her say that, at the same time as he felt so good, so powerful he could have lifted the house with one hand. "It could have been a lot better, but

I forgot myself," he said, without undue modesty. Hell, what did he have to be modest about? He knew he was a good, considerate, and sensitive lover. Most of the time.

"What did you forget?"

"Everything about what a woman likes. The little details. The slow, sweet building of her desires. I didn't take care of your needs very well."

She rolled up onto one shoulder. "I don't think even one of my needs was less than fully satisfied." She ran a hand down his chest. "I feel entirely complete. Satiated." She giggled again and drilled the tip of a finger into his bellybutton. "But I have a feeling you're going to be my chicken chow mien of the week."

"Huh?" He stilled her hand lest it stray into forbidden territory.

"You know, half an hour later?"

"Hah!" His derision was aimed more at himself than at her. He knew his capabilities, and it would take several multiples of half-hours before he could even consider a repeat performance. Not that he'd actually performed, he remembered with a frown. At least, not well, not properly. He'd been like a boy. Like a novice. He'd just leaped on and done it. He cringed inwardly at the memory.

"You're pretty monosyllabic, friend. Tired?"

*Friend?* That simply proved his point, didn't it, he asked himself, trying not to feel hurt.

"Exhausted." But as he said it, he had to reconsider, because it wasn't completely true. He should be exhausted, but he was . . . exhilarated. More than that, he was getting aroused again.

What the hell was going on here? He was forty-five years old, but parts of him were about to forget that. He tried to ignore those parts. They didn't know what they were talking about. Another session like the last one and he'd probably have a fatal heart attack.

He could just imagine Ceil having to phone Crystal and tell her Jed had died making love to one of Ceil's college teachers.

As scenarios went, that wasn't a bad one. He grinned, thinking about it.

"What's so funny?" Karen traced the shape of his lips with one finger.

He eyed her warily, ashamed that he'd let Crystal into Karen's bed. She didn't belong there. She didn't, he realized with conviction, belong anywhere in his life anymore. Not in any way that mattered.

It was as if he had shed pounds and pounds of useless flab. He felt vital, alive, strong. For the first time in more than five years, he knew he was free of the past, that it would never haunt him again as it had for so long. He might think of it, but it would be without pain.

He considered telling Karen that at last he was cured of an old obsession, that he was over wanting his ex-wife back. But even he, as insensitive as he sometimes was to women and their needs, knew better than to mention one woman in another's bed. "I don't think I'd better share that one," he said.

"Okay." The ease with which she dropped the subject surprised and delighted him. She wrapped her fingers around him. "What would you like to share? This?"

He laughed. He couldn't help himself. He felt wonderful! As if she felt just as good, she laughed, too, her eyes shining, her face reflecting the kind of happiness he felt welling up inside him.

How novel it was to make love to a woman who enjoyed every nuance of the experience, who talked and asked questions, told him what she liked, learned what he wanted, and even laughed with him in bed. He buried his laughter against her breasts until it subsided. Then he began—slowly, carefully, expertly—to make love to her.

This time, he swore, she'd see how good it could be when he took the time to do it right.

Karen opened her eyes. It wasn't easy. But at least she was able to breathe again. She didn't know if she could speak, but she had to try. Jed lay beside her, cradling her against him. He had pulled the sheet over them and she tucked it around his shoulder, wishing she had words to describe what she felt. His gaze clung to her face, his expression soft, gentle. Maybe he knew without her saying it.

But maybe he didn't.

In many ways, she thought with aching tenderness, he was terribly vulnerable, unsure of his ability to please. He had such a strange set of notions about what women liked, as if he'd read too many conflicting articles on the subject and ended up a very confused man, outwardly the epitome of the feminist's dream, working hard at being kind, sensitive and understanding. Inside, he churned with all the basic masculine traits—possessiveness, protectiveness, toughness.

His daughter was right. He treated women beautifully.

On the other hand, he could be so forceful, so masterful, that he took her breath away and made her want to be hauled up onto his fiery black stallion and swept away.

He also made her madder than anyone else ever had or could.

Oh, yes, all of those characteristics combined into one

man was devastating, deadly, impossible to resist. And she didn't want to resist any longer. If only . . .

She sighed, unaware of the tremulous sound of it until he cupped her face in his hand and showed deep concern. "Honey? Are you all right?"

"Yes. Oh, yes! Jed." She could have wept with all the turbulent emotion roiling inside her, everything she wanted him to know, everything she was deeply, instinctively afraid to tell him—for all the obvious reasons, she thought as her baby shifted inside, poking her. But some of what she felt had to come out or she would burst.

"Jed," she curled her hand around his jaw. "I have never felt more—" She hesitated, swallowed the thickness in her throat, and continued softly. "More—loved—in all my life."

Jed groaned and choked back the impulsive words that sprang to his lips. Burying his face in the sweet scented hollow of her neck, he held her fast. *You are loved. My beloved. I love you so much, love you to distraction.*

He didn't say it aloud. He couldn't. He could only stroke her back, hold her, feel the warmth of her body resting against his, her hands stroking his skin.

"You have Penny intrigued," she said, startling him. He thought she'd fallen asleep again.

"I do?"

"Yes. She calls you the song man."

"What really happened to her that day?"

"Violence terrifies her. Men terrify her. She's lived through a lot in her eight years."

Jed rolled up onto one elbow. "My God! Was she—?"

Karen shook her head. Her hair tickled his upper arm. "No. But her stepfather was a brutal drunk who mistreated her mother terribly. He never hurt Penny or her two little half-brothers, except once when Penny tried to protect her mother. Her mother ran out of the house, probably to lead him away from the kids. He followed. She'd just gotten into the car when he scrambled in the other side. They crashed not two blocks from the house, according to neighbors who witnessed the whole thing. Both were killed instantly. Penny was running after her mother and saw it all.

"That was over two years ago, and she still reacts that way when she sees any kind of violence. She blames herself for not looking after her mother well enough and tries to compensate by making herself responsible for her brothers, her aunt, even me, in every way she can. The reason her aunt, who has custody, enrolled her in the Big Sister program is to give her a chance to be a little girl, to experience life as a child should, not to feel it's up to her to take care of everyone around her. She needs to learn to let others take care of her."

"Poor little kid. Karen, I wish I'd known. If I had, I'd never have touched her or even spoken to her. I was simply trying to get her to stop hitting me, the same way I'd have stopped one of my own children."

Karen touched his face. "Jed, I know that. I would have told you her story earlier, but I couldn't, not without her aunt's permission."

He frowned. "I assume you have that now? Why?"

"Very soon after I met you, I remember thinking that if any man could get through to Penny, you'd be the one. You know little girls, Jed. Your gentle manner and kindness shines through everything you do. I wish—" She broke off, sighing.

"What do you wish?"

"That you and Penny could become friends. That through you, she could learn there are good men in the world."

Jed thought of the folly of continuing this relationship. He thought of the time when it would have to end. Karen's eyes shone into his, filled with trust and patience and affection as she waited for him to decide. "I'm willing to try," he said at length. "If you think it won't traumatize her further."

"Oh, Jed!" She wrapped her arms around him and hugged him tightly for a moment before rolling to her side and smiling at him. "We'll have to go very, very slowly, very carefully," she said, becoming serious. "She might ignore you completely for days. She might make you feel like a monster if you make any mistakes, even the slightest ones. But I think it's worth the trouble, if you really want to try."

"I do," he said. To him, it sounded like the most solemn of oaths.

"Thank you." She rolled over and switched off the bedside lamp, then snuggled back into his arms. In what seemed like seconds, her breathing deepened, lengthened, and she went limp in sleep.

Still, Jed held her. For a long time, he ran his hand up and down her back, knowing he should go, knowing it was folly to stay and take the risk that he might just blurt out something that would complicate things irreparably. He couldn't be in love with her. He wouldn't be.

Presently, he slept, too, and wakened to a warmth as unfamiliar as it was pleasant. He lay for several moments orienting himself.

Karen. He was with Karen. He breathed in the scent of her. She lay tucked against his back, spoon-fashion. One of her arms was wrapped around his waist, one hand splayed on his chest as if she would keep him at her side forever as she nestled close, her round belly pressed to him. He had made love to Karen not once, but twice.

Her scent clung to him, sweet, musky, filling him with body-tightening need. He wanted more than anything to make love to her a third time.

A faint, almost imperceptible pressure told him her baby was kicking. Slowly, carefully, so as not to disturb her, he rolled to face her, slid a hand over that mound and felt the motion against his palm, strong, then faint, then strong again, moving on as the baby rolled over. He followed it with his hand.

That was more magical, more awe-inspiring, more miraculous and unbelievable than anything else on this earth, he thought. When his own babies had been on the way, he had done the same in the night, felt their movements and lain awake lost in thoughts and dreams and hopes.

Who was this person who was half him? he had wondered. What would he or she be like? What would it feel like to hold his son or daughter for the first time? In moments like that, he had been almost envious of women for their ability to bear young, to hold them within their bodies for nine months, nurture them, to be part of them for so much longer, to have such a deeper involvement than a father could hope to have.

Now Karen's baby, who was not half his, kicked again, as if to dislodge his hand, reminding him suddenly of why he had come there in the first place. He rolled away, again quietly, carefully. Damn it, he'd meant to tell her right away. He'd intended to do just that, but they'd argued. He'd kissed her, dragged her into the house like some kind of wild animal, her neighbor had called the police and—

And then they had made love, again and again, leaving him no time to think, no time to remember.

He wished he could have continued to forget. As if

Crystal were standing beside Karen's bed, he heard her voice in his mind: *When people forget something important, it's because they don't want to remember. Ask yourself, Jed, why did you choose to forget to tell Karen about the phone call?*

He asked himself and didn't like the answer. He'd forgotten because if he'd remembered earlier, chances are he wouldn't have ended up in her bed. No, he did not like that answer, nor, he reasoned, would Karen like it when she knew the truth.

Getting out of bed, he saw that it was dawn. In the faint light coming from between the drapes, he dressed, finding his clothing scattered around the room. He shook his head at the memory of his and Karen's second impetuous journey into her bedroom.

That time, it had not taken her fiery temper to goad him into losing his self-control. All it had taken was her touch, the desire he had seen shining from her eyes, her words, open and candid. Her need. Her need of him.

He sighed silently and crouched to kiss her temple, brushing her hair back from her forehead. The perfume of her skin drew him, made him crave her again, but he knew he couldn't have her. She didn't belong to him— could never belong to him, not permanently. He stood and turned resolutely from her bed, then turned back, to make sure her alarm clock was set. She had to get up for work in an hour or two.

He knew, too, her need would soon fade. She'd said she felt like this, had become wanton and passionate, only because she was pregnant. He frowned as he closed the bedroom door silently behind him.

Crystal had been just the opposite. When she was pregnant, she'd found sex a chore, and he'd soon learned to leave her alone most of the time. She liked to be held, to be stroked, and while it had been torture sometimes, he had done that and nothing more because that was all she wanted—except for the times when the animal in him took over, and then he had suffered a different kind of torture, the torture of overwhelming regret. Crystal had never said anything. She hadn't needed to. Her pained yet patient look of tolerance had said it all.

He thought about that inner animal he hadn't quite managed to subdue. Karen hadn't objected to it. She had deliberately opened the cage.

Why was it so different for her? With her?

There was no answer, of course, except that Karen was not Crystal.

How many times since he'd met Karen had he been caught off guard by the apparent differences between the two women? They couldn't be more than outward ones, superficial, however fascinating he might find them. Inside, they were both women, and what they needed and wanted would be the same.

Its name would not be Jedidiah Cotts.

Soon, Karen would have her baby to care for, would no longer need him. It was pure folly to let himself wish it could be otherwise. He truly wanted no part of raising a child again. He knew very well how small a part of it a man could have, anyway.

It was the book, thick and hardbound, with gilt letters on the black cloth of its cover, that told Karen most of the story. So that was why he'd come—to return it.

The note said the rest of it. Jed had left them both on her kitchen table. He'd been thoughtful enough to make a pot of decaf coffee for her. It was the gurgling of the

coffeemaker and the aroma that had wakened her even
before her alarm rang.

She'd come out to the kitchen expecting to find him
there, expecting his arms and his mouth and his good,
solid body to lean on, to cuddle against. All she'd found
was her copy of *Atlas Shrugged* and his little note, written on the back of an envelope she'd dropped into the
recycling bin the day before.

At least he hadn't wasted any paper.

He hadn't wasted any words, either.

*Karen:*

> *I almost forgot why I came. Yesterday Barry
> phoned and asked for you. I didn't blow your cover,
> simply said you'd call him when you could. I'm sure
> you know how to reach him. Bye, and take care of
> yourself.*
>
> *Jed*

No *I'll call you soon.* No *I'll see you tomorrow.* Not
even *call me.* So what did this note mean? *So long, baby,
nice knowing you?* Maybe not literally, but close enough,
she thought, firming her trembling mouth, clasping a
hand under her baby as it kicked and squirmed as if tired
of confinement.

She laughed without humor. "All right, baby girl. Your
mother has just become a one night stand for the first
and last time in her life. Close your ears. She's about to
cuss."

She sought words suitable to express her mood, but
not one word she knew was strong enough. Not one was
bad enough, foul enough. Not one could ever relieve the
debilitating ache within or fill the hollow. She buried her
face in her arms on the table and howled out her grief.

"That," she said to herself ten minutes later in a tone that sounded strangely like her mother's, "is quite enough of that."

She blew her nose again, sniffed, and picked up the cup of coffee she'd poured. It was cold. Dumping it down the drain, she poured a second one and took it outside to the backyard, where she found another relentlessly bright day to be gotten through.

At noon, she remembered to call Barry. His spirits were at a low ebb. He'd lost a patient, a thirty-one-year-old mother of three. They talked for half an hour until she had to go back to her room for a class, and she told him when he asked that of course he could call her again. It made her sad and angry to know Candice wouldn't listen when he needed to unload his problems.

It wasn't until she'd hung up she remembered he still didn't know the truth about where she lived or who had fathered her baby. Was it necessary to tell him yet? No, she reasoned. There'd be time later. She didn't want to burden him. Her innate honesty brought her up short. Burdening Barry had no bearing on her decision. What she didn't want was to share her baby with him, her joy, her hopes for a shining future. It was as if sharing it with him would somehow dilute her own pleasure.

Right. She was acting like a selfish brat.


"Hi, Ms.—Karen."

Karen looked up from her desk. Ceil Cotts stood before her in the doorway to the cubbyhole she fondly called her office.

"I've come to say good-bye."

"Good-bye?"

"I'm transferring to the University of Oregon. Wes,

my fiancé, is doing his final year down there. I've decided to join him. I'll be living with my mom." She sighed. "It's tough, though, leaving Dad all alone."

"Oh. I see. I'm sure he'll be fine."

"I was, well, kind of hoping you'd—"

"Hoping what?" Karen prompted.

Cecelia looked uncomfortable. "Hoping you'd . . . sort of keep an eye on Dad for me. You know, be a friend if he gets lonely. I thought the two of you would hit it off, but I guess . . ." She shrugged.

Cecelia tossed her long pale hair off her face and, as if in preparation for shaking hands, shifted her load of books from one arm to the other, dropping several in the process.

"Oh, darn," she muttered, dumping the rest of the pile on Karen's desk and crouching on the floor to collect the escapees.

"Thanks, Karen," she said, standing. "You made the course really interesting. And about my dad . . . maybe you could call him sometime?"

"We'll see." Karen hated lying to Jed's daughter, but she'd simply have to put him out of her mind to concentrate on getting ready for the baby and preparing for the fall semester. She wanted to leave things in good order for her replacement when he took over.


A week later, as she and Penny were gearing up for a skate around the nearby park, a burgundy Buick almost identical to the one she'd made Jed wreck wheeled into her drive and came to a smooth halt. Her mouth went dry; her palms grew wet. At her side, Penny stiffened.

"What's *he* doing here?"

"I haven't the faintest idea."

Jed alighted from the car. Karen stood, one hand on Penny's shoulder for balance. "Good . . . heavens!" Her gasp turned into a laugh as she gaped at Jed.

He wore skintight navy Lycra shorts with red stripes angling diagonally across his thighs and an equally tight green pullover. While she watched in stunned silence, he strapped on orange elbow pads and purple knee pads, then topped off his ensemble with a bright yellow helmet. Inline skates dangled from his hand.

"Good morning, ladies," he said. "Ready to go skating? I've taken some lessons and can't wait to show off my newfound expertise."

Penny looked betrayed. "He's going with us?"

Karen couldn't speak. Lessons? He'd taken lessons?

"I'd like to," Jed said, dropping down to Penny's level. "I worry about Karen, about if she fell down and couldn't get up."

Penny's pointed chin tilted aggressively. "I'd pick her up."

Jed smiled. "I know you'd try, but she might be too heavy for you."

"Then I'd get someone else to help."

"Who?" His tone was mild, interested, not challenging.

"I don't know. Somebody."

"A stranger?"

"Yeah." Pure belligerence emanated from her.

"They why not me?"

Penny frowned. She stared at the toes of her skates. Her lower lip trembled. She cut a swift and wary glance at Jed's face, then turned her gaze to Karen. "You want him to come?"

"He's right, honey. If I fall down, you won't be able

to pick me up. But it's entirely up to you. If you don't want him along, he won't come."

Penny took Karen's hand. "He can follow us, I guess. Just in case you fall."

That was they way they skated to the park. That was they way they skated along sidewalks skirting flower beds and playing fields and onto a blacktop path through the woods.

Penny and Karen stopped under a tree to sit on the grass at the side of a pond and rest while they fed a flock of waddling ducks with popcorn from Penny's fanny pack. Jed leaned against a tree near them. He chuckled aloud at Penny's reaction to a duck that got too greedy and took her fingertip in its bill along with the popcorn from her hand.

That was the only time the child appeared to notice his presence, with nothing more than a quick, leery glance his direction. When the popcorn was gone and the fickle ducks trundled back to the pond, she was eager to go again.

Behind her back, Jed caught Karen's eye and shook his head.

"In a few minutes," Karen said. "I need to rest a little longer."

Jed began to sing softly then. It was the first sound he'd made since leaving Karen's house.

> *Penny and Karen went skating one day.*
> *They sat in a meadow that smelled like hay.*
> *They leaned on a tree and fed a duck.*
> *It bit Penny's finger, and she said "Yuck!"*
> *Karen kissed it and then she said,*
> *"I'm tired, Penny. Go skate with Jed."*

He left it at that, folded his hands behind his head, leaned back, and stared up into the branches of the tree.

Penny watched him. Karen watched Penny. Cautious curiosity showed in the girl's eyes, in the tilt of her head.

"What comes after that?" she whispered to Karen.

"I don't know. I guess you'll have to ask Jed. He's the one who made it up, not me."

For a moment, she thought Penny might fall for the ruse, but she didn't. Scrambling to her feet, she held out a hand to help Karen up. "Have you rested enough now?"

They skated on, but this time, Jed moved up beside Karen. With a startled glance at him, Penny whirled away, putting several yards between herself and the adults. She looked over her shoulder frequently as if to make sure Karen wasn't too far away—and was still safe.

"Karen . . ." Jed took her hand, slowing her. "I've missed you. More than I can tell you."

"You're the one who left," she said, "without saying good-bye."

"I left a note."

"A good-bye note." Her voice quavered.

He nodded. "Yes. All right. That's what it was. I was scared. Scared to stay."

She nodded. She understood, Jed thought. Maybe even agreed.

"But you showed up today."

"Yes." He pulled them to a halt. Her gaze was soft on him, filled with a longing he shared, and he knew it wasn't over yet, no matter how hard he'd tried to make himself believe it.

"I remembered I'd made a promise to you about Penny. It's a promise I want to keep."

Karen fought to keep her voice steady. "Good. She's asked about you often since that first day."

Ahead of them, Penny stood still, looking back, not as warily as before, not as suspiciously, but with a certain curiosity. Jed let Karen go and she caught up to her friend, taking Penny's hand as they skated along, leaving Jed to follow.

"You like him, don't you?"

Karen agreed that she did.

"Is he going to be your baby's dad?"

"No, sweetie. Just a friend. My baby's dad lives in Montana."

"Oh."

Back at Karen's house, Jed took off his skates, got into his car, and drove away with only a brief smile and a cheerful good-bye shared between the two of them, and no indication of when Karen might see him again.

# ELEVEN

The following Wednesday Karen and Penny ran, laughing and ducking, trying to shield themselves from a sudden downpour, toward the front entrance of a chain hamburger restaurant. They were halfway to the door when Jed appeared, a golf umbrella opened to cover all three of them. Penny went stock still, a rabbit under the eyes of a hawk. Karen all but tripped on her. Jed steadied her by clasping her elbow. Karen laid a comforting hand on Penny's nape, tugging the child to her other side, away from Jed.

"Good evening, ladies," he said, smiling down at Karen as rain sizzled on the umbrella and danced up off the sidewalk. "I stopped in for dinner. What a coincidence to find you doing the same. Would you care to join me?"

Karen wondered how long he'd been following them. Likely since she'd left her house to go and collect Penny. The door opened before Karen could decide how to handle this. A family of four left the restaurant, the father politely holding the door for the newcomers. There was nothing to do but enter.

The place was crowded, noisy, and steamy. The young hostess chirped a welcome, then said, "I have one table for three left."

Jed looked down at the child. "Okay, Penny?"

Several seconds passed. Penny's shoulders hunched; then she glanced up, sullen. "Yeah. Okay."

She slid into the booth the hostess showed them, and Karen followed.

Throughout the meal, while Jed and Karen kept up a steady conversation, mostly about his daughters when they were children, Penny ate in silence, but Karen knew she was listening to every word. Once, during a particularly funny story about Ceil and a snowy hillside, she even smiled, letting her gaze rest on Jed's face for longer than an instant.

"Well, ladies, where are you off to now?" he asked when the server had brought the bill. He scooped it up and stood.

"To a movie." Karen told him which one and he sighed, looking wistful.

"I hear that's really funny. I haven't seen it yet."

Silence followed his statement. A long, heavy silence. Penny fidgeted. Karen slid out of the booth, allowing the child to follow.

"Good night, Karen. Good night, Penny. Enjoy the movie."

As Jed moved away to pay the bill, Penny said, "I guess he'd like to go with us."

Karen nodded. "Probably."

"You gonna invite him?"

"No. But you can if you like."

Jed was nearly at the door, shrugging into his jacket, when Penny moved. "Mister!" Jed stopped, turned. "You can come with us," she said grudgingly. "If you want."

She stared at the floor while Jed and Karen shared a jubilant smile.

\* \* \*

Two weeks went by before Karen heard from Jed, and
then he phoned before she got home and left a message
on her machine that Barry had called again, asking for
her. His taut voice suggested she should tell Barry the
truth about where she lived.

She knew he was right, but still resisted doing it. Luck-
ily, she couldn't reach Barry. If he called back, she didn't
hear about it from Jed. Maybe Candice had come through
for him, let him unload on her about his troubles in the
hospital. Damn it, the girl was his wife! It was time she
took on some responsibilities, instead of turning her back
on him and forcing him to approach Karen with his problems.

She hoped his failure to call back meant Candice had
begun to act like an adult.

Yet part of her hoped she hadn't, that Barry would call
Jed's house again looking for her. That would force Jed
to contact her again.


Three weeks into the fall semester, as Karen picked
up a stack of folders she'd knocked to the floor, a small
book slid out.

She opened it. "Oh, no! Ceil's diary!"

She remembered the panicked call she'd gotten from
Portland a day or two after Cecelia had left, asking if
she had seen a small, red book. When Karen said she
had not, the girl had groaned loudly. "It's my diary," she
explained. "I must have dropped it somewhere at home
then. Oh, gosh, I hope my dad doesn't find it."

Karen supposed the best thing to do would be to mail
the book to Ceil, but a glance at her watch told her the
administration office was closed. She'd get no help there,
even assuming they had a forwarding address.

If she knew Jed's address, she could mail it to Ceil care of her father.

She stuffed the diary into an envelope, put Ceil's name on the front, sealed it, shoved it into her shoulder bag, and locked her office. The only sensible thing to do would be drive to the Cotts's house and drop the diary through the letter slot in the door. It would only be right to, return it as soon as possible. She glanced at her watch. Jed probably wouldn't be home for another couple of hours.

Karen fanned the driver's door of her truck back and forth, trying to expel some of the ovenlike heat that had built up in it all day. It was Friday. He probably wouldn't be home at all.

That thought made it easier to get into the truck and head it toward West Seattle.


He was watering a bed full of gold and bronze chrysanthemums. Wearing denim cutoffs and nothing else except a splendid suntan, he was magnificent. Little beads of moisture gleamed on his arms and shoulders as if he had sprayed himself with the hose.

Jed thought he saw Karen's rusty little yellow truck out of the corner of his eye and he stared hard at the mums, so as not to turn fully around. He stared so hard he saw black spots in front of his eyes, heard a roaring in his ears that sounded like a leaky muffler.

It wasn't. It simply was not. It was the heat creating auditory hallucinations. But he had to turn. He had to look.

It was her behind the wheel, driving slowly in front of him, her eyes seeming to cling to him. He took one step forward, lifted a hand up several inches before he let it fall back to his side.

"Karen . . ." He didn't know if he'd said her name aloud, or merely mouthed it. As if he had called her, she wrenched the wheel. At that, he did cry out, lunging forward as she executed a sharp left turn across the path of an oncoming car she seemed not to have noticed. Oblivious to the shaking fist of the other driver, she stopped her truck beside his car and sat there, clutching the wheel as if undecided whether to emerge.

She alighted, came around the front of her truck, putting one hand on the hood to balance herself, and glided toward him. Her sky blue dress had wide pleats that began just below her bustline. Seven months of pregnancy made her unbearably beautiful. Her gaze clung to his face beseechingly, as if she were afraid he might send her away.

The weeks since he'd seen her might not have been. Nothing had changed, no cure had been effected. He hadn't stopped wanting her. He wanted to tell her that, but he couldn't. He didn't want to plead.

"Hi." His voice was thick, rough. He cleared his throat. "You look . . . wonderful." Jeez! The language needed fixing. The words he knew were inadequate. There was only one way he could have told her how glad he was she'd come to him, had broken the silence.

She blinked her eyes, and tears shimmered in their depths, turning them silver in the sunlight. "No, I don't look wonderful. I look fat."

"Not fat. Pregnant. Beautifully so." He smiled, wondering if he looked as inane as he felt—like a huge, stumbling pup about to fling himself onto a human he adored, muddy paws and all. "Wonderful," he said. "Beautiful.

Let's go inside and . . ." *And make love.* "And have some lemonade."

Did he have any lemonade? No. He had beer. Lots of that, and lots of lust, but no lemonade.

She hesitated. He knew she was on the verge of refusing. She held something out, an envelope. She was talking, telling him something about its being a book Ceil had left in her office, and that Ceil wanted it, only he could scarcely hear that. What he could hear was his own greedy self clamoring that *he* wanted *her,* even if it was just to talk to, look at, listen to, be with. He wanted her for all of those things, but the only thing he knew how to do was make love.

She continued talking and he bent down, covered her mouth quickly with his, stopping her words and all but stopping his own heart as he tasted her, sweet, sweeter than he'd remembered, better than his nighttime fantasies, more fulfilling than any food could ever be. Karen. His sustenance. Her lips moved under his, answering.

He lifted his head and stared into her eyes, searching for green rays, finding them, and then he had her elbow in one hand and was leading her toward the broad, shallow steps that led up to his front door.

"Jed."

He stopped and stood looking into her eyes again. She was laughing. "What?"

"The water. Turn it off."

"Water?"

"The hose." She took it from him and aimed its nozzle toward the ground.

"Oh." He took it back and twisted it shut, then dropped it. It coiled like a snake down the steps and back onto the lawn. They looked at it for a moment, then back at each other.

"Karen." He put his hand around the point of her shoulder and pulled her up against him as he opened the door. "Oh, Karen. You came to me."

He closed the door and the welcome coolness of the dim house enclosed them, enfolded them as he wanted to enfold her in his arms. He looked at her shoulder where he touched her and saw the edges of a wet handprint on her dress. Oh, hell, he was such a clumsy oaf! He wiped his hand on his shorts, but it was too late. The stain remained on the cotton of her dress. He covered it again, needing that much contact at the very least.

"I brought Cecelia's diary," she said. "I was going to drop it through the letter slot. I wasn't going to see you again."

"Why?"

"Because you haven't called. You haven't dropped by. I thought you didn't want to see me again."

"I wanted to."

"So why didn't you?"

"Because . . . there are too many obstacles."

They glanced down at the most obvious obstacle. Karen smoothed her hands over it as if to soothe her baby, comfort it for the slight he'd offered in referring to it as an obstacle. She raised her chin and met his gaze again. "As I said, I had no intention of seeing you today. I didn't think you'd be here."

"But I am here, Karen. Ceil's not. She doesn't live here anymore. I live all alone."

"I know," she said, still clutching the brown package that contained his daughter's diary, holding it between them as if it might form a barrier. Funny, he hadn't even known that Ceil kept a diary. "She said she was moving to Portland," Karen went on. "Do you miss her a lot? You must be lonely."

The compassion in her tone slathered itself over his self-inflicted wounds like thick ointment. He might have played for her sympathy, but the joy of having her in his home, almost in his arms, was too great. He shook his head. "I've been enjoying the lack of rock music too much to miss her more than just a little."

He let her go and stepped back a pace or two, still looking at her. "But you," he said, having to work hard at maintaining an even tone, "that's a different matter. You, I've missed." His voice was rough, and he looked at her from eyes that burned. "Badly, Karen. More than I can say."

He thought she might cry. Her eyes shimmered again, but she lifted her chin and stared him down. "You're the one who stopped coming around."

He licked his lips and couldn't continue to meet her steady gaze. "I know."

They met in one pace and he held her to his heart, rocking her back and forth, loving the warmth of her body, the scent of her skin, the crispness of her hair against his cheek. A damp streak ran down the center of her back.

He fingered it. "You shouldn't have been driving in this heat." He thought of the comfort of his own air-conditioned car. She needed to be looked after, pampered.

She didn't lift her head from its resting place against his shoulder. It was as if she had come home and nothing could persuade her to move again; at least he could pretend that was what kept her in his arms. It might be something else, not need, just . . . apathy because it was too hot to argue. It didn't matter. He'd hold her for whatever reason.

"It's not so bad," she said, her voice muffled against

his chest. "I had the windows open and got a good breeze going."

He ran a hand into the back of her hair. It, too, was damp, and curled tightly. It had grown a lot. She shook his hand off and unwrapped her arms from around his torso.

"Jed, don't touch me. I'm hot and sweaty and probably smell bad. I wasn't prepared to see you. I didn't think you'd be home yet or I wouldn't have come."

"But since you've found me home . . ." He tilted her chin up and kissed her softly, gently, tenderly. As her lips quivered under his, another massive surge of desire smashed through him, and he came close to forgetting the facts that had to govern his actions. With supreme effort, he forced down the passion and lifted his head, then held her away from him as her child gave him a wicked kick.

Punishment. Deserved punishment.

She looked down at the mass of her belly between them. She grinned. "Sorry about that."

"You need a swim," he said.

A swim in his pool would be the ultimate in luxury. "I don't have a suit." There was no way she could hide the regret she felt.

"You don't need a suit. My backyard is completely private. No one would see you but me."

"Jed!" She laughed and pressed her hands to her front, molding her wrinkled dress to her shape, not that the fabric needed much help to cling. "Look at me! I'm grotesque. I'd hate to have you see me."

He laughed at her, and her heart filled with warmth and happiness. "Grotesque?" he echoed. "You are, as I said not five minutes ago, beautiful. But if it would make you happy, I'll stay on this side of the house, go back to watering flowers, and let you have the pool area to yourself."

"Jed . . ." She swallowed hard. "No, really, I couldn't. Not without a suit, not even if you promised not to look. Even with a suit and your promise of privacy, I'd be uncomfortable."

"Honey . . ." He pulled her dress away from her sticky back. "You're uncomfortable now. Ceil left a couple of suits." He grinned. "What you lack in height, you'll take up in girth. Please, Karen. Stay. At least until the sun goes down and it'll be cooler driving home."

*Let me look after you. Let me care for you.* That was what he needed to do, just for now. She was pregnant, and no pregnant woman should have to be alone. It went against the laws of nature—the laws that said people lived in caves, and the male hunted food for the female, who was busy nurturing the young and needed to be protected.

Laws that had died out a million years ago, yet managed to live on in him.

She nodded. "You're right. I am uncomfortable. Okay, then. I'll try Cecelia's suit, but you still have to promise to leave me alone."

He exulted at her capitulation and tried to hide it, but couldn't stop himself looking for just a bit more. "I promise. But only if you let me fix dinner for you after."

The glow of her smile filled him, and she nodded again. He took her hand, led her into his bedroom and turned on the shower for her before pulling back the drapes to show her the doors leading directly to the pool from the bathroom. Then he rushed to Ceil's room and rummaged for a suit, which he dropped on his bed for Karen. He stood listening until the shower stopped, then all but raced from the room, not wanting her to know he'd been ready in case she fell.

He really had meant what he'd said about giving her privacy, he thought, hesitating inside the patio doors that led to the pool area from the family room. But what if she'd had a cramp? What if she couldn't get out of the pool for some reason? What if she was in trouble and needed help? Needed him?

Ten minutes passed. Another five. He cracked the door an inch but could hear nothing but the grumbling of a bird that wasn't sure it should fly south.

He couldn't see all of the pool. The deck and diving board at the deep end were visible, but from where he stood, the shallow end was hidden behind a bank of rhododendrons. A person could drown in the shallow end as well as the deep end.

Suddenly, the need to protect her overcame the desire to respect her privacy. Jed slid the door open the rest of the way and lunged outside.

The first thing he saw was her lower legs and feet. As he leaped forward, he saw the rest of her, her head at the edge of the pool nearest him.

She lay on her back in the water, elbows hooked around the ladder, arms over her head, which rested on the first rung. Her eyes were closed, her face calm, her lips lightly parted. Little curls of hair floated around her half-submerged ears. Her belly, covered by neon green fabric striped diagonally with cream and yellow, jutted upward like a surrealistic watermelon; her breasts, scarcely covered by the material, were like two blue-veined casabas, rising and falling rhythmically as her body floated free and weightless and she slept.

He couldn't leave her like that. Stepping into the pool, he slid his arms under her, floating her toward him until she bumped against his chest. Her lashes fluttered open and she blinked at him solemnly for a moment before she frowned.

"You promised."

"I lied. I didn't mean to. I didn't know I was doing it. But then I started worrying about you getting a cramp. Drowning. Needing me."

She lifted a languid hand and drew her fingertips along his jaw. "I like having you worry about me."

"Baby . . ." He lifted her out of the water and carried her up the steps, across the pool deck, and laid her gently on a chaise longue. Grabbing a sun-warmed towel off the back of a chair, he carefully rubbed her arms and legs dry.

"You fall asleep in the damnedest places," he said.

"I didn't mean to, but being weightless felt so heavenly. My back aches a lot."

He nodded. "I know. Lie here and rest for a minute. I'll be right back."

"Where—" *Where are you going?* Karen started to say, but his long strides carried him away too quickly. He disappeared into the cabana and returned seconds later wearing a terry robe, carrying another big towel that he spread over the back of her legs to shield her from the sun. He dumped a pool of liquid from a bottle of suntan oil into his palm and rubbed it briskly between his hands before he sat behind her, his hip crowding her over on the lounge, and applied the oil to her back.

Oh! It was heavenly. It smelled like coconuts and was thick and creamy, but what was best was simply having Jed's touch on her skin. Without the oil, that would have been enough.

Working left-handed, his right hand supporting her shoulder, his long, firm fingers soothed her aches. The hard pad of his thumb seemed to know by instinct exactly which vertebrae needed attention. He worked from the small of her back upward to her shoulders, shoved aside the straps of her bathing suit, spent uncountable delicious minutes there and on her neck, then made a slow, studied tour back down to where he had begun, lingering there for many more minutes before moving even lower.

She sighed, a long, tremulous sound full of aching need. If only she could roll fully onto her front.

As her exhaustion began to seep away, she felt the beginnings of heat coil through her, heat that had nothing to do with the late summer afternoon.

Oh, heavens, what was she going to do? It was not his intention to turn her on. He was offering relief from her backache, nothing else. She was fat and ugly. A blimp. A middle-sized elephant. No man could look at her and want her, not sexually. He was simply being kind, but this kindness was a terrible cruelty in disguise.

To her horror, a huge sob burst from her lungs and she bit her arm to try to muffle it, but he heard, rolled her onto her back, and stared at her, his eyes filled with need, filled with a desire that clearly equaled her own.

His face was flushed. His breath, she heard now, rasped as raggedly as hers. His robe had come undone and he seemed not to have noticed as he sat there, staring down at her. He was fully aroused, and when she reached out and touched the bead of cream at the tip, he gasped, jerking away. She sat up and slid both her hands around his neck. "Jed?"

He caught her hands, snatched them down and pressed them against his chest. His gaze glided down over her body, as physical as a touch. She knew the heat rising under her skin would be a bright flush over her chest and shoulders.

"Ah, baby," he said raggedly. "I'm sorry. That wasn't supposed to happen. To either of us."

"No, no, Jed. Please don't be sorry. Just make love to me."

## TWELVE

# TWELVE

Jed squeezed his eyes shut. "Sweetheart, I can't," he said, but he lay down and pulled her against his chest, stroking her damp hair back from her face. His sex was hot and hard against her thigh. "I want to, so much. But you know we can't."

"Why not?" She couldn't believe what he was saying. He could touch her like that, set in motion unstoppable forces in both of them and then turn away? "God . . . Jed . . ." She moaned in despair as she tried to get closer and could not. There was too much of her in the way. She slid one leg up over his. The heat of his skin, the roughness of the hair on his thigh elicited a shudder of need for more. "I'm only seven months. It's safe."

As if the frustration was too much for him, too, he groaned softly and stood, then bent and swept his arms under her and lifted her, carrying her around the end of the pool and into his bedroom.

He lay her down on his large bed and followed her, holding her close to him. The mattress gave under her, the water within conforming to her shape, supporting her as comfortably as had the water of the pool. She rolled to her side, smiled at him, locked her hands behind his head, and drew him to her.

"Jed, I want you so much."

"I've spent so much time, so many nights, thinking

about this." He spoke against her breasts, his face buried between them, then cradled them in his hands, rubbing his cheeks, slightly rough with whiskers, across their sensitive tips. His lips plucked at them again. When she arched to him, he suckled harder and she felt a pulling from very deep inside her, then a hot rush and a spurt of moisture from the breast under his hand.

He drew his head away, looked at her, at the liquid running down her chest, then looked into her eyes, his filled with a startled, disbelieving smile. He licked his lips, then licked the stream coming from her nipple. His laugh was full of amazed delight. "Well, I'll be damned! It tastes *good!*"

She was embarrassed by the leakage, touched that he liked it, and several other emotions that weren't quite clear at the moment. "It does?"

He bent and tasted again, gently, not sucking, merely licking up the beads that continued to well up and spill off. "Very good."

Flustered, she said, "Well, of course, I guess it should, if I'm going to be feeding it to a little baby."

She struggled to sit up, but the waterbed defeated her. So did Jed, with nothing more than a fingertip between her breasts and a whispered, "Stay still."

She managed a small smile as she covered her oozing nipples with tissues. "I guess any kind of a turnoff is better than none, under the circumstances."

"Yeah, right," he murmured, but instead of rolling away from her as she'd expected, he wrapped his hands around her face and kissed her, his tongue plunging deeply into her mouth. Briefly, she tried to resist her own urges, tried to tell herself that the moment had passed, that she was no longer so wildly aroused that it would be impossible to stop, but her resistance was swept away as need rose up with renewed strength.

She met the thrusts of his tongue measure for measure and her protective hands fell from her breasts, baring them to the abrasion of his chest as she wrapped her fingers around his arms. He broke the kiss, looked into her eyes for a moment, then flicked one nipple gently with his fingertip and stroked the other with a thumb.

"Are you turned off?" he asked softly as he stroked her huge stomach and down between her legs.

She clamped her thighs together to bar his hand. If he touched her there, he'd know how far from turned off she was.

He parted her legs with shocking ease and felt her intimately through the crotch of her bathing suit, eliciting a moan, a sound he caught with his mouth as it covered hers again.

"You're not turned off," he gasped moments later. "I'm not turned off. So we have to do something about it."

"Yes!" Karen said as he touched her. Then again, "Yes!" as she lifted so he could slide the suit down over her body and out from under her. She sighed and arched as his fingers curled in between her legs, gently parting her flesh, probing at her moist entrance, pressing insistently.

Her breath caught in her throat, refused to go in or out as he stroked deeper, urging her legs to part and her hips to surge upward. She rolled onto her side, flinging a leg over him, clinging to his back with one hand, the other finding his sex and wrapping around it, eager to guide him home.

\* \* \*

A long time later she awoke and saw through the archway that it was dusk. She'd been sleeping for two or three hours, and Jed with her. She stroked a hand around the angle of his jaw and he opened his eyes and smiled at her, slowly, sweetly. Then, as if remembering what they had done, he bit his lower lip, a look of distress crossing his face as his arms tightened around her. "Are you all right?" he asked.

"I'm fine." She stretched luxuriantly. "This is the first time in months that I've awakened without a band of pain across the small of my back. It feels wonderful. That back rub, your wonderfully comfortable bed, or"— she grinned—"something else was exactly the medicine I needed."

He smiled. "I vote for something else, because I feel pretty damned wonderful, too."

"Good," she said softly. "A wonderful man deserves to feel that way."

"As long as you're sure I didn't do any harm."

She shook her head. "No harm. I feel great." She yawned hugely. "Sleepy, but wonderful." He continued to look doubtful and she nestled close to him, wrapping an arm over his chest.

"You glow," he said, his tone marveling. "You shine in the darkness."

"You're responsible for my glow, Jed, but you were not responsible for what happened between us. As I remember it, you were the one who tried to stop it. I was the one who insisted we continue." She lifted her head for a moment. "That seems to be becoming a routine. Am I too aggressive?"

He laughed, and all his tension seemed to fly away. "Honey, if I'd wanted to make you stop, I would have. A man can always walk away. The trouble was, while my mind told me one thing, my body told me the opposite. Like any greedy man, I went with what my body wanted."

She smiled again. "I'm glad your body wanted." For a moment, they stared into each other's eyes, reliving the ecstasy of their joining. Karen shuddered.

"Lord, Jed. I still can't believe it really happened like that. To you, I mean. Getting aroused by this tubby body. Yuck!" She smoothed the sheet over her shape. "I mean, look at me!"

He buried his face in her neck for a moment. "I was looking at you, and that's why it happened. Looking and touching and wanting, because you're so damned sexy I lose my head completely around you."

She rolled away from him because she wanted to cry, because his sweet lies touched her right where it mattered, in the middle of her heart, and made her ache unbearably. She wanted this kind of joy with him to be a forever kind of thing, but he wanted something else.

He caught her and rolled her back, forcing her to face him. He caught one tear that escaped and held it on the tip of his finger before he licked it off. "What's this for, Karen?"

"I'm not sexy. You shouldn't pretend."

He threw back his head and laughed. "It is physically impossible for a man to pretend something like that. I wanted you. You are very, very sexy."

"Jedidiah Cotts," she said shakily, "you are a sick man. A sweet one, but sick. Definitely not sane."

She poked him in the nose with one finger. "Pregnant women are not sexy," she went on. "Limber, skinny women who can play tennis and hike up mountainsides without panting and puffing and getting red in the face are sexy. Women who can tie shoes and go roller-blading without losing their balance are sexy. Women who can stay awake for more than half an hour and who don't leak milk all over the men they love are sexy. But I—"

His openmouthed stare, his fingers biting into her shoulder, cut off her words.

He leaned over her. His blue eyes glittered hotly. "What did you say?" It was a rough whisper.

Oh, hell, what had she done? Her mouth felt dangerously tremulous. She firmed it. The words had slipped out and she'd give anything to be able to recall them. Her emotions were her problem, not his.

"Karen. Answer me."

Stubbornly, she kept her mouth shut. She damned well wasn't about to repeat what she'd said, to lay it out before him so the two of them could analyze it and pick over all the reasons why it shouldn't be. She knew why it shouldn't—couldn't—be. That didn't alter the facts, but it didn't make them easier to bear, either. "I said I'm not sexy."

"After that."

"I'm not skinny?" It was a challenge. She dared him to persist in this line of questioning. He returned her angry stare, so she added, "Not limber?"

"Karen, damn it all—"

"Jed, please," she interrupted. "Drop it. It's not important."

"It is important!" He was close to shouting. His brows were drawn together over his nose. His face looked gaunt and hawklike as he stared at her.

"No. Forget it. Let me go."

"Karen." His fingers relaxed minimally. He shook her gently. "Are you in love with me?"

She shrugged and tried to turn away from him. "Our lives aren't compatible. I know that. We both know that."

"Do you love me?" His voice grated, his eyes burned into hers.

He was furious. He clearly hated knowing she'd been so stupid as to lose her heart. Damn it, didn't he realize she was paying him a compliment? Did he think love was something she gave lightly? Or did he see it as a trap?

This time she managed to roll free of him, to sit up against the resistance of the waterbed and fling her legs over the side. It took all the strength in her arms to thrust herself to her feet. She snatched up the robe he'd been wearing and jammed her arms into its sleeves before she turned to face him.

"All right. Yes, I do love you. But so what? It doesn't mean I'm looking for anything in return, Jed. I like my life just fine the way it is. I'm going to have my baby, raise her, and be the best parent I can be. A single parent, because that is what *I* want, what I *choose.* My baby and I will be happy together. I'm not asking anything of you or anybody else. I don't *want* anything from you or anybody else."

He rolled to his feet and stood looking down at her, searching her eyes as if trying to read something in there that she might not be saying.

"You should want," he said harshly. "You have a basic right to want things, to have all you should have. Oh, God, I hate the way this world is going!"

"Jed, please. I don't hate what's happening to me."

Slowly, he drew her against him and rocked her back and forth, his cheek on top of her head. "I know you don't." His arms tightened, holding her fast as she tried to move. He didn't want to look at her, she realized, didn't want her to look at him. "I respect that about you. Your independence. I know it's important to you. I'd never try to take it away from you because I want—need—my own freedom too badly not to understand how you feel."

"I know," she whispered. She did know. She hated it, but she knew it.

For her, it was independence.

For him, it was freedom.

For several moments, he continued to hold her, running his hands up and down her back, then he pushed a fist under her chin and tilted her face up and smiled crookedly. "I envy you and your baby, you know that? And your future. I'd like to be at a point in my life where I could be starting out like you, fresh and eager and full of plans."

Suddenly, she was filled with a terrible desire to ask him to join her in those plans, to share her future and her baby's life, to start out again, fresh, to let the love she felt for him. She wanted for herself what he thought she should have, a complete family.

She parted her lips and would have dared all, would have spoken from her heart, but he went on.

"But I'm not where you are, Karen. I'm at a different stage. You're in springtime, I'm in autumn. And even when I was at that point in my life, I blew it. I can never forget that."

The doorbell rang. Almost simultaneously, the door opened and a voice called out, "Hi, Dad! You home?"

Jed set Karen back from him. "Willi," he said, clearly rattled. He spun quickly and hauled open a drawer in a tall mahogany bureau dragging a pair of shorts on over his naked body, zipping them quickly. He glanced nervously over his shoulder, as if expecting his daughter to burst in on them.

"Would you like me to hide in the closet?"

He frowned slightly, as if Karen's irony bothered him, but his focus was aimed elsewhere. "Just stay here, okay?" he asked. "I'll see what she wants and—"

*And what? Make sure she doesn't see that you have a woman in your bedroom?* Karen wanted to ask, but he had slipped out the door and closed it securely behind him.

She stood feeling ridiculously hurt for several moments before she picked up a pillow that had ended up on the floor and straightened the blue and gold bed cover that matched the blue and gold drapes over the windows. From elsewhere in the house, she could hear rising and falling voices, a feminine laugh, a baby's squeals of delight, as if he were being tossed high into the air and caught securely on the way down.

Jed's family. His daughter. His grandson. Whom he clearly did not want her to meet.

She went into the bathroom, dressed without bothering to shower, and slid her feet into her sandals. Then, quietly, she stepped out the open door to the pool deck and followed a flagged path and a flight of stone stairs back around to the front of the house. Her purse and keys were in the truck where she'd left them and she started the engine, backed out, and pulled away without looking back.

But at least the sun had gone down, and now it was cooler driving.

"You couldn't have waited for five minutes?" Jed demanded when Karen answered her door.

She'd considered ignoring his ringing and knocking, but he was at least as stubborn as she and would keep it up all evening, if necessary.

He still wore the shorts he'd pulled on when his daughter arrived, but had added an unbuttoned short-sleeved shirt and thongs. It was cool outside now, blessedly cool to Karen's way of thinking, but goose bumps stood the dark hair on Jed's arms on end.

She wanted to brush it flat. "I thought it would be better for you if I left. I didn't want to embarrass you."

He took a step forward, and she had to take one back. This placed him inside her house, but there didn't seem to be a lot she could do about it. If she hollered and tried to force him out, sure as blazes Mrs. Harrison would get agitated and call 911 again. He kept on walking, pausing only to kick the door shut behind him, cutting off the welcome breeze its opening had created. "Why would you have embarrassed me?"

She continued to back up. He came with her, steering her toward the sofa. The feel of his callused skin on her bare shoulders sent shafts of heat stabbing through her. "My presence was an embarrassment to you."

"Like hell." He sat her down as if she were made of spun sugar, and crouched before her. For a moment, he buried his face against the legs of her pink overalls, then lifted his head and looked at her. "Is it hot in here, or is it just me?"

"It's hot in here." She wiped her brow, then sat on both hands to keep them from straying and touching him. "Jed, if I wasn't an embarrassment to you, why did you tell me to stay hidden in your bedroom? Why not introduce me to your daughter?"

He looked pained and let out a long, gusty breath. "Oh, hell, if you could have seen yourself, Karen, you'd have understood. I thought *you'd* be embarrassed. Your hair was a mess. Your face was flushed. Your lips were swollen and you had a whisker rash on your throat. You were in my bedroom and you looked as if you'd just been well and truly—" He bit his lip, then shrugged helplessly. "There's only one word for it," he said, and finished softly.

That he'd used the term didn't shock her. What did was how that particular choice of word, used in that particular context, sent a shaft of heat through her.

She had to smile. "I had been, Jed. Truly and very, very well." She knew her eyes must be shining with the memory. She felt as if she shone all over. "Oh, brother, had I been!"

He groaned and drew her against him, pressing her face to his chest. "Honey, I suggest you don't look at me like that. I also suggest you don't call me brother again or I'll have to show you I'm not."

"Mmm. I'm awfully glad of that, too."

"Karen? You broke your word, you know."

"I did?"

"You did. You promised that if I let you have your swim alone, you'd have dinner with me. Have you eaten yet?"

She shook her head, feeling the hardness of his muscles against her cheek, wishing she could nudge the front of his shirt away and press her lips to his skin.

"Then come home with me. Let me feed you. Let me—just come home with me, Karen."

She lifted her gaze to his, and there was no way in the world she could refuse him. "Okay," she said, and he looked as if having a fat, pregnant woman in his house for dinner was as good as winning a million-dollar lottery.


"What did you tell your daughter?" Karen asked as she perched on a stool in Jed's kitchen, watching him prepare dinner. She dipped into the jar of olives he'd left too close and plucked out just one more, licking the deliciously salty juice off it before sucking it into her mouth. When she'd savored it and swallowed, she continued. "I mean, about why you didn't stay and visit with her. Obviously, you didn't spend much time here after she arrived. Either that or you broke every speed law in the city when you followed me home, because I'd barely showered and changed before you arrived." She took another olive almost without noticing.

"The minute I heard your truck start and saw you driving away, I told her I had to leave, and fast, but she'd only come to tell me she couldn't water my garden next week. Her husband had to switch vacations with another man, so they're off on a camping trip as of tomorrow morning."

Karen felt a sense of foreboding. "What happens next week that you can't water your own plants?"

He finished breaking lettuce and feta cheese into a bowl and reached for the olives, tipping the jar up and looking in. "Little pig. You've eaten them all."

"I have?"

He angled the jar so she could see in. "Oh. I'm sorry. Why didn't you stop me? I mean, you stood right there watching me do it."

He grinned. "Someday take a look in the mirror and watch yourself eating olives. No man in his right mind would stop you."

She got that delicious little fluttering feeling again but refused to let it distract her. "Jed, what happens next week?"

He lifted one shoulder and dropped it as he set the salad in the fridge. "Singapore. I need to check out some silk stocks. One of my clients, a wholesaler, needs a large

order and an Asian contact of mine has made an offer
that may be too good to be true. The price sounds great,
but I have to see the quality for myself before I decide
to put in a bid to supply the wholesaler."

"I see." What she really wanted to say was *Don't go.
Don't leave me. I need you to rub my back.*

Of course, she couldn't say that. He respected her independence. She respected his freedom. Only right now,
independence wasn't all it was cracked up to be. Right
now, she felt ugly and fat and pregnant, and Jed seemed
to be the only person in the world who could make her
feel worthwhile.

Oh, sure. So worthwhile that he was eagerly planning
a jaunt to the other side of the world. It was an unfair
statement, but she couldn't deal with it just then. It was
simply the way she felt. She also felt like crying.

"That sounds like an interesting trip. How long will
you be gone?"

"Probably until Sunday. Maybe Monday or Tuesday,
depending on how business goes. It will be an interesting
trip," he said, apparently not hearing the sour note she'd
detected in her own voice. "I like Singapore. It's one of
the few Asian cities I feel fully at home in."

He took the steak from its marinade and laid it on a
plate. "Want to come outside with me while I barbecue
this? You can bring the French bread."


Karen batted at a moth that persisted in dive-bombing
her head. "Your hair in the torchlight must look like a
candle," Jed said, reaching out and brushing the moth
away. "Let's go inside."

She sighed and dropped her feet to the flagstones of
the patio from where they'd been propped on a low cedar

block railing. "I have to get home, Jed." It was late, but she hated to leave.

"No, Karen. Please stay."

"I wish I could. I love your house. I love your view, the . . . wideness of it."

"I'm glad you like my eagle's nest," he said. "When I found it fifteen years ago, I felt as if I had come home. I had to have it. There's a purity in the air up here, and the sweeping view makes me feel as if I'm in charge of a vast domain."

He gave a self-deprecating chuckle. "I suppose that's my male ego, wanting to feel like the ruler of all I survey."

"I understand. I feel it, too."

"Don't leave," he said again softly, and for a minute she thought she'd detected a plea in his voice, but of course it was only an invitation. His next words showed that. "Stay the night. You're right, it is late. Didn't you say that your sleep this afternoon in my bed was the first one you'd awakened from in a long time without a backache?"

"Well, yes. But . . ." But what? Even thinking of the drive home was daunting, though Jed would be doing the driving. Contemplating sitting that long in a car made the idea of simply falling into a nice, resilient waterbed five minutes from now more attractive than she should admit even to herself.

She looked down at the pink cotton overalls she'd put on after going home earlier that evening before Jed came to get her. They were wrinkled and she'd dropped a bit of lettuce leaf from her salad onto the protruding front, leaving a slight oil stain. The striped blue and white T-shirt that she wore under them was limp and damp under the arms. If her clothes looked this unappealing to her tonight, what would it feel like having to climb into them come morning?

Jed turned her, tilted her face up, and looked into her eyes. The flickering torches on the patio wall sent shadows across his face. "Don't think of dumb excuses like clothing and a toothbrush and stuff like that. They can be overcome. And don't think I'm planning to keep you awake all night repeating this afternoon. I'm not asking for anything, Karen. I'll sleep in the spare room if you prefer it that way. I just want you to be comfortable, to have a good sleep."

His thumbs touched the dark arcs under her eyes, so lightly they could have been moths fluttering against her skin, and he added, "Just stay in my house with me. This once."

For a moment longer, she hesitated, then nodded. "I'd like that, Jed. Very much."

His smile was the kind of reward she thought people should receive only rarely lest it begin to lose its immense value. It filled her until she thought she must be spilling over with happiness.

"But I don't want to deprive you of your own bed." She wanted to laugh at the silly, girlishly shy note that had crept into her voice. Really, this was ridiculous. Only hours ago, she had begged this man to make love to her. Couldn't she come right out and ask him to sleep with her after all that?

He looked down at her, expressionless, waiting, and she was forced to put it into words.

"Could we . . . share?"

His arms came around her tightly as his breath left his

lungs in a shuddering whoosh. "We could. Oh, yes, we could."

*I love you. I love you. I love you.* Her heart chanted the words, sang them, wanted to burst with them as she nestled against Jed, but all too soon he had relaxed his grip and was steering her into the house. She yawned. It was very much time for bed.

# THIRTEEN

Pure delight filled Karen when she woke to find Jed curled around her back, his hand cradling her belly as if he loved the child within as much as she did. Carefully, she placed her hand over his, matching her fingers to his, feeling the difference in size, enjoying the quiet intimacy of the early morning. She wanted to turn and hold him tightly, but did not dare. *I love you,* she told him silently, sliding her fingers between his, caressing his hand as she drew hers up and over his wrist.

He half woke, captured her hand and pinned it against her stomach, holding it there, and she heard his soft chuckle as the baby responded to the touch with a vigorous kick. *I love you, too,* she told it, and then her eyes fluttered closed and she drifted into sleep again.

Jed was gone when she woke. A carafe of coffee stood on the bedside table nearest her, along with a glass of orange juice, a bran muffin, and a big, shaggy bronze chrysanthemum in a bud vase three sizes too small. It fell over when she reached for the coffee.

As she picked it up, she saw the note folded under the coffee cup and quickly opened it.

*Good morning. You and the baby were sleeping, so I didn't disturb you. You have bathroom privileges and pool privileges, and you are to stay put until I get back. To make sure, I've confiscated your clothes.*

*P.S. You still snore.*

"I do not!" She laughed and leaned over to pour her first cup of coffee. There was a lot to be said for being pampered, so she'd make the most of it while she could.

It was very early Monday morning. Jed was dressed in a gray raw-silk suit and carried a bone-colored raincoat over his arm as they arrived at the airport. Over the weekend, the weather had done a complete turnaround and a wet, blustery gale now lashed the entire Pacific Northwest coast. He looked at Karen as she pulled his Buick to a halt outside the terminal in the passenger loading zone. They would have only moments before she had to move the car.

"I guess I won't need to water your garden," she said, and he found himself resenting her cheerful tone. He felt distinctly glum, which was unusual. Normally, he was eager to go on a trip like this, his whole focus rushing forward to what lay ahead, but not this time. This time his mood matched the gray day too well.

Cupping her chin in his hand, he kissed her, very quickly, in case he gave in to the temptation to prolong the agony. "Go to my place anyway," he said, releasing her. "Please, Karen. Stay there. Sleep in my bed."

"No," she said for maybe the tenth time since they had arisen long before dawn. "I have to go home, Jed. For one thing, I like to be where Penny can reach me."

"Penny knows my number."

"So she told me."

"You look disapproving. I wanted her to have it in

case she was with you and something happened. She could call for help."

"I understand that, but Penny knows how to dial 911."

"If you need help, I don't want her calling some uncaring stranger unless there's no alternative. Or you either, for that matter. Damn it, Karen, haven't you figured out yet that I care about you?"

*Do you?* she wanted to ask, *or do you just feel responsible for me because I'm pregnant, and you think some man—any man—must take responsibility for a pregnant woman?*

Jed scowled at her silent face as he got out and struggled against the wind. He tugged on his raincoat before opening the back door and grabbing his suitcase, which lay on top of the one he'd packed for her at her house Saturday morning. His high-handedness had worked then; she had spent the weekend with him, sleeping in his bed, in his arms, and he had somehow managed to let her get all the rest she needed. Damn it, he'd treated her right, hadn't he?

So why wouldn't she do what he wanted now?

He looked at her as she sat half turned to look over the back seat, watching him, clearly ready to zip away the minute he shut the door. Deliberately, he checked the locks on his suitcase, ignoring the rain beating down on his back.

"Why do you *have* to go home?" he asked. "So you can sleep in a bed that makes your back hurt?"

"It's not forever, Jed. Until a few weeks ago, I found my bed perfectly comfortable."

"So why not spend the next few nights in my house? Or even the next few weeks. That's not forever, either."

She met his gaze levely. "I know it's not. Good-bye, Jed. Have a good flight."

He paused for another moment, feeling the rain begin to soak through his coat. He didn't give a damn! So he'd be wet all the way to Singapore. Other things were more important.

Karen met his stormy gaze, staring him down. She would not give in. She couldn't. Why didn't he understand that? Damn it, she'd been stupid enough to let him know she loved him. Where was his compassion? Didn't he see how hard it was for her, having to be strong, having to curtail her foolish, pregnant-female inclination to let him take over her life? To pamper her and make things easy for her? She didn't dare get used to that, because soon she'd be a mother, and she'd have no one to smooth her path. As a mother, she'd need to become the path smoother.

"I'll phone you, Karen." His eyes were dark, hardly blue at all as a result of the stormy skies and his stormy mood. "At my place."

"I won't be there," she said stubbornly. He had to understand. He had to believe her. Her independence was important to her.

"If you want to talk to me, you will," he retorted.

"If you want to talk to me, call me at home," she said, but doubted if he'd heard her, because he'd shut the door and was rushing inside the terminal, suitcase banging against one leg, briefcase tucked under his arm, head bent against the force of the gale. She also doubted that he'd call her at home.

"So I guess that's that." She checked the mirror before pulling out. "You can phone your empty house, and phone and phone, but all you'll do is run up a huge bill when your answering machine kicks in."

The decision was hers alone. She knew that. He knew that. If only she could convince her heart it was the right one, but she couldn't. A very important part of her wanted to spend the next week living in his house, sleeping in his bed. The next week? The next lifetime wouldn't be enough.

Only he had been right. He *wasn't* talking forever.

Jed sat on his hotel balcony sipping a drink, making a silent toast to himself for his forty-sixth birthday. The steamy heat of the Singapore night hung thick around him. The sights, sounds, and scents of the swirling alienness had once pleased him. This time, they failed. Not even knowing that this could, if he chose, be his last trip overseas could make him enjoy it.

He missed Karen. He longed to see her, to hear her, to touch her, to taste her. The need for her lived inside him like a heavy weight and he didn't think it would ever be relieved.

Except by finding a way to keep her in his life.

Staying home was one way. That he was more than willing to do. This time, leaving had been hard. It would get harder the longer he knew her, the deeper he let her burrow into his heart, into the fabric of his life. It was time for him to trust someone else to take care of business, time for his assistant to take over the bulk of the foreign travel. That would be the easy part.

The baby. There was the big stumbling block. Lord, but it scared him, the thought of trying to be a father again, trying to get it right this time. With Karen's help, could he?

A vision swam before him—a little doll of a girl, slender like her mama, with dark hair that shone red in the sun, learning to walk, a little girl with freckles across the bridge of her nose riding a tricycle, a little girl with big gray eyes, looking up at him trustingly, calling him "Daddy" as he taught her to—to what? What kinds of things did fathers teach their little girls? What had he taught Willi and Ceil? Not a hell of a lot.

Through most of the years they could remember, he thought, taking a long swig out of his glass, he'd taught them Dad was the guy who went to work before they got up and got home after they were in bed. As older children and teens, he'd taught them they couldn't rely on him for birthday dinners out on the town, because he'd probably be on the far side of the world. He'd taught them Dad was the guy who came home with gifts in a futile attempt to make up for his not being there for them, that Dad was the one Mom looked at with silent reproach in her eyes.

He thought, too, of a little girl to be born before long, a little girl whose mother was so determined to have her independence, to raise the child alone, that she hadn't even told the baby's father whose child she carried. Yet who was he to suggest it could be otherwise? Hadn't his wife had to raise his children all but alone? And hadn't she done an exemplary job?

He was a fool to think he could horn in at this late stage and at this time in his life. When Karen's little girl was starting college, he'd be collecting Social Security.

As if he had the right to do it, he spent an entire afternoon shopping just for Karen—dresses in every imaginable color, loose and roomy for the next few weeks, form-fitting and sleek for when she was her normal slim self again. He bought bolts of silk, too, telling himself they were for Willi to make clothes for herself and her sister, but it was Karen he visualized in the intense jewel tones he selected—sheer silk for lingerie, silk satin for gowns, washable silk for blouses and slacks, nubby raw silk for jackets. Caftans, ready-made kimonos, shoes, slippers, even a fancy parasol—he couldn't stop buying, couldn't stop picturing Karen in the things he found for her, couldn't stop aching inside because he couldn't reach for her in the night and find her beside him.

He'd lingered in a jewelry store, then left without making a purchase. The next day he'd gone back and picked up beaten silver bracelets for his daughters, jade earrings and pendants, and fine gold bangles he told himself would look nice on Willi's wrist. But it was Karen's he kept envisioning.

He bought toys for Timmy, then found himself picking up bright mobiles to hang over a crib.

Now he crushed the suitcase shut and fought the zipper. The thing was so stuffed it bulged, dangerously close to splitting. Enough was enough. He could buy no more.

He picked up the phone and called Karen's number. It rang and rang without a reply. What was the time at home? He should know, but his head was fuzzy with fatigue and the jet lag he still hadn't licked.

He awakened in the middle of the night, called her number again, and once more, there was no reply. Maybe she was spending the night with Penny and her brothers, giving their aunt a break.

Frowning, trying to force down the unease that persisted in prodding him, he dialed his own number. It rang until his machine picked it up and, as he had several times since his arrival, he left a message for Karen, the same one as all the previous times.

"I miss you. I'm thinking about you. I love you."

Funny how much easier it was to say that to a tape than to her face. He'd never told her. He wished now he had. He wondered if she was there, listening to him, too stubborn to pick up, or if she'd meant what she said, that she wouldn't go to his house at all, not to sleep in his bed, not to use his pool, not to wait for the phone to ring.

This time, impulsively, without bothering to reason out why he felt the strongest urge he had ever felt in his life, he added, "I'll be home tomorrow."

Then he dialed again, this time a local call, to tell Kuan Lee he'd been called back early and he was trusting him to see to the details of the shipment.

It was good, Karen told herself, that Jed had impressed on her the code to his security system. It wouldn't have done at all to have Barry, who had followed closely behind her all the way from the college, and who was even now pulling into the driveway behind Jed's car, discover her fumbling it, or, worse, to have the thing blaring like a banshee because she'd forgotten the numbers to punch.

She turned and watched Barry step out of his rental car, watched him look, clearly impressed, at Jed's house. She felt a stupid flicker of pride, as if it were her house in reality—which of course is exactly what Barry thought. That was why she'd brought him here.

It had been a shock to find him driving into the parking lot at the college as she was driving out. Both of them had slammed on the brakes upon recognizing each other, and his eyes had swept over the sleek lines of the car she drove as they came to a halt, the drivers' windows only two feet apart.

"Very nice," he'd said as she rolled hers down. "Beats the hell out of your old truck, doesn't it?"

She hadn't bothered to explain that it wasn't hers, that her truck had died an untimely death on the freeway in rush-hour traffic on Wednesday afternoon. That had forced her into driving Jed's car, as he'd practically ordered her to do anyway, if she was to get to and from work. Saturday she planned to buy herself some decent transportation. Jed would need his car when he got back.

All she'd said was, "Barry! What in the world are you doing here? Where's Candice?"

He'd shrugged and his gaze had shifted away. "I'm in town for a few days. Alone. It's a . . . a seminar."

She'd gotten the distinct impression he was lying, an impression that intensified as he reluctantly met her gaze again, asking, "How are you, Karen?"

"I'm fine." This time, she'd managed a smile. "How about you?"

"I wanted to see you." His throat worked. "Talk to you. It's important. Could we go for coffee, or something, or is Jed expecting you home right away?"

"Jed's in Singapore."

"Oh. Well, would he mind if I came home with you for an hour or so? I'd prefer to talk in private."

"I . . ." Home? Her home? But then Barry would know that her marriage to Jed was nothing more than a sham. If he knew that, he'd figure out the rest of it. Suddenly, she knew she was nowhere near ready to tell him that her baby was also his. She bit her lip as she scanned his face. He wasn't ready to hear it yet, either. He looked totally miserable and her heart went out to him as it always had. "Barry, what's wrong? Is it Candice?"

He nodded and shrugged again, a hollow little laugh forcing its way from his throat. "Yeah. Please, Karen? I know this is going to sound stupid, but you're still the one I need to talk to when I've got a problem. You're still my best friend. Right now you might be my only friend."

A car had pulled up behind her, waiting to get out of

the parking lot. She had to move. "All right. Pull into the lot and turn around. Follow me. I'll wait just up the road."

He'd followed her all the way to Jed's house and now was about to follow her inside. Karen's head ached with tension, her back ached with pressure, and her heart ached because the house was so terribly empty without Jed to make it live.

She opened the drapes to let in the bright, fall day and waved Barry to a seat, hoping he wouldn't notice the four day's worth of fine dust that covered all the surfaces, clearly showing no one had been in here since she and Jed had left Monday morning. She also hoped he wouldn't notice how neat the place was. Barry knew her habit of dropping books and papers and shoes and coffee cups all over. He'd often grumbled at her lack of neatness.

"Would you like some coffee, Barry? Or a drink?"

He hitched up his pant legs and sank onto one of the couches for a moment before getting up and pacing again. "Rum," he said. "Light on the Coke."

As she fixed his drink, she watched him from the corner of her eye, recognizing the signs of suffering in his face, his rounded shoulders, his forward-thrusting head. He'd been like this when he was losing a patient and unable to discover why, unable to find a way to save a life.

*Talk to me,* she wanted to say, but held her tongue. Prodding him wouldn't work. She knew Barry would have to bring up his problems in his own way. There was no point in trying to rush him.

He walked to the window, looking down the curving road at another large house in its well-maintained grounds, eyes sweeping over the broad view where the wind-whipped waters of Puget Sound sparkled blue and white in the afternoon light. "Nice place you've ended up in."

He sounded resentful. Presently, he turned back to her. "Are you happy here?"

"Of course." She handed him a short glass clinking with ice cubes and raised her own, filled with ginger ale, in a salute. "To good friends," she said, before sliding gratefully into a recliner and putting her feet up.

He strode to the far corner of the room where a red light blinked. "There are messages on your machine." He bent. "Quite a number."

She could guess what those messages were, and she wasn't going to play them back with Barry listening. "I'll get them later. Sit down, Barry, please. I'm too tired to watch you pace."

He smiled. "That sounds like my old wife." He sat across from her, elbows on his knees, glass dangling precariously, between finger and thumb, gently swaying. He stared at it.

"Aren't you here to talk about Candice?" she prompted him gently.

To her dismay, his shoulders heaved. A heavy, tearing sound came from him and he set the glass between his feet to bury his face in his hands as he wept harshly.

"Barry!" Awkwardly, as quickly as she could move her ungainly body, Karen struggled out of the depths of her comfortable chair and went to him, sitting beside him, sliding an arm over his back. "Honey, tell me what's wrong."

He lifted his face and looked at her from streaming eyes. She drew him forward until his face rested against her shoulder. "I have to tell you. I can't tell anyone else," he said. "God, Karen, everything's gone so wrong! I've moved out of our apartment and everyone thinks I'm the worst rat in history, leaving my poor pregnant wife only three months into our marriage, but I had to! I can't forgive what she's done to me, Karen. I can't forget it, can't pretend it doesn't matter. Everyone hates my guts—my parents, her parents, probably even yours. I'm treated like a pariah at the hospital. I'm—"

He broke off, choking, fighting to regain control of his emotions, but then, as if this grief had built in him for too long, he held her tightly and continued to weep in the ugly, difficult way of a man. The sound of it tore Karen to shreds.

"Hush, now. Don't," she murmured, stroking his head, his shoulders. "Barry, please talk to me. Tell me what happened."

"The baby," he said. "Her baby. It isn't mine! I'm not its father and God, how I wanted to be that!"

Candice's baby wasn't Barry's? In shocked silence, Karen continued to hold him, feeling the tenuous control she'd taken over her own life begin to fray and slip from her grasp. For the first time, she fully realized just why she had kept putting off telling Barry the truth about her child, just how deep had run her hope that even after she'd told him, he'd be so involved with his and Candice's child that he'd want nothing to do with hers. Somehow, tangled up with that hope had been one that someday Jed would want to be part of her life, would want to help her raise a fatherless child.

But if the baby had to be shared, Karen would have to be shared. She would have to continue her contact with Barry, however limited. And what hope could there be of a man who doubted his own abilities in both the role of a parent and of a husband wanting to be put in the position of second husband, secondary father? What he needed was to be the center of someone's universe.

That the hope of Jed's changing had been foolish made no difference. Now that it was to be snatched away, she finally understood its hold on her, understood why she had kept coming back to him when everything told her she was destined to be hurt. *This* hurt. It was like having her soul torn out, watching the future fade away.

Some small remnant of her secret hope made her say, "No, Barry, no. That can't be true." It was a plea for him to tell her he was joking, but he was too wrapped in his grief to hear hers. Slowly, she came to accept what he told her was true.

Candice's baby was not to be Karen's way out of future involvement with Barry.

# FOURTEEN

Presently, Barry began to recover. He lifted his head and turned his face away from her. "Bathroom," he said thickly.

Karen guided him to the one off the hall and returned to the living room to wait for him, hardly daring to think. Too many frightening images kept crowding in on her. Protectively, her hands wrapped around her baby. Hers—and Barry's. No! No, hers, hers alone. That was the way she'd wanted it, whether she'd known it or not.

But that wasn't entirely true either. For the past couple of months, she'd secretly begun to want this baby to be hers and Jed's.

Barry stayed in seclusion for nearly ten minutes. When he returned, he had regained much of his composure. He gulped his drink, and she fixed him another one, much weaker, then sat away from him.

"What makes you think the baby isn't yours, Barry?"

He looked at her balefully. "Candice told me. She had to. She got so big so fast. I thought she must be carrying a double load and started insisting on a sonogram. She refused again and again. Then she broke down and confessed she was afraid to go in, because the minute she had the ultrasound, the whole hospital would know she was going to deliver eight weeks before I expected her to. She said she was glad it was finally out in the open, because she couldn't live with lying to me. She *loved* me."

He laughed harshly. "Loved me. So she married me with another man's kid in her belly."

"Whose?"

He winced at the question.

"That's none of my business," Karen apologized.

"Oh, what the hell. You may as well know it all. It's my brother's," he said. "Ross's."

She stared at him in disbelief. Ross was married, had been for ten years. He and his wife, Vicky, had two kids. Karen and Barry had envied them not only their children, but their obvious closeness and happiness. Was it all a sham? At least on Ross's part? She knew Candice had worked for Ross in his furniture store in Helena. "Oh, good Lord," she said. It seemed totally inadequate.

"Yeah. A regular little soap opera we've got going back there, isn't it? You're lucky to be out of it."

Karen could remember likening the situation to a soap opera herself, and Barry didn't know the half of it! Would her news be yet another blow to him? Why hadn't she found the courage to tell him months ago? It might have made this easier for him to bear.

She wished, stupidly, that she'd been there for him, that he hadn't had to come all this way to find comfort and solace, alone until he got to her, where he could unburden himself. He hadn't been able to tell anybody at home; he'd have destroyed his brother's marriage, torn his parents between their two sons, and ruined his wife's reputation.

Oh, Lord! If she hadn't left him, none of this would have happened. She would have gotten pregnant anyway, probably even sooner than she had, and she and Barry would be parents now. They'd be together and happy.

Or would they? No, of course not, she reassured herself, feeling sick to her stomach. It wasn't merely a child their marriage had lacked. There had been so much more missing. Even with a baby, it would have been over by now, and a baby would have made it that much harder.

She pushed her own concerns down and asked him gently, "Are Candice and Ross in love with each other? Is Ross going to leave Vicky?"

He shrugged. "I don't know. I suppose not. I mean, if he'd been going to leave his wife for Candice, if he'd wanted to be with her, she wouldn't have married me, would she? She says she was just infatuated with Ross, that she loves me now, that she's glad I fell in love with her when I did."

His mouth twisted. "Which was really convenient for her, wasn't it? She probably knew she was carrying Ross's baby before I ever touched her. Looking back on it now, I can see she's the one who made the first move, came on to me, the one who . . . orchestrated our whole affair."

He laughed bitterly. "Smart little devil, isn't she? I mean, if the kid looks like my side of the family, who's to wonder? So she goes around town, her belly out as far as yours is, looking like an injured angel, and I get to be the village heel."

"Oh, Barry." She choked, wanting to weep for the pain he endured. Then she sighed. Her tears wouldn't heal him, wouldn't help him. "Do you think Ross knows the baby is his?"

He shrugged. "I don't know. I didn't stop to ask Candice details like that. I—hell, who am I kidding? Of course he knows. He has to. Why wouldn't he? He knew what he was doing with her there in the back room of the store, and the bastard knew what the consequences could be. He can see she's pregnant, but he's all right, secure in his marriage, while his kid brother's the talk of the town because he's just blown marriage number two. He's probably laughing up his sleeve at me now, the sucker who's taking the fall for him."

His face contorted again and he covered it with his big, capable hands. His fingers trembled. "The sucker who was so damned proud of himself for finally having managed to knock a woman up."

Again, Karen forced her reluctant body out of her chair and went to him. "But Barry! It has to be more than that. You love Candice."

He looked at her. "Do I?" he asked bitterly.

"If you didn't, you wouldn't be suffering so much."

He shook his head slowly from side to side. "I didn't know a man could suffer like this and live."

She waited.

"I love her, sure, at least—hell, Karen, I think I do, but I hate her, too, so damned much it sticks in my throat. How can I love her after this? I don't know what I feel except betrayed. Sick at heart."

He jammed a hand into his hair and shot to his feet to stride away again. "I think I loved her most *because* she was carrying my baby. She'd made me feel like a real man."

He broke off, his face flooding with color. "I'm sorry. That was a filthy thing to say to you."

Karen shook her head. "It's okay. I understand."

Barry slumped down onto a bright chintz cushion that sat on the black slate hearth. Picking up one of its tassels between two fingers, he played with it while his eyes remained fixed on her face. "You always did, didn't you?"

"Did what?"

"Understand me. Understand that I felt so lousy about our not being able to have kids that I was letting it ruin our marriage. That's why you left me, isn't it? You figured maybe I could have them with somebody else."

He shut his eyes for a moment as he leaned his head back against the stones of the fireplace.

Opening them again, he looked at her. "And that, when it comes right down to it, is why I let you go without putting up a fight. I thought, even though none of the tests showed you to be barren, that with someone else I'd make it."

His eyes filled with tears again and he rose, pacing away. "As a physician, I knew that wasn't necessarily true. As a man, I wanted kids so bad I let myself believe it."

When he turned again, he was steadier. "It's rough, you know, learning I'm not the hotshot stud I figured I was when Candice told me she was pregnant after we'd been together just a couple of times. For the first time in my life, I begin to understand people who shoot themselves in the head."

She rose quickly. "Barry!"

"Oh, don't look like that. I'm not going to. But I'm not going back to her, either. I wanted that kid, Karen. I wanted him real, real bad. But not when he isn't mine. Do you understand that? I needed to know that baby was *mine.*"

Karen drew a deep breath as she lowered herself to the couch again. Then, sitting forward, her feet planted squarely on the floor for steadiness, hands wrapped around her belly, she faced him.

"Barry," she said, "there's something I have to tell you. Something I should have told you a long time ago. I don't know why I kept putting it off, but I found all sorts of excuses. Now I've run out of them." She bit her lip, fighting the urge to run away and not tell him the truth he so desperately needed to hear—the truth she could no longer deny him.

"What?" he said, his brows drawn together. "Karen, you're awfully pale." Suddenly, he was as much doctor as ex-husband. He crouched before her, touched her face. "Lord. Look at you. You're shaking. What is it?"

She tried to form words, but her throat locked down on them and she made a small mewling sound, shaking her head from side to side.

Barry laid a hand on her belly. "Are you having contractions?"

She shook her head and tried to talk again. All that came out was a squeaky laugh. It was hysterically funny how difficult this job was, once she'd decided to go ahead and do it. She giggled again.

"Cold, moist," he muttered, brushing his hand over her forehead, talking to himself, his eyes sweeping over her. "Damn it, what's wrong?" He took her wrist, fingertips going unerringly to her pulse. "Are you sick?"

She drew in a deep breath and shook her head. "No. But . . . Barry, *this* baby *is* yours."

He sat back on his heels. "No," he said, his eyes filled with confusion. "No, Karen. You don't have to . . . I mean, I know it's not possible. It's—"

"It's your baby," she said again, controlling her queasiness, pushing it out of the way of this very important task. "It's due the about the eighth of November, not late December as Jed told you. I conceived in February, that night you came to my house after dinner."

Hope rose in his eyes, only to die out as he made himself deny it with a rueful shake of his head and a forced laugh. "Come on, Karen, get serious. I'm not a kid who needs to be appeased, you know. And I told you I had no real intention of taking a gun to my head. You don't have to do this."

"Barry, it's true."

He searched her face, and she saw the slow belief dawn. He swallowed audibly. "Why didn't you tell me right away?" he asked in a whisper, then again, "God, Karen! *Why?*" It was a howl of anguish, of accusation, as the full impact of the truth struck him. "Holy sh—" He clamped his mouth shut on the curse. "Why did you let me marry Candice?"

Tears poured from her eyes, partly in response to his pain, partly from her own. "I didn't know, Barry. You have to believe that. I didn't just *think* I couldn't get pregnant, I *knew* it, and since I couldn't get pregnant, I couldn't *be* pregnant, so it never occurred to me that I was."

"Symptoms, Karen. The symptoms? You must have recognized them, for the love of God!"

She wiped her face on the hem of her maternity blouse and looked at him again. "Barry, are you forgetting how irregular I've always been?"

He sighed deeply. "Yeah. I guess I did forget that. Sorry. I can see how you might not figure it out right away. Were you sick?"

She nodded. "But I put that and the weight gain and the breast tenderness, everything, down to all sorts of other causes. By the time I knew I was going to have your baby, Martina had phoned and told me Candice was pregnant and you were getting married."

He stared at her in horror. "Do you think for a minute I'd have married her if I'd known *you* were carrying my baby first?"

She sat back, pulling away from him. "Yes, Barry, I

do, because you and I were finished, over with, all done. You were no more in love with me than I was with you. You were in love with her."

"You couldn't have known that then," he said. "You could have given me the choice."

"Be reasonable. I'd made *my* choice nearly two years before. And if I'd told you, it would have put a real damper on your celebration."

He managed a twisted sort of smile. "And how."

"Besides," she went on, "even if you hadn't been engaged, I didn't want . . ."

He closed his eyes. "Didn't want me back."

She reached out and touched his face. His cheek was cold, clammy, as hers had been. Now, her face felt as if it burned with fever. "You wouldn't have wanted me back, either, Barry."

"How do you know that?" he demanded, leaping up and pacing across the room to pound his fist against the solid wood of the mantel. "God, Karen! How could you do this to me? To us? If you'd told me at the very beginning, none of this would have happened, and now it's too late for us! For you and me and our baby. We could have made it work. We could have made a family."

He lifted his head and stared at her. "Jed. Does he know the truth?"

"He knows the truth."

"Then he's a better man than I am! Oh, sweet Jesus! What are we going to do?"

He reeled away from the end of the room, returned to where Karen sat, and knelt before her, burying his face in what remained of her lap, his cheek pressed to her stomach, his arms wrapped around her. "My baby," he wept. "My child. You can't keep him from me, Karen. He's mine. You're mine! Come home with me, darling, please come home with me. Please. Let's make it up to each other. We were so much in love once. Why can't we have it all again? You said you'd always love me as a friend, so let's build on that. Dear God, Karen, don't deny me this, not now, not when I need you so much!"

"Barry, don't do this to yourself." She bent forward and wrapped her arms around his heaving shoulders. "Please, Barry, listen to me. I love you, of course I love you, but—"

*"No."* It was the thud of the dropped suitcase as much as the swiftly aspirated word that cut Karen's voice off in midsentence.

She whipped her head up, her heart nearly coming to a stop. She shoved an equally stunned Barry away from her and tried to get to her feet, but the terrible look on Jed's face kept her pinned where she sat.

"Jed . . ." she began, choked, then tried again. "You're home early!"

"Yes," he said, his tone harsh, his face like gray stone. "If you'd picked up the phone or listened to my messages, you'd have known I'd be home today, Karen." He slammed down a second suitcase, one Karen hadn't seen him take with him, and its zipper broke, spilling bright colors across the cream carpet.

"That's for you," he said, glancing at it as if it were no more than a spot of lint. He kicked the tumbled garments. "Take it and go. And take your husband with you."

"Jed, no, please! This is not what you think!"

"It's not? 'I love you, Barry, of course I love you,'" he quoted. "I've been through this kind of thing before, remember? But at least she had enough integrity not to bother pretending to be something she wasn't. She just pulled the sheet up over herself and asked me to leave.

I'd do that this time, but this happens to be my home, not yours."

"Jed!" She managed to get to her feet and run toward him. "Damn it, give me a chance—"

But he wheeled away, strode from the room, and a door slammed deeper in the house.

"Jed," she said again, a soft, weak whimper, her hand going to her mouth. She went after him, but his bedroom door was locked and he refused to answer her calls. Through the singing in the water pipes, she heard his shower running.

"Leave him," Barry said, placing a hand on the small of her back, turning her from the door where she leaned, weeping convulsively. "Give him a few minutes, then I'll have a talk with him. I'll make him understand."

Karen wiped her eyes with the backs of her hands. "He won't understand," she said heavily. "He thinks history's repeating itself. He came home from a trip a few years ago and found his wife in bed with someone else, and now he thinks I've—"

She bent her head, unable to go on.

"All right, stop now, come away from the door. Come back into the living room," Barry urged her. "Come on, hon. We'll sit down and wait for him and you can tell me all about it."

"No. No. I just want to go . . . home."

"This is your home, Karen."

She shook her head "No, it's not. And now it never will be. He doesn't want me." She cradled her baby between her hands. "He doesn't want us."

"You think not?" Barry asked. "Look what this suitcase has in it."

Karen blinked her eyes and stared down at the spill of fabrics—a pale, embroidered bonnet with ruffles across the front; a tiny dress in apricot silk with cream lace; a pink plush teddy bear. A bright butterfly mobile poked from tissue wrapping. She knew who those gifts had been meant for, and her heart shattered as she bent to lay them tenderly back into the suitcase, which she closed and shoved against the wall.

"It was all a pretty fantasy," she said, as she rose and turned to rest her forehead against Barry's shoulder. "Take me home," she whispered. "Please, Barry, just get me out of here."

By the time they reached Karen's house, Barry was up to speed on her life. "Lady-love," he said, using the old name he'd given her years before—and then stopped using, though neither of them had noticed when it happened—"we've really screwed things up, the two of us, haven't we?"

She nodded and gave him her key so he could unlock the door.

Exhausted, Karen let Barry take her into her bedroom and pull her blouse off over her head. He unzipped her skirt, dropped it to the floor and efficiently stripped her of her panty hose and shoes. "Turn around," he ordered, then unhooked her bra.

Flipping back the covers, he said, "In with you," then covered her up to her chin.

She looked at him in alarm when he headed for the door. "Where are you going? Barry, please don't leave me."

He glanced over his shoulder, an owlish look. "I'm going to get my bag out of the car. I'm worried about you."

She subsided back against her pillows, ashamed of her panicky outburst. "I'm all right."

"I want to be sure. It's either me or your own doctor. Just vital signs, Karen."

She didn't argue further.

"Now," Barry said, taking the blood pressure cuff off her and stowing it in its black leather case. "You can have something to eat."

"I'm not hungry." She knew better than to ask him how her pressure was, but if it had been threatening, he'd have called an ambulance.

"You will be."

He was right, she found, when he returned a few minutes later with two mugs of chicken noodle soup and a large stack of toast oozing butter.

"Comfort food," she said, sniffing back a fresh spate of tears that threatened. "You remembered."

"I remember a lot of things maybe I should never have forgotten, Karen. Like how important you once were to me."

She spooned up some soup and ate half a slice of toast before saying quietly, "You were important to me, too, Barry."

He nodded. "I know that. We go back too far to let it get away from us."

Karen ate another triangle of toast and a few bites of the noodles from the bottom of her mug, then set it aside.

In brooding silence, he drank the liquid off his soup, then finished the rest of the toast. As he lifted the last spoonful of noodles from his mug before setting it down, he said, "Have you had enough?"

She nodded, and he took her mug to finish what she'd left. Looking at her over the rim, he said, "I've got a portable profession. I can live anywhere in the world.

We can. We wouldn't have to see anybody we didn't want to, and if we went where no one knows us, we wouldn't have to try to hold our heads up against the pointing fingers and wagging tongues. We could—"

"Barry, Candice is your wi—"

"Candice has a problem that's not of my making." His tone was hard. "It's one she's going to have to work through without me. I meant what I said. I can't go back to her—not because she lied to me, tried to cheat me, but because of you, Karen, and what's right for you. I owe you something, and I mean to make sure you get it. Because of this little creature here."

He stroked a hand over the mound under her covers. "Because of my son. Or my daughter. It doesn't matter to me what it is. All I know is I want it, and I want you, too."

He touched her lips when she would have replied, and said, "No. Sleep on it, okay? But think about this while you're doing it: Do you want to send your child to wherever I am every second weekend, miss out on Christmases and Easters and Thanksgivings with her or him? I'll want my fair share of my child's time, Karen. I mean to be its father in every way. Wouldn't it be easier for all three of us if we lived under the same roof?"

With that, he stood, collected their dishes, and left her alone.

To think.


Jed wasn't surprised to see the rented Cavalier by Karen's house. He mounted the steps slowly, hesitated for a moment before ringing the bell, and then stood back. He wasn't surprised, either, when Barry Renton answered the door.

"If you came to see Karen, she's asleep," Barry said, stepping back. "I'll wake her if you insist, but let me tell you that not only are her temperature and her heart rate up, her blood pressure is elevated. Not dangerously, but enough that I'm prescribing bed rest for the next two days and freedom from stress. If you think you can talk to her without upsetting her, then by all means do so. After all, she's not my wife now, so I can't very well stop you."

Jed set down the suitcase full of gifts. "She's not my wife, either."

"So I understand. Your loss, Cotts."

"Yeah. And where, might I ask, *is* your wife, Renton?"

"At home. Her home."

Jed felt the impact of those last two words deep in his gut. "Which is no longer your home?" He didn't have to ask. He chose to. He wanted it all out on the table. It would be easier to deal with if he could see all the pieces, figure out which ones fit, which ones didn't.

"That's right. Oh, I'll have to go back to sort things out, but not yet. Not until after my baby's born."

Jed nodded. "And then? Will you and Karen be staying in this part of the world?"

Barry lifted one shoulder. "We haven't discussed that."

"But you mean to?"

"I mean to."

Jed shrugged. "Then all I can do is wish you the best of luck. Both of you. All three of you." He turned for the door, then paused, looking back. "Tell Karen that. And tell her there's a gift in there for Penny."

Barry cocked his head, his eyes narrowing. "Who's Penny?"

"A little girl who learned a valuable lesson that a bunch of do-gooder women, Karen among them, are trying to make her unlearn. I hope to hell they fail," he added harshly on his way out the door. "And you can tell Karen that, too."

"Barry?" Karen came out of the bedroom.

He jumped at the sound of her voice. "I want you to stay in bed, Karen. Tonight and all day tomorrow. Maybe the next day, too. And I'm going to stay here and see that you do."

She sat on the sofa. "That was Jed, wasn't it? Did he ask to see me?"

He shook his head. "Before he had a chance to, I told him your pressure was up. I guess he decided not to bother you." He got the suitcase and set it on the coffee table. "He brought this."

Karen clenched her icy hands on her lap, remembering the small garments she had seen spilling out of it, the toys. "I don't want it," she whispered. "Any of it. Take it away, please."

"He said there's a gift in it for Penny. Who is she, Karen? He said something strange about her."

"She's a child I know. What did he say that was strange?"

Barry frowned as he tried to remember. "That she's a little girl who once learned a valuable lesson that you and a bunch of do-gooder women are trying to make her unlearn. He hopes you fail."

"She's my Little Sister." Pain made it hard to force out the words.

"What's the lesson he hopes she never forgets?"

"That trusting isn't a smart thing to do."

* * *

The phone warbling on her nightstand woke Karen and for a moment she didn't remember, only smiled. *Jed.* At last! But as she rolled over, the memory of the previous evening came crashing down on her and she picked up the phone reluctantly, not because she knew who it was, but because she knew who it wasn't.

"Karen? It's Martina."

She sat up, groggy. "Marti? Are you in town?"

"No. I'm sorry to bother you so early on a Saturday morning but—"

Not quite with it, Karen said, "What time is it?"

"Six. No, five, I guess, your time. Look, I know you don't wake up easily, but concentrate, Karen. This is important. I've got to find Barry!"

"Barry? But he's—"

"Just listen. He's out on the Coast at some kind of medical seminar, but he's not in his hotel room, the hospital where the seminar's being held doesn't know where he is, and you're my last hope. If he gets in touch with you, have him call me immediately. Please, Karen."

Karen was waking up. Shoving her hair back, she sat higher in the bed. "What's wrong?"

"It's Candice. I'm at the hospital with her. Karen, she needs him. He left her last week, moved right out of their new apartment, and she's been going crazy—not eating, not sleeping, crying all the time—and she won't tell anybody what happened between them, not even me.

"I know it's all over between you and Barry, but he's been acting really weird since he moved out on her, and you're the one he's always run to if he's in trouble, ever since we were kids. Since he's on the Coast, I'm sure he'll get in touch. Just give him my message. Tell him that Candice's bleeding, threatening a miscarriage. Whatever went wrong between them can't matter more than that. Candice needs her husband."

"Yes. Of course she does. He's here, Marti."

There was dead silence before Martina said in a cold tone, "There? With you? At five o'clock in the morning?"

"Marti, give me a break, will you?" Karen said disgustedly to her friend. "I don't mean he's here in my bed. He's here in my house. On my sofa. Hold on and I'll get him."

But Barry had heard her voice and thrust the door open. "Are you all right?"

Karen nodded and handed him the phone. "It's for you."

"She lost the baby." Barry reeled out of Karen's bedroom a few minutes later, his face white, his hands clenched into fists, and she handed him a cup of coffee.

"No, Barry, Marti said she was threatening to abort, not that she—"

"While I was talking to her, John Lefski came out and said it was all over. I didn't even get a chance to talk to Candice. She's bleeding badly. They're taking her down for a D and C." He drew in a shuddering breath. "I have to go to her, Karen. She's just a kid, really, and she needs me."

"Of course she does. And of course you have to go to her. I'll call the airport while you get dressed."

"I already called." Barry's agitation seemed to be easing. "They've got me booked on a flight that goes out at eight. I won't have time to go back to my hotel for my bag. They'll have to send it. Can you take care of that for me?"

"Of course."

He ran a hand into his hair, leaving it all on end except

for the part that was still squashed from sleep. "With luck and a chopper from Helena, I can be there before she's fully out from under the anesthetic."

"Right," said Karen, swinging into action. "Grab a shower. I'll run an iron over your shirt and pants. You may not be really clean, but at least you won't look wrinkled."

"Thanks, hon." He kissed her on the cheek, obviously having forgotten the bed rest he'd prescribed the night before. He took two long strides away. Then, pausing in the doorway, he turned back.

"Karen? About the things I said last night . . ."

She laughed softly. "I had no intention of going along with any of that. I was simply too tired to argue."

He looked at her for another second before smiling wryly. "And that," he said, "is *tired!*"

Before he left, he stood for a moment looking down at her, one hand resting atop her stomach. "I meant part of what I said. I do want to be a father to this child, no matter how many more I might have in the future. This one will always be special. My firstborn. Will you let me share it with you? At least part of the time?"

"Of course, Barry. All along, that was my intention. I just let myself pretend sometimes it could be otherwise. The baby will need a father."

"It'll need a full-time father as well as the one it'll have on the other side of the Rockies. Jed loves you."

She shook her head. "He's never said so."

"Still, I think it's true." He smiled as he tugged at the back of her hair, the way he had when she was fifteen and had worn a pony tail. "Funny, isn't it, how we can see the different sides of other people's problems better than we can see our own? You knew I'd go back to Candice. You knew I'd have to."

Karen nodded. She wished it would be that simple for her and Jed, but she knew it wouldn't be. The different sides of their problems were too far apart.

"I'm not going back because she's not pregnant anymore," Barry said. "Not because there's no more baby to stand between us. I'm going back because she's sick and bereaved and will need me. And because I love her."

"I understand that, Barry."

He sighed. "I know. But will Candice?"

She patted his shoulder. "It's up to you to make sure she does."

"How?"

"Love her. Be there for her."

"Like I wasn't for you."

Working around the huge lump at her front, Karen stood on tiptoe and kissed him on the cheek. "Good-bye, Barry."

He swept her into an awkward hug. "So long, my dearest friend. Take care. And call me when the baby comes."

# FIFTEEN

"Omigod! Not now!"

"What? Karen, what's wrong?"

Penny winced as Karen gripped her shoulder. Realizing what she was doing, Karen let the child go, then stared in dismay at the spreading wet stain on her huge, tentlike witch costume. Penny jerked her foot away from the flood of water running off Karen's metal folding chair and gaped at her friend.

"Karen!" Penny's face was slack with shock. "You're peeing your pants."

Karen laughed and clutched at her belly. "I'm having the baby, I think. Penny, go and get that lady over there. I can't remember her name. The gray-haired one who's in charge of the apple-bobbing."

She was also the coordinator of this community Halloween party.

Penny stared at Karen and the widening pool between her feet for another second then ran across the room, tripping and skidding in the litter of orange and black streamers and broken balloons.

"Lady! Lady!" she shrieked as she ran toward the woman. At least a dozen ladies turned, along with half that number of men and many children. "Hey, you gotta help Karen. She's having her baby *right now!*"

Karen breathed through another short contraction then

assured everyone she was fine. She asked that someone call Esther, who was to be her labor coach, only to learn moments later that Esther wasn't home. Contrary to what she'd been told about first babies taking a long time, this one seemed determined to hurry. The contractions were coming thick and fast, getting stronger and stronger, and it was difficult not to groan aloud. She refrained, though, not wanting to frighten Penny, who stood clutching her hand.

"Then you'd better call an ambulance," she said, wiping sweat off her face. "I think things are happening pretty quickly. I'm going to Women's Hospital."

A man crowded forward and slid his hand under her arm. "I'll take you there. It's quite a distance and you're better off getting there as soon as possible. You're right. It looks like you're well on your way. My wife has had four, so I'm something of an expert," he added, heaving her to her feet. "Speaking of which," he added, "three of my kids are here. Can somebody get them home?"

"And Penny," Karen gasped to the apple-bobbing woman. "Look after Penny."

"I want to go with you!" Penny howled, trying to fling herself on Karen, but someone caught her and held her back as the man walked Karen out of the hall and into his car. As he drove rapidly toward the hospital, lights and color and sound whirled around her and she bit back the cry that her heart echoed.

*Jed! Jed! I need you now!*


Jed picked up the phone on the third ring. He'd been going to leave it to the machine, but it was as if an unseen hand had pushed him toward it. He frowned at the tearful child's voice he heard, not recognizing it for a moment, then said, "Penny! Hold on. Slow down. Start again."

"I'm at a Halloween party and Karen's gone to the hospital. She peed herself a whole bunch, then a man came and took her away and they wouldn't let me go, too, so I could look after her."

Jed's head spun for a moment before he managed to steady himself and say calmly, "But he's her husband, Peanut. It's all right. He'll look after her."

"No, no!" she said insistently. "He's not her husband. She doesn't got one, remember? He was just a guy at the party. He told somebody to take me home and his kids, too, but I'm scared, Jed. Karen and me, we gotta look out for each other 'cause we promised, and they wouldn't let me go with her. You said you'd help her if she ever needed it and I couldn't do it by myself. You promised!"

Jed drew in a deep breath, felt it run life-giving oxygen into his blood, clearing his head, making his thoughts sharp and finely drawn, slowing motion down so he could get a grip on himself, on events. Not her husband? Barry wasn't with Karen?

Where the hell was he, the jerk? Why the hell wasn't he doing his duty and looking after his wife and baby and. . . . He sucked in another of those oxygen-laden breaths, needing it badly.

"Okay, Penny," he said. *"I'm* going to take care of her. Did you hear anybody say the name of the hospital?" To his relief, she had. "Right, I'm on my way, and I'll call you at home as soon as I can. Give me your number."

She did and he wrote it down carefully, knowing he wouldn't be permitted any slipups. "All right. Is some nice lady going to take you home?" he asked.

"Yeah." She still sounded tearful, but then she said, "You know, I think I like you."

He laughed. "I like you, too, Peanut. For sure. I'll call you as soon as I've talked to Karen."

Jed rammed his arms into a yellow gown. Somebody shoved a cap over his head and another person grabbed each of his feet and pulled cotton boots on over his shoes. "This way."

"Jed's here, Karen," said a woman, ushering him into the delivery room, standing him at Karen's side.

She was chanting, "Jed, Jed, Jed," under her breath and at his touch, rolled her head back and forth, her dry lips pulled back over her teeth as she fought a contraction. She muttered, "Jed. Jed. Jed. Help me."

He slipped his hands around her face and bent to kiss her brow. She was drenched with sweat. "I'm here, Karen."

She opened her eyes, looked at him, and started to speak, but was caught up in the next huge contraction. Jed steeled himself not to cry out with her, held her tight, and said, "Breath with it, honey. Don't fight it. Work with your muscles. Concentrate. Come on, you can do it. I'll help you."

She wrapped her hands around his wrists, nails digging in. When she could talk, she said, "Oh, Jed. Jed!" Tears spangled her eyes and she smiled through them. "How?"

"Penny called me."

Karen's smiled widened. "Good . . . kid."

"The best," Jed agreed, taking a cool, moist cloth from a nurse and wiping Karen's face. "And so are you, my darling. You're doing a wonderful job here."

"Tired." She groaned loudly. Jed let her nearly break

his hands with her grip. Another massive contraction built, and she arched into it.

"That's it, here we go! Push!" the doctor told her. "Push now!"

"Push, love," Jed said, holding her gaze with everything that was in him, willing her to do it, to get this baby born. "Push."

"Push yourself, you stupid bastard!" she shouted, tearing his hands from her and baring her teeth, glaring at him, letting out an awesome sound as her nails scored his wrists. "I . . . can't! I can't! I—"

Her nails bit into him again. Her eyes squeezed shut and her face contorted. She made the same unearthly sound as she pushed for all she was worth and her baby popped out into the doctor's hands.

Karen laughed. She cried. She clung to Jed as he lifted her up so she could see. The doctor cleared the baby's airway and the enraged cry that rose up made everyone in the room laugh. The doctor laid the baby on Karen's belly and said, "Boo!"

"Boo?" she repeated.

"All Halloween babies say *boo* to their moms."

"Boo, yourself, little boy," Karen said, curling her hands around her baby. "Oh, Jed, isn't he beautiful? Isn't he perfect? Didn't I do a helluva good job?"

"Superb," he agreed. "What's his name?"

"Penelope May," she said distractedly, stroking her baby's dark, wet hair, and everyone burst out laughing again. "Oh!" Karen looked startled. "No. I guess it's not, is it?"

The doctor cut the cord and a nurse wrapped a towel around the baby, placing him right in Karen's arms. "How about Andrew?" Karen asked the baby, smoothing a finger down his cheek. He turned instinctively toward it, mouth seeking. "That's a good, strong name. And all the Andrews I know are nice. Do you want to be Andrew, little boy?"

"He wants to suck," said a nurse, helping Karen adjust her position.

Jed still held her from behind, and over her shoulder, he looked down at the child she had borne. He reached out and touched a small, crumpled ear, then stroked Karen's cheek. Slowly, he eased her back onto the fresh pillows a nurse held ready, then he bent and kissed her forehead.

Karen, enraptured by these first moments with her baby, didn't so much as look up.

Aping holding a phone to his ear and dialing, Jed asked directions and was shown from the room. He took off his gown, shucked the boots and the cap, then walked slowly down the long, bright corridor.

He decided to call Penny from home.

"This is 555-3214. Please leave your message after the tone."

Karen complied. "Jed, it's Karen. Please call me." She'd said that, and other things, over and over, but he never called back. The first week, she'd told herself he was briefly out of town again. The second week, she tried to believe he was out of town for a long time. By the third week, she knew he wasn't going to answer her. Yet some kind of determined perversity kept her trying.

"I could just send a thank-you note," she said to Andrew as he nuzzled and pummeled to hurry his breakfast along. "But I don't have any and I keep forgetting to buy them. Do you suppose there's something significant in that?"

No, she thought, it was easier to keep making calls. That way, she could keep making excuses for his lack of response. That way, she wouldn't be forced to give up.

She sighed. "Somehow, Andrew, I'm going to get through to the man. There's always a way to solve a problem. It's a matter of basic logic, applied where necessary. All you have to do is think it through, decide what you want the outcome to be, detect the hitches and snags that are holding things up, and then come up with a creative solution to smoothing them over so everything slides nicely together. Simple."

She smiled at her son as she detached him from her breast and sat his hunched little form on her lap, one hand under his chin, the other supporting and rubbing his back.

"Think of it, little boy. You've just attended the intro to your first college class. Aren't you advanced for a kid only five weeks old today?"

Andrew belched, and a week later attended his first college class for real.

"This is my son, Andrew," Karen said, lifting him from his portable crib. "He'll be joining us for the foreseeable future. My having him here in class with me is something of an experiment. If things go the way I hope, it will prove that creative thinking can find solutions to problems that at times seem insurmountable. If it doesn't, if he cries the place down so we can't hear each other or think straight, then we'll have to get creative and think of a different solution to my problem, that of two conflicting needs: The need to earn a living, and the need not to be separated from my son for eight hours a day."

It was good to be back, she thought.

If only she could solve her other problem so easily.

The solution, or at least a part of it, presented itself to her just as she and Andrew were about to leave at the end of the day.

"Hi, Karen."

"Cecelia!" It was insane how happy seeing the girl made her. "What are you doing here? Did you transfer back?"

"No. I took a day off so I could come and see my dad. My sister and I have been worried about him. He's had pneumonia. He's been out of the hospital for two weeks, but he's still coughing pretty bad and won't go back to the doctor. We figured maybe if we got on his case together, we could make him do it."

Karen sank back down onto her chair. "And did you?" she asked weakly. Pneumonia? Pneumonia killed!

Cecelia shook her head. "Not so far. We were hoping you might help."

Karen shook her head. "Me? Why me? I haven't seen him for ages."

Cecelia looked at her for a long moment, then smiled and plopped herself down in the visitor's chair. "He was delirious the night Willi and Kevin took him to the hospital. He talked. And then there were all your messages on his machine. When he was in the hospital, Willi played his tape back in case there was something important businesswise. We think you're the only one who can help my dad."

Karen sighed. "If you heard those messages, you know he's ignored all the previous ones. He doesn't want to see me, Ceil. I don't know why I haven't given up."

"Because you love him, maybe?"

Karen shrugged, and Cecelia asked quietly, "Can you tell me what happened?"

She shrugged again. There was no reason not to. "Andrew happened," she said, patting the baby. "Of course, all along, we knew Andrew was going to be a problem. You see, your father thinks he was a bad parent."

Cecelia looked stunned. "But he was a wonderful father! The greatest!"

Karen nodded. "I'm sure he was. But he suffers from the great male guilt factor."

In response to Cecelia's mystified expression, she explained.

"Women's equality is something I don't want ever to live without, but I really hate what it's done to the good men, the ones like Jed, who think and reason and truly care and don't respond only with their hormones. It's been wonderful for modernizing the dinosaurs, but hell on the men who didn't need all the reeducation. He's taken all those lessons he learned somewhere and tried to apply them, but they conflict terribly with all the things he knows instinctively are right, to the point that he's become completely unsure of himself and his own value as a man."

Ceil looked as if she might burst into tears. "I've known him all my life, and I never really understood what he was going through. But in just a few months, you picked up on it."

She swallowed, looking pensive. "Oh, poor Daddy. Please, won't you help him? I think he needs *you* more than he needs any doctor or medicine."

"But he doesn't want me," Karen said quietly.

"I think he does. He just won't admit it. Darn! There has to be a way to get through to him."

"I've been looking for one, but I haven't found it."

Cecelia's eyes narrowed as slowly, she nodded. "Okay, then, I guess it's up to me and my surefire top-notch Daddy breaker."

Karen wasn't sure she liked the look in the girl's eyes. "What's that?" she asked warily.

Cecelia grinned. "Tears. My dad can't tell me no when I cry. It's simply impossible for him. That's how I got him to go to Montana with you. I don't do it very often. That wouldn't be fair."

"No," said Karen slowly smiling. "No. I don't suppose it would. I found getting mad at him worked. Yelling."

"Oh." Cecelia nodded, her blue eyes wide. "Yes. I guess it would. He's not used to that at all. My mom never gets mad about anything. She *discusses* stuff. I don't suppose she ever cried, either. That wouldn't have been dignified. My mom's a great one for dignity."

Then, biting her lip as if realizing that she shouldn't be discussing her mother in this context with Karen, she said, "Is that Andrew in there?" She tiptoed closer to the car seat where the baby slept, all bundled up to go out into the December afternoon. "Could I see him? Maybe hold him? I don't have any bad germs that I know of."

Karen lifted off several blankets, picked Andrew up and held him close for a moment before passing him across the desk.

"He's beautiful!" Cecelia's praise was clearly genuine. "I wondered for a bit if he could be my dad's, but then I figured the dates were all wrong, considering when it was I started throwing you together."

Cecelia bounced Andrew gently as she perched on the corner of Karen's cluttered desk. "You're not going to ask me what I mean about throwing you together?"

Karen shook her head. "I know what you mean. I wasn't fooled for a minute after I met Jed. A man like your father could have had a date any weekend of the year if he'd wanted one, as well as a place to stay."

"Maybe he *could* have," Cecelia said, "but he *didn't*.

He didn't want to be with a woman. Until you. I know he wants to be with you, but something's holding him back." She frowned. "If getting mad at him works, why aren't you doing that?"

Karen stared down at her messy desk. "Because, like your tears, that's not something I want to overdo. And I'd much prefer him to come to me of his own free will."

"But if he doesn't?"

Karen looked up. It was time to face it. Jed might never come to her of his own free will. "Cecelia," she said, "how'd you like to drop another diary for me?"

After a moment's shocked silence, Cecelia burst into laughter. "Oh, no! You knew?"

"The instant I found it. It only took me a few minutes to convince myself to act on it once I had it in my hands, and I knew what you'd been up to."

"I should have known better than to try to put one over on a logic teacher. I'll drop a diary or whatever it takes." Ceil's eyes danced. "What do you want me to do?"


Jed looked at the huge greeting card he had pulled from its oversized envelope. It was the third one in as many days from Ceil. Stacked on the table at his side were others from Willie, one purportedly from Timmy filled with I-love-you-because messages, and one from Bunny.

Even Kevin, his son-in-law, had gotten in on the act with a brief, awkward phone call during which he had said most unexpectedly that he loved Jed like he did his own father that he had learned a lot from him about how to be a man and hoped he'd go on learning, that he just wanted Jed to know that.

The girls' cards were full of utter mush—long, flowery verses about what a wonderful person he was. On every unprinted surface of each of them was a list of things the kids remembered he had done for them, from teaching Willie to tie her shoes to helping Ceil with her math to giving Bunny horsey rides. Each list on each card was numbered. Checking the last one from Ceil, he found that her list ended at four-fifty, even. Curious, he checked Willi's third card. It, too, ended the same. Bunny's lists totaled ninety, along with ten I-love-you-because messages from Tim.

He smiled as he shook his head, then coughed until sweat popped out on his forehead. That was nice, really, when he thought about it. One thousand things they were thanking him for, and it wasn't even Father's Day. He wondered when he'd actually had time to do a thousand nice things for his kids. Their memories were better than his, that was painfully obvious. He figured they'd probably been repeating themselves; someday when he was less tired, he'd read every word and see.

Jeez! They'd gone to a lot of work, those two. What the hell was the matter with them? He'd had a bad cough and a bit of a fever. The doctor, who was an alarmist, insisted on calling it pneumonia and sticking him in the hospital for four and a half days before he managed to sign himself out. The damned fool had scared the girls half to death.

These cards and the sentiments they expressed made it obvious they still thought he was going to die, even though he was out of the hospital and on the mend, and wanted to get their thanks in before that happened. He was going to have to talk with his doctor, get him to speak to the kids and reassure them.

That decided, he got wearily to his feet and went to

bed, though it was only eight o'clock in the evening. There was nothing else he wanted to do. Tomorrow, he'd take care of talking to the doctor—tomorrow when he felt better. Maybe tomorrow he'd even go to work, though his assistant seemed to be handling things pretty well.

The phone rang. Once, twice, three times, and four. He lay there looking at it and then rolled over as it quit. The answering machine in the living room had picked it up and he couldn't hear the voice speaking into the tape. He wondered if it was Karen.

Tears stung at the insides of his eyelids, but he breathed deeply and evenly until the sensation went away. He couldn't talk to Karen. If her baby had been a girl, it might have been different. Then they might have had a chance. But a boy?

He shook his head back and forth on his pillow, then shoved the pillow to the floor, pressing his cheek to the cool sheet. He rolled over. He did a lot of that, until the bed was so tangled and uncomfortable that he had to get up again. What the hell. It was too early to sleep anyway.

Dragging on a robe, he went out to check his answering machine. Maybe he could at least hear her voice saying what it so often said: "Hello, Jed. I have things to say to you. Please call me when you have time."

Other times, she got mad and said stuff like "Damn it, Jed! Talk to me! It isn't time to say good-bye!" It was those times that most tempted him to say to hell with what he knew was right and sensible. When he heard her angry tones, he could see her eyes all stormy and gray, with those intriguing flares of green that beckoned him closer, closer. He could see her face flushed and her nipples on high beam. Those times he ached to go to her, to say he wanted to take a chance, to beg her to let him try to be what she needed in a man.

To be what Andrew needed in a father.

He hoped, as he rewound the tape, that she'd be in one of her quiet, pensive moods.

It wasn't Karen's voice he heard. It was Ceil's. She was crying. Her voice—how long ago had she recorded that message? When the hell was it the phone had rung? Five minutes ago? Ten? Fifteen? Her voice said, "Daddy, please pick up! I know you're there! Please, Daddy, please! I'm at Karen's and I need you! And—" The click came, cutting off her message.

"And what?" he shouted. "Damn it, Ceil, and what? Karen? The baby?" He dialed as fast as he could punch the numbers, but the line was busy at the other end and he smashed the phone down and raced back to his room.

Traffic was light, but the rain was heavy. Christmas lights glittered and glared through the wet windshield, reflected off wet pavement, and shone from every house in suburbia. The cheerful scene grated on Jed's nerves as much as every red light he came to, every stop sign that barred his rushing progress.

Karen's house was not decorated, but in the living room window he saw a tree between the panels of the drapes. The lights in the kitchen were on. The tree lights were on. A strange car stood in the drive, not Ceil's, and Karen's truck wasn't there. As he braked to a stop, he thought back frantically to that message. Had he heard what he thought he'd heard? Had she really said she was at Karen's place? Could it have been Carrie? Did she have a friend named Carrie? What if—it was too late for speculation.

He leaped out of the car and up the steps, where he hammered on the door. What in the hell was Ceil doing back in Seattle when she should be in Portland taking exams?

He hammered again. Nobody came to the door.

With a groan of dread, he tried the knob and found it open. Stepping through, shouting "Karen? Ceil?" he ran inside and came to a halt halfway through the doorway into the living room. His car keys fell from his hand to the floor.

Ceil looked up from the Monopoly board on the coffee table. "Oh, Daddy, you didn't even put on a jacket!"

Karen looked up from counting off the squares and shifted the baby in her arms. His mouth was fastened securely to her and Jed could, in the utter silence that followed Ceil's greeting, see the round pink cheeks working as Andrew suckled. Calmly, Karen rearranged the small blanket over baby and breast.

Willi sat there, holding Timmy on her lap. Tim chewed happily on the nose of a pink plush teddy bear from Singapore, and beamed around it at his grandfather. Bunny jumped up from where she sat nestled against Willi and flung herself at him. He lifted her with effort, spinning her around. She buried her face in his neck. She might be twelve, but he knew she still loved that. In fact, it had been one of the things she'd written in her cards: "I always loved the way you spun me till I was dizzy. No one can make me laugh like you, Daddy."

What in the hell was going on?

On the fourth side of the board, his back to Jed, but neck craned around so he could look over his shoulder, was Kevin. He gave Jed a jaunty grin and turned back to the game. "You owe me seven hundred dollars rent, Karen."

One-handed, she counted out the money and passed it across the table.

"That's it, gang," said Ceil, standing up. "Game's over."

"But I'm winning," Kevin objected.

"Too bad. Fold it." Ceil's tone held no sympathy for her brother-in-law. "Dad, please sit down."

Jed took another step into the room, then shook his head. "What the *hell* is going on here?" He stood Bunny back on her feet and she curled up with Willi again, playing with one of Timmy's hands, grinning at Jed.

"We all—each of us, that is," Ceil said, "have something to say to you. We want to say it where everyone can hear, because we're a family. But we aren't going to start until you sit down."

"Why here?"

"Because Karen asked that it be here. She knows you maybe better than even Willi and Bunny and I."

"Differently," Karen corrected Ceil, and Jed felt his face heat. Oh, jeez! He was blushing like a callow kid in front of his daughters.

Ceil seemed not to notice. "She said you were being noble and needed a push to get you off your self-imposed pedestal, that when you were off balance was the only time she could catch you. Sit down, Daddy. Please?"

Jed looked around the room. The only place left to sit was beside Karen on the sofa. It wasn't a case of choosing the opposite end to where she sat. She occupied the middle.

He ran a glance over her. She didn't smile. She didn't frown. She didn't look as if she expected anything at all, but when he let his gaze rest on her eyes for a moment, he saw, in the clouds of gray, the faintest hint of green.

On legs that felt like stumps, he circled the coffee table, brushing a hand over Timmy's head in passing, and took the place they all seemed to want him to take.

Karen's scent filled his head and made him weaker and dizzier than the so-called pneumonia had. Her warmth clung to him, wrapped around him, and he wanted very badly to burrow against her the way her son did. He could hear her heart beating—or maybe it was his own.

The blanket didn't cover her from this angle. The baby had stopped sucking and his cheek rested now against her nipple, hiding it from Jed. Gently, she eased him away and pulled her nursing bra shut before slipping the front of her silk caftan closed and tossing Ceil the blanket.

Ceil draped it over her shoulder, stood and took the baby, cradling him on the blanket, rubbing his back as she resumed her seat.

"Hey, I want a turn," Bunny objected. With a sigh of resignation, Ceil transferred the blanket to Bunny's shoulder, then carefully put Andrew into her arms. She held him tenderly, patting his back.

His baby, nearly thirteen years old, holding Karen's baby, less than two months. Couldn't any of them see what he saw—the disparity, if not in ages, then in the stages of life? He'd told Karen she was in springtime, and he was in autumn. They *couldn't* make a lifetime out of what was left.

"Did you read the cards we sent you?" Ceil asked. She seemed to be in charge of this meeting.

He nodded.

"Every word?"

Still not trusting his voice, he shook his head.

"I told you he wouldn't, Ceil," Willi said. "But I bet you checked out the bottom line, didn't you, Dad?"

"One thousand." His voice sounded rusty.

"One thousand what?" Ceil asked.

He shrugged. "Things. Stuff you guys remember. Stuff I don't recall."

Timmy slithered off his mother's lap and came to Jed, leaning against his knee. Automatically, he reached down and picked the little boy up, curling an arm around him, holding him securely. Tim stuck his thumb in his mouth and snuggled.

"Why don't you recall it?" Kevin asked, curiously.

Jed snorted. "Because it wasn't important!"

"Who wasn't it important to?" Ceil asked.

He frowned. "Willi stayed because Kevin was a big part of her life. You stayed because at the age you were, friends and familiar surroundings are very important to a kid."

Ceil laughed softly. "Dad, you never have been able to see it, have you? We loved you, Willi and I. That was why we stayed with you. All of us here in this room love you and need you. That's what we wanted to tell you, that you are important to us."

"Maybe so, honey, and I thank you for saying it, but the things I did for you, the things you put on those cards, none of those were important things."

"If they weren't important, Dad, why do you suppose we remember them all?"

"Hell, Ceil, I don't know. Because you're all girls? Because girls are sentimental about stuff like that? I mean, jeez! Shoelaces? Who cares about being taught to tie shoelaces?"

"I did," Willi said. "It made me feel very grown up and independent to be able to tie my own shoes. Proud of myself. I hope you'll teach Tim to do his."

"Hey, wait a minute! That's going to be my job," Kevin said.

"Andrew will need someone to teach him things," Karen said, speaking to Jed for the first time since he came in.

He looked into her eyes. "Andrew has a father, too," he said. "Like Timmy does."

She shook her head. "Andrew has a father, yes, but not like Timmy does. His father lives on the other side of the state and has never seen him."

Jed was silent for several shocked seconds. "Why not?"

"That was his choice."

He closed his eyes for a moment against the anguish he expected would flood Karen's face as she admitted that terrible truth to him. "I'm sorry," he said, daring to touch the back of her hand where it lay on her lap. It felt smooth and satiny and warm, as if she had just rubbed lotion into it. That whirled him back to the first time he'd touched her.

"I'm not sorry." He heard the smile in her tone and looked back at her face. He detected not the slightest hint of sorrow. "Not at this point, anyway. He may change his mind later, and if he does, I'll deal with it. We'll deal with it."

"What—" He began as Willi lifted Timmy off his lap, but she smiled and shook her head. She bent to kiss his cheek.

"Say, *See you later, Grandpa,*" she told her son, and Timmy gleefully babbled something that sounded like *bompa,* as he planted a wet, open-mouthed kiss on Jed's nose. Bunny handed Andrew over to Ceil and kissed Jed, too, as, to his intense surprise and partial embarrassment, did Kevin.

His eyes stung again and he had to shut them. When he opened them, he and Karen were alone with the soft lights of the Christmas tree. He leaned forward and buried his face in his hands.

"Just tying their shoes was enough? God, how could

they settle for so little? I never did any of the big things I wanted to do—should have done—for them."

He felt the warmth and weight of Karen's hand on the nape of his neck and raised a hand to cover it, to draw it down and around, where he could place his mouth against her palm. He felt her trembling and looked up to see her eyes shimmering in the subdued lighting.

"I love you," he said, and the shimmering drops splashed out.

"You never said that before."

"I said it. A million times, I said it."

"But not to me."

"I think every time I ever said it I was saying it to you. Even when I didn't know there was such a person as you."

"I love you, too."

He smiled. "I know that. And I'm grateful. It makes me feel humble, because I don't think I deserve it. I have never done anything to deserve you."

"Haven't you? What about agreeing to take a total stranger to her ex-husband's wedding so she could save face? What about pretending to be her new husband so she wouldn't be embarrassed by her pregnancy? What about the night you came to me when I needed you as I've never needed anyone before, Jed?"

He snorted. "You didn't need me that night. You were doing fine. By the time I got there, it was almost over."

She slid her hands around his neck. "I needed you, all right. I couldn't very well call the doctor a stupid bastard, could I?"

He laughed and buried his face against the warmth of her neck. "Andrew's going to have the kind of vocabulary you were trying to protect him from, isn't he?"

She looked around. "Andrew's safe in his room where Ceil put him."

"Ceil," he said wonderingly. "She's quite a girl."

"She's quite a woman," Karen corrected him. "You raised a pair of very fine adults, Jed, and your Bunny is a good-natured, well-adjusted little girl who adores her dad. I only hope I do as well with Andrew."

He looked at her for a long moment, then frowned. "Why doesn't Barry want to help you raise him? He told me he wasn't with his wife."

Karen explained, finishing with, "Until she recovers from the loss of her baby, he doesn't want her to know that Andrew is his son. He doesn't want to risk hurting her. He may, someday, feel the time is right to tell her, but I'm leaving that entirely up to him. Whatever happens, custody will not become an issue. I have that in writing. If and when I ever marry and my husband wants to adopt Andrew, give him his name, Barry won't object."

"I . . . see."

Jed released her and rose to his feet, pacing to the other side of the room. He stood, his back to her, holding a curtain open so he could look out into the decorated night.

"The night Andrew was born, I left because suddenly I was more afraid than I've ever been in my life. I wanted you—and him—so much that it was all I could do not to gather you both up and carry you home with me. I wanted to keep you safe. I wanted to hide you from everything that could ever hurt you and—" He broke off, coughing deeply, then turned to face Karen. "I wanted to hide you both from Barry, but I didn't have that right. So I went home."

"And worked yourself into a case of pneumonia."

"That's all better," he said, shrugging one shoulder.

"Sure it is," she said, rising and walking toward him, a slender figure dressed in a royal blue silk caftan from Singapore, with an embroidered belt drawing it in over her flat tummy, under her big breasts.

He blinked and a delighted smile spread over his face. "Jeez! Have you ever got a great shape! You're a knockers—I mean a *knockout!*"

Karen laughed. "Why, thank you for that wonderful Freudian slip."

He slid his arms around her and pressed her flat belly against his hardness. Drawing in a deep breath, he said, "And what would your reaction be if a construction worker said that as you walked by?"

"I'd belt him." She wriggled against him. "Why, Mr. Cotts," she said in mock surprise. "And I haven't even gotten mad at you yet. Does merely thinking about my belting a construction worker have that effect on you?"

He groaned and flattened his palms on her neat little rump. "Merely thinking about *you* has that effect on me."

Her arms looped around his neck. "Plan to do anything about it anytime soon?"

"Don't tempt me," he whispered raggedly.

"Why not?"

"It's too soon after the baby."

"No, it's not."

"I . . ." He could scarcely breathe. "I didn't bring anything with me."

She slid her hand down between them. "You *didn't?* Then what is this? I sure didn't notice it around here earlier."

"I'm talking about protection! I don't have anything

to protect you. Karen, damn it will you stop that? Please, sweetheart, don't."

"Jed, trust me. I don't conceive easily."

He thought about it for all of two seconds before he moaned and strained her closer. "Ah, hell, that's good enough for me! Besides . . ."

He didn't get to finish the thought, but that was all right. Thought wasn't required.


"Honey?"

Karen ran her fingers down Jed's chest. "Hmm?"

"Look at me." He curled his fingers around her jaw and tilted her head up. "Will you marry me?"

She smiled. "Of course, silly. Do you think I want Penelope May to be born without my having you there for me to yell at?"

He looked horrified. "God! What if you are pregnant? Jeez! I can't believe my irresponsibility! How could I have done that? How could I have listened to you? I know your not conceiving for a long time before is no guarantee that you wouldn't do it this time and—"

"Jed. Shut up."

This time, he looked startled. "What?"

"You talk too much. You worry too much. You take too much on yourself. Am I here, naked in this bed beside you, because I want to be, or because you forced me to do it?"

He considered for a moment. "If I reconstruct it rightly, I was the one backing up. You were the one pushing me this way. If anybody was forced to do anything . . . hmm." He nuzzled her breasts. "Food for thought."

She drew in a shuddering breath. "That, my love, is

food for Andrew. But I think he might be willing to share."

Jed raised his head, grinning. "If I ask politely?"

Karen laughed. "Try a little *im*politeness, Mr. Cotts. Sometimes it gets even better results."

"Yeah." He laughed, too. "Boy, will I have a lot to teach our son."

She wrapped her hands around his face. "Sons," she corrected, "or sons *and* daughters. Jed, will you give me more babies?"

"I dunno," he said. "I'm pretty old. But maybe I can manage it—if we start right now."

Karen laughed. "I thought we already had."

Cradling her close, listening to her breathe, drawing in the scent of her skin and hair, Jed knew they already had—and that they were never going to finish.

# BOOK YOUR PLACE ON OUR WEBSITE AND MAKE THE READING CONNECTION!

We've created a customized website just for our very special readers, where you can get the inside scoop on everything that's going on with Zebra, Pinnacle and Kensington books.

When you come online, you'll have the exciting opportunity to:

- View covers of upcoming books
- Read sample chapters
- Learn about our future publishing schedule (listed by publication month *and author*)
- Find out when your favorite authors will be visiting a city near you
- Search for and order backlist books from our online catalog
- Check out author bios and background information
- Send e-mail to your favorite authors
- Meet the Kensington staff online
- Join us in weekly chats with authors, readers and other guests
- Get writing guidelines
- AND MUCH MORE!

**Visit our website at
http://www.zebrabooks.com**